ROBERT DOHERTY

BODYGUARD OF LIES

TOR®

A TOM DOHERTY ASSOCIATES BOOK
NEW YORK

This is a work of fiction. All the characters and events portrayed in this book are either products of the author's imagination or are used fictitiously.

BODY GUARD OF LIES

Copyright © 2005 by Robert Doherty

A Tor Book
Published by Tom Doherty Associates, LLC
175 Fifth Avenue
New York, NY 10010

www.tor.com

Tor® is a registered trademark of Tom Doherty Associates, LLC.

ISBN 0-765-34057-7
EAN 978-0-765-34057-3

First edition: March 2005
First mass market edition: March 2006

Printed in the United States of America

0 9 8 7 6 5 4 3 2 1

To Craig & Corey

BOOKS BY ROBERT DOHERTY

The Rock
Area 51
Area 51: The Reply
Area 51: The Mission
Area 51: The Sphinx
Area 51: The Grail
Area 51: Excalibur
Area 51: The Truth
Area 51: Nosferatu
Area 51: Legend
Psychic Warrior
Psychic Warrior: Project Aura
Bodyguard of Lies

AS BOB MAYER

The Novel Writer's Toolkit:
A Guide to Writing Great Fiction and Getting It Published
Who Dares Wins: Special Operations Tactics for Success

BODYGUARD
OF LIES

CHAPTER

1

THE OLD MAN sat alone in the darkness contemplating failure on a scale that historians would write about for centuries, and the subsequent inevitable need for change. He was one of the most powerful people in the world, but only a few knew of his existence. His position had been born out of failure over sixty years previously, as smoke still smoldered above the mangled ships and dead bodies in Pearl Harbor. For over six decades he had given his life to his country. His most valuable asset was dispassion, so he could view his own recent failures objectively, although *recent* was a subjective term. He realized now it had all begun over ten years ago.

His office lacked any charm or comfort. There was a scarcity about the room that was unnerving. The cheap desk and two chairs made it look more like an interview room in an improvised police station than the office of a man so powerful his name brought fear throughout the government he served in Washington. The top of the desk was almost totally clear. Just a secure phone and a stack of folders.

There were, naturally, no windows. Not three hundred feet

underground, buried beneath the "crystal palace" of the top-secret National Security Agency at Fort Meade, Maryland. And not that he could have used windows. The few who knew of the organization sometimes wondered if this location was what had led to its name. While the CIA made headlines every week, the Cellar was only whispered about in the hallowed halls of the nation's capitol. It might have been located underneath the NSA building but it was an entity unto itself, answerable only to its founding mandate.

The room was lit only by the dim red lights on the secure phone. They showed the scars on the old man's face and the raw red, puckered skin where his eyes had once rested. There was track lighting, currently off, all three bulbs of which were over the old man's head and angled toward the door. When on, they placed his face in a shadow and caused any guest to squint against the light. The few who had the misfortune to sit across from him didn't know whether the lighting was meant to hide the severity of the old man's wounds, or simply blind them as well.

He was not a man given much to sentimental reflection, but he knew his time was coming to an end, which made him think back to his beginning, as he knew all things were cyclical. He opened a right-side desk drawer and pulled out a three-dimensional representation of an old black-and-white photograph. He ran his fingers lightly over the raised images of three smiling young men dressed in World War II–era uniforms—British, French, and American. He was on the right. The other two were killed the day after the photo was taken.

He left the image on the desktop and reached for the files. The ones he wanted were the first two. He placed them on his lap. Paper files, the writing in Braille. He'd never trusted computers, even though there were ones now that could work completely on voice commands and read to him. Perhaps that was part of the problem. He was out of date. An anachronism.

They were labeled respectively Gant, Anthony; and Masterson. He ran his fingers over the names punched on the tabs. He was patient. He had waited decades for plans born out of seeds he had sown to come to fruition. Quite a few similar plans had failed, so there was no reason to believe this one would succeed. But this plan was in motion now, initiated by an event he had had nothing to do with, the way the best plans in the covert world always started to allow deniability.

Despite his gifts of dispassion and patience, he felt a stirring in his chest. It puzzled him for a few moments before he realized he was experiencing hope. He squashed the feeling and picked up the phone to set another piece of the puzzle in motion.

CHAPTER

2

NEELEY HAD NOT anticipated that waiting to kill people could be so boring. Staying well back in the darker shadows, out of the dim reflection of the few working streetlights, she scanned the ghostly quiet alley. She used the night vision portion of her retina just off the center of vision as Gant had taught her. There was nothing moving. A dumpster, an abandoned car, and intermittent piles of refuse dotted the pitted concrete between the two abandoned tenements. There was a way out on either end. She could hear the rumble of traffic from the Bruckner Expressway a few hundred yards away.

Neeley had been here for a day and a half and she could superimpose from memory the details that the night refused to divulge to her naked eye. Looking right, a couple of miles to the east, she could see the aircraft warning lights on top of one of the towers of the Bronx-Whitestone Bridge crossing Long Island Sound.

She picked up a bulky rifle and pressed the scope on top to her right eye, twisting the switch to the on position. After a moment's hesitation, the black night gave way to bright green and she no longer needed her memory for the details the technology provided. Completing a second overall scan from her location in a corner apartment in the abandoned tenement, Neeley then zoomed in on the three locations she had noted during thirty-six hours of observation.

Two of the three men had arrived together four hours ago, just as darkness had slid like a curtain across the alley. Neeley had watched the two set up in separate rooms, on the second floor of the derelict building across the street.

The third man had shown up twenty minutes after the first two. If he'd tried the building, he might have bumped into the first two, but this last man wasn't very smart. He'd positioned himself inside the dumpster on the alley floor, leaving the top wedged open so he could observe the street, south to north. She gave the man an A for effort, getting among the moldy garbage inside the large container, but an F for tactical sense. True, the dumpster had a good ground-level field of fire, but the man was trapped in a steel coffin if it became necessary to relocate. The two men in the building had the high ground, always a tactical advantage, and the ability to move. Of course, they lacked the element of surprise but Neeley mentally gave them a few points anyway.

Through the scope, she could easily see the glow of one of the men across the street covertly smoking a cigarette, obviously thinking he was secure since he was well back from the window in the darkness of the room. The burning glow, barely visible to the naked eye, showed up like a searchlight in the night-vision scope. She shifted left two windows. The second man was watching the dumpster through a pair of older-model, army-issue night-vision goggles. PVS-5s as near as Neeley could tell at this distance.

Nothing else was moving in the street and Neeley didn't expect to see anything until the deal went down. Alleys in the South Bronx were places even most bad people stayed away from at night. A few blocks to the south, prostitutes haunted the streets and docks of the Hunts Point section but this area was a no-man's-land. Which was why the two sides had chosen it.

The man across the street put out his cigarette. Neeley lay the rifle down and slid back from the window. Pulling a poncho liner over her head, she completely covered herself. Only then did she peel back the Velcro cover on her watch, and check the glowing hands. Twenty minutes to twelve. She considered the situation. At least six hours of darkness left. Neeley hadn't allowed herself to sleep since arriving here a day and a half ago. She'd drunk the last of the coffee from her thermos a while back and now her eyes burned with fatigue. Given the presence of the advance guards, odds were the deal would go down soon. She decided to take a calculated chance and pulled a pill out of her pocket. Popping it into her mouth, she washed it down with a swig from a water bottle. Four hours of intenseness. She would need at least an hour, preferably two, on the flip side of the deal to get out of the immediate area and be reasonably secure. Neeley reaffirmed the decision she had made during mission planning: 0300 and she was out of here, deal or no deal. Survival first and stick with the plan.

Her pulse quickened as the speed hit the blood stream. Neeley pushed aside the poncho liner and crammed it into a stuff sack, placing the sack inside a small backpack. She felt around the floor with her hands. Nothing left out. Just the pack and rifle. Methodically, she did a mental inventory of her actions of the past day and a half and all the equipment she had brought with her. The room was sterile, everything accounted for. Rule number four: Always pack out what you pack in. There were some rules you just couldn't break and the remembrance of one of Gant's rules brought a wry smile to Neeley's lips.

Neeley laid the pack down three feet inside the window and sat on it, laying the rifle across her knees. She was used to waiting. She'd spent most of her thirty-two years learning that patience was a virtue; a life-saving one.

She picked the rifle back up, the feel of plastic and steel a familiar one. It was an Accuracy International L96A1, a venerable sniper rifle of British design, firing NATO standard-

size 5.56mm by 51mm rounds, each of which Gant had reloaded to reduce velocity to subsonic speeds. A bullet that
broke the sound barrier made a cracking noise as it left the
muzzle and the special load eliminated that noise. On the end
of the barrel was a bulky tactical suppressor which absorbed
the other large noise source for the rifle, the gasses that came
out of the end of the barrel upon firing. In essence the suppressor was a series of washerlike baffles around the end of
the barrel that took the force of the expelling gasses. It was
good for about ten shots before it had to be retooled. The
combination of the two made the rifle almost noiseless to operate although they did drastically reduce the range and
change the trajectory of the rounds, both of which Neeley
was prepared for after many hours on the range firing it.

A pair of headlights carved into the northern end of the alley. Neeley tried to control the adrenaline that now began to
overlap the speed. She watched the car roll slowly down the
alley and come to a halt, the dumpster and its hidden contents thirty meters ahead.

Looking through the scope, Neeley saw one of the men in
the building across the street, the one on the left, speak into
his hand.

The car was an armored limo. Another pair of headlights
came in from the south. This one was a Mercedes. Not obviously armored, as it rode too high for that. It came to a halt
thirty-five meters from the limo, headlights dueling. The
dumpster flanked the Mercedes, to its right front.

The doors on the limo opened and four men got out, two
to a side. Three had submachine guns. The fourth a large
suitcase. The Mercedes disgorged three men, all also heavily
armed. One went back and opened the trunk.

"I want your man out of the window up there," one of the
men from the Mercedes yelled. The guy in the dumpster had
seen the glow from the same cigarette that Neeley had. This
also confirmed that the man in the dumpster had communication with the Mercedes.

After a moment's hesitation, the man with the suitcase

pulled a small Motorola radio off his belt and spoke into it.
A minute later, the man who had been smoking walked out
of the building and joined the other four.

"Satisfied?" the suitcase man yelled back.

"Yes," the chief Mercedes man answered.

Neeley adjusted the scope's focus knob, zooming in. The
remaining man across the way was now resting the bipods of
an M60 machine gun on the windowsill. She shifted back to
the standoff in the alley.

The men from the Mercedes unloaded two heavy cardboard boxes from the car's trunk and stacked them ten feet
in front of the headlights. The five men from the limo side
moved forward, fanning out, the man with the suitcase in the
middle.

Neeley placed the crosshairs of the night-scope on the
head of the suitcase man. She began to note the rhythm of
her heart. The tip of her finger lay lightly on the trigger, almost a lover's caress. She slowly exhaled two-thirds of the
air in her lungs, to what Gant had called the natural respira-
tory pause, and then held her diaphragm still. In between
heartbeats she smoothly squeezed the trigger and, with the
rifle producing only the sound of the bolt working in concert
with a low puff from the barrel suppressor, the 7.62mm subsonic round left the muzzle. In midstride the target's head
blew apart.

Reacting instinctively, not knowing where death had
winged its way from, the other four men swung up their submachine guns and fired on the Mercedes crew. The dumpster
man replied, only to be lost in the roar of the machine gun in
the window. In the ensuing confusion, and on the same
paused breath, in between new heartbeats, Neeley put a
round into one of the limo men.

After ten seconds of thunderous fire, an echoing silence
enveloped the street. All the Mercedes men were down. The
M60 had Swiss-cheesed the dumpster. Two of the limo men
were still standing.

Neeley took another breath and slowly exhaled, then
paused. In between the next three heartbeats she fired three

times. First round, a headshot blowing the M60 gunner backward into the darkened room across the way. Second and third rounds finishing the two left standing before they even realized that death was silently lashing out of a window above their heads.

Satisfied that all were down, Neeley pulled out a red lens flashlight and searched the dirty floor of the room. She collected the five pieces of expended brass and placed them in a pocket on the outside of the backpack, ensuring that the Velcro cover was tightly sealed. She listened to the earpiece from the portable police scanner in her pocket as she swung on the backpack and started down. She was on the street before the first call for a car to investigate shots fired came over the airway. The police would not respond with any particular alacrity. Shots fired were common calls in the South Bronx at night. Cops tended to band together here and only became excited if the radio call was "officer down."

As she headed toward the Mercedes, movement from one of the bodies caused her to swing the muzzle up; one of the men was still alive. Neeley watched the figure writhing on the ground for a few seconds. She stepped forward, and with one boot, shoved the body over, keeping the muzzle pointed at the man's head. The man's stomach was a sea of very dark, arterial blood: gut shot. Neeley's training automatically started scrolling through her consciousness, outlining the proper procedures to treat the wound.

The bulky barrel of the rifle mesmerized the man's gaze. Looking above it, into Neeley's dark pupils, his own widened with surprise. They searched for mercy in the depths of Neeley's thickly lashed eyes. Neeley's entire body started sweating and the adrenaline kicked up to an even higher level. The muzzle didn't waver.

The round entered, a small black dot between the man's eyes. The bullet mushroomed through the brain and took off the entire rear of the head, spraying the dirty street. Neeley watched the body twitch and become still. She automatically scooped up the expended brass casing and stuffed it into her pocket.

Moving to the cardboard boxes, she pulled a thermal grenade out of one of the pockets of her loose-fitting, black leather trenchcoat, and pulled the pin. She placed the grenade on top of the boxes and released the arming lever, pocketing both it and the pin. Acting quickly, trying to make up for the seconds lost dealing with the wounded man, she tore the briefcase out of the limp hand still holding it and jogged to the end of the alley. A subdued pop and a flicker of flames appeared behind her as two million dollars worth of cocaine began to go up in flames.

Satisfied that she was out of immediate danger, and before reaching the corner, Neeley twisted the locking screw and broke the rifle down into two parts. She hung the barrel on the inside right of her coat and the stock on the left, securing them with specially sown-in bands of Velcro.

Turning the corner, Neeley settled into a steady, swift walk. From the confused babble on the scanner she had six to eight minutes before the first police arrived.

She made three blocks and then turned left. Here were the first signs of life. This area was more populated, but still well within the urban battle zone known as the South Bronx. Covert eyes watched her as she moved and Neeley slid a hand up, loosening the 10mm Glock Model 20 pistol she wore in a shoulder holster.

Her purposeful stride and appearance deflected any thoughts of evil intent from those lurking in the shadows. Neeley was tall, an inch shy of six feet. She had broad shoulders and a slender build. Her short, dark hair had seen better days and could use styling. Her face was all angles, no soft roundness, with two very dark eyes that took in everything in her surroundings. She moved with a sense of determination, her long overcoat half open, allowing her easy access to the weapons inside.

Two more blocks, no interference encountered, and she reached her parked pickup truck, nestled among other battered vehicles. She unlocked the door and threw the suitcase in. The first sirens were wailing in the distance as Neeley got behind the wheel and cranked the engine.

For the first time she paused. She held her hands in front of her face. They were shaking slightly. Neeley took a deep breath and held it. The vision of the man looking up at her flickered across her eyes, then was gone. She shivered; shaking her head in short violent jerks, then was still again. She put the truck into gear and drove off.

Sticking with the route she had memorized, Neeley drove, keeping scrupulously to the speed limit. After ten minutes of negotiating side streets, she reached an on-ramp for the Cross Bronx Expressway and rolled up it, heading northeast for New England.

The suitcase on the passenger seat nagged at her. Neeley held her patience for two hours, until the city was over eighty miles behind her, and she was well into Connecticut, just south of Hartford. Finally, she pulled into a rest area. Parking away from other vehicles, Neeley turned on the dome light and put the suitcase on her lap.

She checked the exterior for any indication that it was rigged. Nothing. Flipping both latches, she slowly lifted the lid an inch. She slid a finger in and carefully felt the edges. Then she opened it all the way. A wadded piece of cloth lay on top, covering the contents. Neeley peeled the cloth away. Stacks of worn hundred-dollar bills greeted her. She didn't count it. She knew exactly how much was there.

Finally accepting that she was safe, Neeley allowed herself to think of Gant. She wondered how it would have been to open the suitcase with him. She knew he would have been proud of her. Gant had talked about this mission endlessly. He had a source, someone he called his Uncle Joe, although he said the man was not family by blood, who had called him just two weeks ago with word of this meet. Somebody who must have owed Gant a lot, but Neeley understood owing Gant.

She remembered all the nights she had lain with her body curled into his. Talking about it and perfecting the plan. Every ex–Green Beret's dream, he'd called it.

Neeley closed the suitcase and with it the memories of Gant. There was still much to do.

*   *   *

THE DAY HER LIFE as she knew it came to an end, Hannah
Masterson forced herself to stroll casually down the carpeted
hallway. They were all trying hard not to stare but Hannah was
certain they were. She doubted that they knew about John, but
she'd always known that people could sense bad news. Hannah had an urge to walk the length of the long hallway, stopping at every desk, and explain in great detail to every person
that she had been a good wife, never shirked her duties, always smiled and appeared happy, and that John wasn't really
gone. He was just away for a little while. On business.

Of course they wouldn't believe her. She didn't believe it
either. Not that she hadn't been a good wife, but that John
was really gone. Men like John, with six-figure salaries and
power jobs, didn't just dump the wife, career, house, and two
cars for no reason at all. Something had happened to him,
she was convinced of it. Well, she had been. The day-old
postcard in her purse had forced her to acknowledge other
possibilities.

With relief she found the door to Howard Brumley's office open and aimed herself toward a vacant char. One look
at Howard's face told Hannah that there was to be no re-
prieve during this appointment. His normal ruddy complex-
ion was pale, the dancing, flirting eyes were gone, replaced
by shaded "I hate to tell you this" pupils.

Howard picked up a file and tapped the corner nervously.
"You look good."

Hannah's wasn't a natural beauty, but more the result of
money meeting good bone structure. Her blond hair was
thick and shiny, flowing to her shoulders in natural waves.
Her eyes, hidden now by the dark glasses, were the color of
expensive chocolate left in a hot car. The few worry lines
around her eyes and mouth were deepened by the stress of
the past week and were the only thing that made her look
older than her thirty-one years. She was a shade under five
and a half feet and weighed what any self-conscious woman
of means would weigh.

Howard, the family lawyer, was dodging. Hannah knew it was difficult to talk to a woman whose husband had apparently taken the perpetual golf trip. That was how John had done it. Left early on a beautiful Saturday morning the previous week with his golf bag and whistling a happy tune. Glanced back once. Whether to look at her, or the house, maybe both, she would never know. The Country Club had returned the car on Monday. John had taken his clubs. Even with the car back in the garage though, Hannah couldn't believe he was gone.

Howard put down the file folder and leaned back in his chair. "Have you heard anything else from John?"

"Just the card from the islands. If it was John who sent it," she amended.

"Is it his handwriting?" Howard asked.

Hannah reluctantly opened her bag and handed the card over. "It looks like his writing, but it could be a forgery."

Howard shook his head, staring at it. "I can't believe he would do something like this."

"Maybe the card is just—" Hannah began, but Howard was shaking his head again and his attention was no longer on the card.

"No." Howard gestured to the file folder. "I mean I can't believe he would do anything like this."

"You think he's really gone?" Hannah asked. "Off to some South Sea island like this card says?"

Howard sighed. Hannah was watching him carefully. John was hurt. That was it. "He's been in an accident, hasn't he?" She picked the postcard up from the desk. "This was John's way of trying to keep me from knowing, isn't it?"

"He's not hurt, not that I know of." Howard blinked. "Hannah, I've known John a long time and two weeks ago I would have trusted him with the lives of my children." Howard took a deep breath. "I don't know what to say."

Hannah sat still and waited to hear something so bad it would render a lawyer speechless.

Having taken the plunge, Howard continued. "Evidently

John was planning this for some time. He cleaned out every-thing: IRAs, mutual funds, stocks, real estate, you name it. You should have had your name on all of it. It was too easy for him. He did leave you fifteen thousand in your household account. But here comes the bad news."

Hannah's head snapped from an imaginary upper cut. She was a little behind Howard, taking it one step at a time. "He's gone? He's really gone?"

Howard was in a rush to get it over with. "The house, Hannah. It's the house."

"No. That's mine." Her voice was level and hard. "When we paid the note off last year John filed a quitclaim deed and put the house in my name."

She remembered the night well. John had said it was a symbol of his love and devotion. Hannah who had spent most of her childhood in a succession of foster homes felt safe for the first time that night. Her house, it would always be her house.

"John forged your name and took out a new note on the house. It's mortgaged to the max. If you sell it now you can pay the bank. As it is you have a payment of a little over six thousand dollars due in seven days. You don't have enough money to stay there more than two months."

Hannah shook her head. "John wouldn't do that. He wouldn't do that with the house. Not the house."

Howard must have seen too many war movies with shell-shocked victims as he slapped Hannah with his words. "Hannah, John's gone. He left you and stole everything that wasn't nailed down. And what was nailed down he sold out from under you."

Hannah held up a thin, manicured hand. "But that's ille-gal." It was beginning to sink in. "What about the cars?"

"Both leased," John said. He glanced in the deadly folder. "The Volvo is five hundred and forty. The BMW is eight-twenty, both payable the first of the month."

Howard cleared his throat. Could there be more? Hannah wondered.

There was. "I also received mail from John yesterday." Howard was holding several legal-size pieces of paper. "It's a marital dissolution agreement."

"You're joking," Hannah sputtered. "John wants to divorce me after stealing everything?"

Howard looked distinctly uncomfortable. "Apparently so."

"But . . ." Hannah shook her head. "I don't . . ."

"It's an unusual situation," Howard said.

The understatement of the year, Hannah thought. She found it strange that the only thing that resounded in her mind was that she hadn't seen it coming. She didn't really care about the cars or the money—the house, of course, was a different matter, for a different reason—but she hadn't seen this coming.

Howard's voice took on his professional lilt. "You have to realize that some of what John did *is* illegal and not just toward you. The bank he took the new mortgage out from will not be very happy either. You're probably going to have to divorce him to keep the bank and others he defrauded from coming after you, Hannah."

"Coming after me?" she repeated. "I didn't do anything."

"Divorcing him, and a thorough check of your lack of assets, will help convince them of that," Howard said. "But as it looks now, you're a party to everything he did. Divorcing him will be the best thing you could do."

"Divorcing John is a good thing?" Hannah pressed her hands against her temples. "I don't understand. Until a week ago I thought I had a good marriage. John seemed as happy as ever. Something's wrong with this picture, Howard. Either something awful happened to John or my entire adult life has been a sham. After all these years for him to do this now means I'm an idiot."

Howard's voice softened. "No. You're a lovely, lovely woman who married a snake. But now's not the time for pity. Now's the time for action. You have to rise above this, Hannah. We have to take care of the dirt John left you. Then you can start a new life."

Hannah stared. *A new life? She didn't even know how she'd lost the old one yet.*

Howard kept the words coming. "Hannah, you're a beautiful woman with lots of talents. You can get a job or another husband in no time."

Even through the numbness, that struck a painful chord. "I can't believe you said that, Howard."

He held up both hands, defensively. "I didn't mean it like that."

"How else could you possibly have meant it?"

"Hannah, please!" Howard was standing. He had an envelope in his hands that he was running one thumb along the edge of. "Do you need help?"

Hannah was puzzled by the inane question.

"Haven't you been seeing someone? A professional?" Realizing he wasn't getting through, Howard cut to the chase. "A psychiatrist?"

How did he know about Dr. Jenkins, Hannah wondered. John must have told him, she immediately realized. Hannah gave a bitter laugh. "How can I pay for a psychiatrist now?"

"You're still covered by John's health plan; for a while at least. I think you really should go see him. Get some help."

Hannah stood. "I have to go."

Howard started coming around his massive desk. "I'm sorry, Hannah. Please don't leave like this. With everything you have to worry about I'd hate it if I were the cause of any more trouble. I was just trying to help."

Hannah didn't say anything. She walked quickly out the door. As the elevator doors shut Howard was still calling after her, telling her they had to take care of this now. Clear it up before it was too late.

Hannah leaned against the brass wall letting the cool surface soothe her forehead. She was still willing herself not to faint when the doors slid open. The man in front of her shot an appreciative glance as he entered the elevator.

"Nice day."

She stared at him as she pushed by him into the lobby, awed by the fact that the world was going to go on.

Hannah fumbled her way out of the office building and stood in a daze on the sidewalk. All around her office workers were hitting the streets of St. Louis for lunch. After she was bumped a few times she realized it was time to move on. She couldn't quite remember where the car was parked and it didn't seem to matter. The car John had brought home one day. She hadn't even asked if he'd bought it or leased it. Those were questions that simply had never occurred to her after so many years of allowing John to take care of everything.

Hannah wondered if anything was ever going to matter again. This morning her main concern had been John and his safety. Clutching her purse to her chest, she now knew that John was never coming back. Beyond that was dangerous territory for her mind to go.

The Adam's Mark was just ahead. Two weeks ago she might have wandered into the hotel bar and waited for her successful husband to join her for lunch. Today she didn't know if she had enough money for a sandwich and a Coke. She fumbled with her purse and checked. She had a couple of dollars in cash. She had no idea what the status of the credit cards was.

The bar was cool and dark and occupied by a lone female bartender. Hannah took a seat at the bar and waited. She noted that the bartender was about her age but looked it. Hannah's carefully tended thirty-one years had been shielded from the direct hit of aging, until this week of course.

"Are you okay?"

Hannah was startled by the bartender's sudden question. She nodded.

"How about a cup of coffee?"

Hannah indicated in the affirmative, thankful that she would have a moment to compose herself before the woman returned. Hannah noticed that the woman's nametag pronounced her Marty. She was eyeing Hannah suspiciously from the end of the bar as she poured the coffee. She carried the cup the length of the bar and set it carefully in front of Hannah.

"Let me see if I can guess: man trouble."

Hannah tried to smile and failed. "Yes. He left me."

Hannah surprised herself. Even though John had been gone a week, this was the first time she had uttered those words aloud. It was as if by refusing to say them she had been able to negate the fact that he was no longer there. She had simply refused to consider the possibility. Even the postcard's intent had been ignored.

"He left you?" Marty emphasized the latter pronoun as the look on her face passed from sympathy to incredulity. "I don't mean to be funny but if you got left, I don't figure any of us are safe."

Hannah took a sip of her coffee. The scalding liquid bit at her lips and she put the cup back on the polished surface of the bar. "Maybe nobody is safe."

Marty was leaning on the bar. "Was this guy your husband?"

"Yes. Next month would have been our tenth anniversary."

"He just up and left? Took his stuff and split?"

"Not really. He didn't even take a change of clothes. He just never came back home. For the past week I was afraid something terrible had happened to him and then yesterday I received a postcard with palm trees all over it saying he wasn't coming back. I went to our lawyer and he had the divorce papers all ready."

Marty wiped the bar top. "Sounds like he went a little bit nuts. Maybe he's gonna come back after he gets regrooved and everything will be fine."

"He can't come back now. He forged my name on some real estate papers. He left me with nothing."

Marty wore a mask of outrage. "Oh man, that's the worst thing I ever heard. Don't sign the divorce papers. Nail the asshole. Get your own lawyer."

Hannah wondered why she was sharing this with some woman she would never speak to again, and realized that was the reason. She could hardly talk about this with the women in her limited social circle. She had kept John's disappearance as quiet as possible, telling only Howard and calling the people at John's office trying to find out, without saying *she* didn't know, if they knew where John was. But no one had had a clue as to his hereabouts. Hannah had even considered calling the police, but Howard had told her to wait a little bit. Howard's position had been that John's sensitive job at the company should be protected.

Hannah watched as Marty returned her thoughts to the bar. Hannah drained the last of the coffee and decided that it was time to go home.

She left the three dollar bills that were all she had and mumbled some polite words to Marty. She passed through the hotel foyer focused on the green marble floor, ignoring the businessmen of assorted ages checking her out, noting the rings that marked her as taken and bagged by one of their own. They all gave her the soft smile and nod that they expected from other men for their own wives. They didn't expect Hannah to notice them just as they didn't expect their own wives to alert to the nods of other men.

She found the car around the block from Howard's office. The big black BMW that John had loved to drive. It was odd to discover that she didn't own it; that she didn't own anything. She thought about that for a minute, feeling the anxiety that threatened to overwhelm her. She pulled up to the garage attendant and panicked, realizing she had no money to pay the parking fee. She flipped open the console and slid quarters out of their holder. She had to go halfway down the dime column before she had enough. She was relieved when the gate released her and she burned rubber pulling away.

That little incident was more telling than anything Howard had said. Hannah moved some numbers around in her head and knew she needed a plan. The money that John had left would be swallowed by house expenses in no time. Howard was right: she was going to have to sell the house and then turn in the cars. But that left her without a job, home, car, anything. Hannah's mind was churning. She could sell the contents of the house. Maybe she could generate enough to lease an apartment.

She had to get a job. The very thought brought a tightness

to her throat. Not because she didn't want to work, but because she felt she had nothing to present a future employer. She had dropped out of college to put John through graduate school, working two jobs, one as a receptionist and the other waiting tables. Instead of going back and finishing her degree, she had become a full-time wife. John's career had been so demanding and financially rewarding that she had simply never thought that she would need to support herself one day. That was the deal—the word stuck in her consciousness—the deal they had made without even bothering to verbalize it. It had just happened.

CHAPTER

3

"DAMN!" Neeley hissed as she walked into the cabin. It was colder inside than it was out. The wet weather of the Green Mountains gnawed into the bone worse than any cold she had ever experienced.

She wondered, not for the first time, why Gant had lived here. He'd hated the cold. A few years back he had insisted that she needed some high-altitude training. At the time Neeley was already exhausted. Her days were filled with physical and mental lessons that were threatening to break her. Her nights were filled with Gant's hard body and his soft voice. She gave in when she saw there was no bridling his childish enthusiasm over the new adventure. One of Gant's many contacts in the shadow world had provided the aircraft for transportation.

Neeley and Gant had flown to the Rockies. They had jumped with skis strapped to their sides and one hundred and twenty pounds of gear in their rucksacks onto a small drop zone located at 10,000 feet of altitude. They'd dumped the parachutes and skied farther into the mountains, to almost 14,000 feet. The wind chill had hit sixty below, but Gant had sworn it felt better than plus twenty degrees in the Green Mountains of Vermont. The dry cold in the Rockies had hurt on the surface but this wet cold of New England was an inner bone ache.

Neeley looked out the window of the small cabin at the patch of late snow that blanketed Gant's grave. He had known the ground would be impossibly frozen now and had insisted they dig the hole in autumn. They had dug it together, he tiring easily and sitting a lot, sipping a beer and making awful, morbid jokes.

It had been the first time she had allowed herself to contemplate life beyond Gant. She'd asked what she should do once he was gone. His lined face had folded in on itself as he turned to look at her, the setting sun filling it with shadows.

"Do you know what dead time is?" he'd asked her, and when she'd shaken her head, he'd continued. "That's what the past ten years or so have been for us: a condition of balance among various forces. We should have been dead these last ten years, but we've managed to keep things in stasis."

"I don't understand," Neeley had replied.

Gant had sighed, rubbing his wasted hand across his face. "There are even parts that I don't know, that I'm not supposed to know because of the deal I've had. And even from what I know, I can only tell you so much without jeopardizing you before you are ready. The rest you are going to have to find out on your own. My dying is going to upset a balance and I don't know what is going to happen. People are going to react to my death and there's a good chance that will put you in danger."

She had known from her first meeting with Gant that her life would never be the same, but that had not been his fault. She could remember that day as most women remembered their wedding day or the birth of their first child.

Sitting alone in the cold cabin, she went back to the event that had brought her here, not willing yet to move on with the actions demanded of her for this new phase of her life.

On that day over ten years ago, she had been a teenager

and her journey against the flow of the terminal crowd with a large gaily wrapped package in her hands had been handled well by the locals. Templehoff Airport was in the very center of what had been West Berlin and the few words spoken had the lilting Berliner accent that marked the speakers as natives. Since the end of the Second World War, West Berlin had tolerated the noise and energy of a major airport in its midst as graciously as it tolerated the foreigners who ruled it. Even a half century later there were still many in the city who remembered when their survival had depended on the goodness of foreigners and the noise of the planes overhead. Those planes had brought the food that had enabled the city to endure the Russian blockade. And for many years afterward this airport had taken them from their small democratic island to the outside world, something their fellow Berliners to the east could only dream about until the Wall came down.

So in Berlin, as nowhere else, Neeley had not been scolded for bumping and pushing, but rather given a wider berth and even a smile by those who had noticed the T-shirt pulled taut across her breasts. A few of the men looked past the shirt and continued to stare downward, taking in her lean, tanned legs that the cutoff Levis exposed. It was the first week in October, too cool for such attire, but Neeley remembered how she hadn't felt the chill. She'd made her way past the waiting line into the center of the terminal.

Gant told her later that it was her obvious confusion and agitation that had first drawn his attention. In a place packed with people carrying bags and extra coats, she had seemed oddly out of place, clutching only the package and not even a purse.

Gant's row had been called ten minutes ago, but he had waited to board, another one of his rules he had given her as he told her the story of their meeting from his point of view. The last few passengers of the boarding flight had paid Neeley the most attention, but it had been more a matter of perspective and not the girl's action that had drawn the notice. They were Americans, young soldiers who even in their

civilian clothes still bore the trademark short hair and overall healthy fitness of the Army's finest. They had ogled her
with relish, their togetherness granting them a certain
anonymity. Some of the other passengers had turned at the
sound of the catcalls, recognizing the blatant intent, if not
the language. The soldiers noticed the looks and quieted in
unison.

Unspoken among the soldiers and those around them was
the knowledge that this was not the time for noticeable behavior by Americans. It had been on the news nonstop: all
the world now knew that just two days before the United
States had failed in its humanitarian effort in Somalia.

The images from Mogadishu had been horrible and
broadcast around the world: helicopters shot down and soldiers dead, the bodies of some dragged through the streets
by angry mobs. A pilot captured and the most powerful
country in the world trying to negotiate his release from a
warlord. It was a tragedy of the first order and a terrible blow
to the Clinton administration that had ordered the mission.
As if remembering all that, the newly silenced soldiers
joined the end of the line.

Neeley remembered standing alone, not knowing what to
do next. That was when she had met Gant, at that time just a
strange, tall man who had stopped right in front of her. His
eyes had been hidden by dark aviator glasses. He'd smiled at
her. She would always remember that first smile.

She'd handed him the package with the first words she
ever spoke to him: "It's a bomb."

He didn't seem at all surprised about the bomb. His attitude implied a familiarity with such incidents that produced
an immediate sense of confidence within her. She had been
stumbling about with that horrible betrayal for what seemed
like hours, but had in reality been only minutes. She had for-
gotten her knapsack and baggage in her haste to get out of
the confining space of the plane's cabin with the bomb.

The passion of the previous night, which Jean-Philippe
had spent reassuring her that he would miss her, had appeared genuine. Even the simple request to deliver the pack-

age to a man in Heathrow during her layover there had seemed normal and inconsequential. She had been a courier for him before, transferring the important documents of his trade to various cities around Europe and the Middle East and even to the States on occasion.

When had she known? She would always worry about that simple question in the years to come. When had she finally known that the man she loved had handed her a bomb to carry onboard a plane full of people?

She had been sitting in her assigned seat waiting for the plane to take off and get her the hell away from Berlin and all the sleazy people Jean-Philippe knew. She had welcomed the trip, even the idea of seeing her mother in New York was more welcome than the thought of another night in the business house on Oncle Tom Strasse. The package had been in her lap and she shuddered to think how casually she had handled it.

She had been told it was important documents. But when she picked it up, the weight indicated something of more substance than paper.

Jean-Philippe had handed her the plane ticket and given her instructions on the method of delivery during the layover at Heathrow. He would be joining her later, he'd told her. There was business to attend to in Berlin that required his attention. He had just flown back from the Middle East and she had picked up his extreme unease the minute she'd met him. Something had gone wrong with the "big deal" he had been working on for over a year now.

Perhaps it was the overly wrought explanation that had first triggered Hannah's suspicions after she'd boarded the plane and had a chance to think. She and Jean-Philippe were lovers, had been for two years. But they had known each other since childhood and as Jean-Philippe had entered the shadowy world of high level, black market oil trading in Berlin, Neeley had blindly followed. He'd never bothered to explain himself before so why the change?

It came to her as clearly as if the elderly man seated next to her had shouted it in her ear. *It was a bomb.* Neeley knew it with a certainty that pulsed through her stomach. She had to clench her teeth to prevent herself from screeching out her knowledge.

Many of the people Jean-Philippe was affiliated with had Middle Eastern names and the Arab world was frothing at the mouth to strike at the Americans. And the plane she was sitting on was an American carrier with many American passengers, most of them servicemen. And there had been much talk among Jean-Philippe's associates of a major deal in the works and the concern that the Americans would mess it up and if that happened, then there had to be payback. Had that just happened in Mogadishu? And was what she held in her hands the payback?

She'd looked up the aisle. The pretty American stewardess was greeting passengers hurrying through the door. Once that closed, there would be no way out.

Neeley stood, carefully holding the package under her arm. She mumbled apologies as she forced her way to the aisle and then to the front of the plane.

"We will be departing shortly," the stewardess said as Neeley approached.

"I don't want to go," Neeley muttered, her thoughts focused on getting off the plane.

She felt the weight in her hands. Jean-Philippe. His name rolled through her brain with the accent she had acquired from her summers in France. He had betrayed her and she didn't have a clue why.

There was nowhere she could go in the city. The only people she knew were Jean-Philippe's. All she had was the plane ticket. And what could she do about the bomb? It had to be several kilograms of explosive from the weight.

That was when Gant had appeared and changed everything.

Gant had simply reached out and taken the box. Neeley at first couldn't obey his simple command to follow, so frozen were the muscles in her legs. She finally walked empty-handed behind the tall American soldier. His face was leathery from exposure to the sun, his eyes bright blue. He wore a black leather coat and carried his bags and the box effortlessly even though his body looked gaunt, the skin tight against his cheekbones.

She remembered noting all these details of his appearance while she followed him out of the airport. She also remembered the lack of fear, now that the bomb was in his hands. She asked no questions and, when they arrived next to the battered Volkswagen in the long-term parking, she allowed herself to be tucked into the front passenger seat. She dimly remembered not being surprised as Gant squatted next to the open door and carefully opened the package, confirming her worst fear as he revealed the explosives. Without hesitation he began humming as he defused Jean-Philippe's lethal package.

No one approached them or even seemed to notice the oddly humming man hunched intently over his prize or the young girl rocking slowly to and fro inside the car. She guessed he was finished when he tossed the once again closed carton into the back seat. He was still humming as he walked around and climbed behind the steering wheel.

He reached out one large warm hand and clasped her knee. Neeley knew at once there was nothing sexual in the touch. He just wanted to give her some firm, physical contact, something to snatch her back from the mindless shock. Then he backed out of the parking slot, aimed the car for the American sector and asked if she was hungry.

Over ten years later, sitting alone, his grave nearby, she still remembered his first touch. It was as familiar and powerful as the last taste of Jean-Philippe's smiling lips.

Neeley shivered. There was much to be done before she left.

Gant had told her that he would find her something like the Bronx meeting for her to get money. She'd always wondered where his money came from but all he would say was that the government paid him every month for past services rendered. With his death that income would be gone and she'd be on her own.

Gant had talked of his root family rarely, telling her he had a mother and a brother. The mother lived somewhere in New York but Neeley had never met her and as far as she

knew neither had Gant in the time they were together. Of his
brother, Gant had also spoken sparingly. She sensed something dark between Gant and his brother Jack and she had
not pried. Gant's given name was Anthony, but she had
never referred to him by it or any derivation of it or heard
anyone else do it either.

He'd told her once his father had disappeared when he
was twelve, an odd choice of words that left many unan-
swered issues that Neeley had not probed into. He also had
someone he called his Uncle Joe, although Gant had indicated the man was not really blood, but a surrogate father
that had raised him in the years after his father's disappearance. This uncle had been the one to call Gant with the information on the drug deal.

"Then there are three other things you have to do," Gant
had added. He'd reached into his pocket and given her a key.
"This is for a locker in the bus terminal in Hartford, Connecticut. Go there. Get what's in it."

She'd taken the numbered key.

"Then go to Boulder." He'd smiled, recalling better days.
"Remember the climb we made in Eldorado Canyon? The
first route you led?"

Neeley had nodded. "Thin Air."

"There's something up there that you will need."

"And the third?"

Gant had pulled out a letter. "It's for my brother."

"How do I find him?" Neeley had asked.

"You'll meet someday. Trust me on that."

"How will I know him?"

Gant had given a wistful smile. "That won't be a problem."

And that had been it. He'd offered no explanation or hint
of what she would find in either location or how she would
find his brother. When she'd pushed him for more, he shook
his head. "I can't tell you what will happen to you once I'm
gone, all I can give you is what I had to keep the dead time
going." He'd paused and reached into his pocket, pulling out
a slip of paper. A phone number was written on it with a 212
area code—New York City. He'd given it to her. "That's Un-

cle Joe's number. If you really are in trouble and need help, call him. He knows your name. He's very"—Gant seemed to search for the word, then he smiled wistfully—"resourceful."

Then he'd tossed his empty beer into the grave and turned for the cabin. The gaping hole and his words had filled her thoughts those last few months. The hole became a symbol for the cancer that was killing Gant and she hated it. But she had always hated the dark small places that Gant insisted were really refuge. He would spend endless hours staring at the hole through the wide front window, wrapped in the big comforter as Neeley fought to keep the fire blazing. Gant had lost so much weight that she could easily carry him, but his voice remained strong as ever. He could no longer partic- ipate in her physical training but she still learned through his voice. He had tried to teach her everything he knew and had almost succeeded.

Last week she had finally filled the hole. He had died in her arms, his last words full of sorrow that he was leaving her alone and in some unnamed danger that she would have to work her own way out of. She had sat by the grave a day and a night, her voice a keening cry that echoed through the snow-covered mountains and stopped only by vocal cords too swollen to move. Then she had gone to the South Bronx and set up surveillance on the alley to do the first of her tasks.

Looking at the suitcase helped her forget the cold some- what. Everything had gone as expected, which surprised Neeley. She could hear Gant's voice: No matter how well you prepared and planned, there was always "Murphy" wait- ing to screw things up. Expect the unexpected and a whole slew of other sayings that Gant had harped on. The rules that he had given her one by one over the years, like other men gave the women they loved jewelry.

She checked the small pile of wood next to the fireplace. Enough to get it going. Then she'd have to break some out of the frozen stack outside and let it thaw in the fire. She looked around for paper to start the fire with.

After a moment, she quietly laughed. For all the preparation, she hadn't laid in any paper to start a fire when she got back.

She tramped outside the cabin to the pickup, opened the door and grabbed the newspapers she'd bought in town on the way through. She also retrieved the overcoat with the rifle attached inside.

On the way back to the cabin, she paused to appreciate the view. Gant may have hated the cold but he had loved the scenery. The cabin stood on the west slope of Mount Ellen. The glow of the rising sun glanced through the trees one hundred meters above, at the crest of the mountain. Laid out below, like a toy town, down over a thousand meters of altitude and about four kilometers to the northwest, she could discern a few twinkling lights in the tiny village of South Lincoln.

The town was where the paved road ended. To get here from there, Neeley had to put the truck into four-wheel drive and negotiate an old, overgrown logging trail that switched back and forth up the mountain. Gant had enjoyed the isolation.

The cabin didn't have much in the way of conveniences. Water came from a mountain stream, not more than ten feet outside the door; the quick flowing water didn't freeze, even in the coldest winter. Heat came from the fireplace.

Neeley stomped inside and laid the papers on the table. The light from the kerosene lamp highlighted her chilled breath as she quickly scanned the news. She had the late edition *New York Times* and the *Burlington Free Press*. The *Times* had a brief mention about the incident in the Bronx that must have made it in just before press time.

Neeley scanned the article and was satisfied that the official police statement was the usual doublespeak, which basically meant the cops didn't have the slightest idea who had done it. Which they shouldn't, Neeley reminded herself.

Curiously, the article didn't mention the destroyed drugs. Neeley had thought the police might have said something about that, but, on reflection, she realized that tidbit might be something they'd keep to themselves for a couple of reasons. It was their little secret to play against any suspects they might come up with; another might be because it would generate some sympathy for whoever had walked away with money. Cops were always afraid of self-styled vigilante killers: bad publicity and a bad example.

The local Vermont paper held nothing on the story. Killings in New York City were common and not especially newsworthy up here in God's country. Neeley crumpled the local, sheet by sheet and lined the bottom of the fireplace. She threw in some kindling and then laid a pair of logs on top. She squirted lighter fluid over the whole mess. Maybe not what Daniel Boone would have done, but she was too cold to worry about style. She threw in a kitchen match. Neeley quickly retreated as the fireplace exploded in flame. While she waited, she reached for the locker key that hung from a chain around her neck. She stared at it, knowing that she would have to be back on the road soon. There was much to do in the next several days.

The cabin was warmer and she finally took off her gloves and sat at her laptop computer. She hooked the modem to her cellular phone. They were the only modern conveniences on the hilltop. When they needed recharging, she plugged a special adapter into the truck's lighter outlet.

Gant had been impressed with the technology but had shown no inclination to spend time hooked into the machine. As much as Neeley had been willing to learn everything and anything from Gant, he had not been so inclined with her. Besides, as he'd put it, he trusted her to do those things that she knew how to do. Neeley had done work like this before, moving money and managing deals for Jean-Philippe in the gray world beyond national boundaries.

Neeley shook away those memories and settled to the work. For the next several hours Neeley immersed herself in the world of electronic banking and legalese.

When she was done, Gant's half of the money was ready to be dispersed to the various accounts that she held for him under different names once she deposited it. The people who depended on Gant would continue to get their monthly

stipends: his mother, his ex-wife, and the son that Neeley
had seen but never met.

Gant had so removed himself that beyond the checks,
there was little connection between Gant and the people he
left in his past. Neeley knew it had been his only fear at the
end other than leaving her alone. That he was shirking a responsibility. As though his death were his fault.

Late one night, half asleep since the pain injections she
was giving him were getting larger and larger, Gant had
talked about his son with her, more than he had ever talked
about it in all the years she'd known him. She had listened,
then told him she would continue his financial responsibili-
ties for the boy—now a young man—and that she would
covertly look in on him every once in a while as she and
Gant had done over the years. He had said nothing further,
but before she fell asleep with his thin, tortured body pulled
close to her, she felt a single tear slide onto her breast.

The fire had died down and Neeley knew it was time to
go. She packed her few things, and then went through the
cabin one last time. Gant's personal effects she had burned
in the fireplace right after he died. It was what he had
wanted.

His professional equipment was a different matter. That
was his legacy to her. The rifle she had used, night-vision
goggles, and the other gear that had been so useful in the
Bronx were just part of it. A dozen weapons' cases were
lined up near the wall and Neeley carried them out, carefully
tying them down in the bed of the pickup. A footlocker and
two duffel bags full of more gear she also hauled out and
lashed down. She covered the whole thing with a tarp, and
then locked the door to the camper shell.

Neeley closed the door of the cabin that had been her
home for so many years and knew she'd never return. She
surveyed the familiar landscape and felt the sharp catch in
her throat as her sight lingered on the patch of raw earth. She
had sanitized the cabin, thereby obliterating all traces of her
life with Gant.

Whoever came looking, and she knew from what Gant

had told her that someone would come, would find nothing. Neeley piled her bags in the passenger seat and climbed in. She slowly made her way down the cutbacks on the hill, her thoughts on what she knew, and more importantly, wondering what she didn't know.

Shivering from more than the cold, Neeley turned to the southeast, toward Boston where she would deposit Gant's half of the money. And from there—the small weight of the locker key pressed against her chest.

HANNAH MASTERSON OPENED THE DOOR and walked to the mailbox, a routine she had done for years. She returned clutching a wad of envelopes and newspapers. A quick check turned up no new postcards or letters from John. There were several bills, objects she would have carried to John's desk but now felt heavy in her hands.

She paused on the stoop to the large Tudor house and looked around, as if seeing the neighborhood for the first time. There wasn't a home in the Cedar Creek subdivision that was under half-a-million dollars and the lawns were all taken care of by professional services. She knew the people who inhabited each house on her street but she wouldn't consider any of them friends.

She had done the Cedar Creek social routine simply because it was what she was supposed to do as John's wife. She had made no special effort to cultivate friends after moving onto the street over three years ago. Now there was no one she could turn to, no shoulder to rest her head on and cry.

Hannah swung the front door open and walked inside. She headed directly for the kitchen, throwing the mail on the counter and pulling the bottle out of the dry bar. She poured herself an ample amount of alcohol then slumped down in her favorite chair, facing the large front windows.

She was surrounded by books. Thousands of them. John had always joked that if a nuclear blast went off anywhere, they were more than adequately protected from the nuclear fallout by the interior wall of books in the house. They had been Hannah's refuge over the years from a different kind of fallout from the world outside. John had supported her in building the walls of paper, constantly bringing home new books for her to read. They brought scant comfort now, though, as trouble had penetrated into the household.

Hannah thought about John. She had been nineteen when she met him in college. A sophomore, she had felt worldly and wise, especially since they met in an Elizabethan literature class, her turf, not his. John had been a major in graduate engineering; she an undergrad comparative literature major. He had immediately attracted her when he spoke of how important a classical education was for everyone. He was older than most of the other students, in his midtwenties and he never really spoke about how he'd spent the years before school, only telling her he'd been in the military. The mystery had deepened her attraction.

In John she had sensed a man who not only knew the concrete facts of how to live his life, but also was aware of the abstract ideas that would make life worth living. She had fallen for him quickly, especially since he projected such strong emotion toward her and wanted her so badly. She had never felt so needed.

Hannah laughed out loud, the sound echoing through the empty house. *Needed. What a word.* Her shock from the meeting with Howard was fading and anger was seeping through the cracks. She drained the glass and hurled it against the wall of the house that was no longer hers. "You son of a bitch!" she screamed.

CHAPTER

4

NEELEY WAS PARKED outside the Greyhound Station in Hartford, Connecticut. She looked at the thin manila envelope she had retrieved from the locker. She peeled away the tape and slid the contents onto her lap, wedging them up against the steering wheel. On top, there were two photos, a man and a woman. The man was a typical businessman in his gray suit. A little soft-looking with a red blush to his checks. A drinker, Neeley thought. The woman was more interesting, sharp looking with blond hair and dark eyes.

Neeley stared at the photos for a few moments, committing the details to memory.

There was a third item in the envelope. A piece of notebook paper with Gant's handwriting scribbled across it.

Dearest,
There are three things you must know in order to maintain the dead time: <u>Who</u>, <u>What</u>, and <u>Why</u> of something that happened years ago, just before I met you.
The man in the photo, John Masterson, knows the

What. Find him. He is in St. Louis working for Tyro
Technologies. The other person is his wife, Hannah.
  Who and Why will come out if you follow the right
path.
  Be careful. I've done my best. I'm sorry.
                                                    Gant

Neeley read the note once more. For all the years they'd
been together, there was still so much she didn't know.
There were no tears staring at Gant's writing. She'd spent
them on the mountain. She put the note and the photo on the
passenger seat and then weighed them down with the pistol
Gant had given her on her birthday two years ago.

The Glock Model 20 had been Gant's weapon of choice
and although initially Neeley had preferred the Model 17,
the smaller 9mm version, Gant had finally convinced her to
go for the larger caliber. His point was that 9mm was a
magic number in pistols and many variations of body armor
were designed for the magic number and that the 10mm slug
would penetrate and kill where the 9mm would just piss
someone off.

The Model 20 held 15 rounds of 10mm ammunition. It
had an integrated laser sight built into the gun, replacing the
recoil spring guide assembly, just below the barrel. Touching
the trigger activated the laser. With no external hammer, the
gun could smoothly be drawn without catching, and the
safety was built into the trigger allowing rapid fire. The finish was flat black, designed not to absorb light.

Gant had also taught her that the gun was only 50 percent
of the equation. The bullets were the other half. The rounds
in the gun had been hand-crafted by Gant for high muzzle
velocity and penetrating power. She had several spare magazines loaded with the same. She also had his loading equipment in the bed of the truck and had spent many hours at his
side practicing the art until her efforts matched his.

Neeley threw the truck into gear and headed for the interstate. She had a long drive ahead of her. As her tires rum-

bled, she kept her eyes on the road but her mind drifted to more memories of Berlin.

After defusing the bomb and leaving Templehoff, Gant took Neeley to a part of Berlin she had not seen during the time she had been there with Jean-Philippe. The sticker on the car windshield brought them a wave through at the base security checkpoint and suddenly they were no longer in Berlin or even in Germany. The American sector could have been any American army post back in the States.

They drove past large housing complexes and schools, small shops and administrative offices. Gant slowly pulled into a large parking lot and took an empty slot close to the building marked commissary. He left her the keys and promised to return quickly. She watched him disappear into the cavernous building and began to shiver. Jean-Philippe had urged her into the cutoffs and T-shirt that morning and she was beginning to understand why. He had hoped any suspicion would be allayed by the promising scenery of her bare skin. Now her skin was mottled by goose bumps and she felt more alone than ever before. She had no idea who the stranger was, only that she trusted him so far.

She watched the shoppers leaving the grocery store and felt her isolation grow. Who were all these women in khaki slacks and ponytails, their toddlers clutching tightly to hands or pant legs, any surface that offered protection? The people Jean-Philippe had associated with had all flashed large amounts of money and wouldn't have been caught dead in the outfits these people wore.

When Gant walked back through the electronic doors, Neeley studied her benefactor as he strode toward the car. He appeared to be in his early thirties and was large and powerfully built. He toted the bags as though they were empty, all the while scanning the area to his front and side. She supposed he was handsome in a masculine, rugged fashion but to Neeley that was no comparison to Jean-Philippe's delicate features and long curling hair. The thought of her lover's face rising above her brought tears to her eyes and she was using her fingers to wipe them away as the car door opened.

If Gant noticed her crying, he said nothing but he did nod toward the food as if it would banish her sorrow. "I wasn't expecting any company so the house is kind of bare."

Neeley grew nervous at the mention of his house.

As if sensing this, he offered her a large hand. "My name is Anthony Gant, but everyone just calls me Gant."

She took his hand with trepidation and mumbled, "Neeley."

"Well, Neeley, it seems we've been tossed together for a while. If it makes you feel any better, what happened this morning will be our secret. I've had stranger mornings."

Neeley looked at him. "If that's supposed to make me feel better, it doesn't. It's definitely been the strangest morning of my life and strange isn't even coming close. I could have been responsible for hundreds of deaths today. Do you have any idea how that makes me feel?"

Gant stared at her hard. "Actually, I do."

The conversation ended with that and they avoided even glancing at each other during the short trip to Gant's house.

Gant's home turned out to be part of a large multifamily dwelling made from the same yellow stone as the commissary. There were children everywhere. As Neeley and Gant walked the chalk streaked sidewalk to his door, they dodged bikes and skates and curious glances.

"This is the last place I'd expect a man like you to live," Neeley said. "Isn't your wife going to be surprised?"

Gant paused as he unlocked the door. "My wife's not here."

He pushed her through the door into the living room of the small apartment. "She left a few weeks ago and went back to the States with my son." He continued to talk as he carried the bags into the kitchen and unpacked them. "I can't really blame her. I've been gone eleven out of the last twelve months. Her note said if she was going to live alone, then she wanted to live alone. I was going to fly over and plead my case when I saw you at the airport."

He shook his head at her look of surprise. "Don't worry.

You haven't altered my family's life plan or anything. She wouldn't have come back and I was just going for myself. You know, to say I did, that I tried. My son barely knows who I am and the only way that would change is if I became someone I'm not. Sometimes it pays to know one's limitations as much as one's capabilities."

Neeley sank down on the Swedish modern couch and closed her eyes. There was something disturbing about what he said and yet he had saved her life and many more. She leaned her head back and was sound asleep when he returned with eggs and toast. He gently woke her. After eating, he took her to a small bedroom and she immediately crawled into the bed he offered and fell asleep once more.

She slept a long time, waking only once to note her surroundings. She was in a child's room, in the bottom bunk. She could distinguish the outlines of toys and spaceships and when she lifted her head to adjust the pillow, the faint moonlight fell on the happy faces of the most recent Star Wars characters. She fell back asleep as easily as throwing a switch.

When she awoke again it was light outside and there was a persistent tapping at the door.

Gant's voice was muffled but audible. "Neeley, are you awake?"

She threw back the comforter and tried to sit up but banged her head on the top bunk in the process. In the daylight she could see the entire room was an homage to Star Wars. Neeley felt sadness for the little boy who had left everything he loved. She knew exactly what that boy was feeling.

She walked out of the room. Gant was seated in a chair facing the front window, his fingers steepled, a cup of steaming coffee next to him, and one for her on a small card table.

"Do you know why you were given that bomb?" Gant asked.

Neeley suddenly felt tired despite her night's rest. She told Gant about Jean-Philippe, the strange people he associated with, and the last couple of years of her life. If he was surprised at any of it, he didn't show it.

"I don't know why Jean-Philippe wanted me dead," she concluded, which brought a ghost of a smile to Gant's lips.

"I doubt you were the objective of the bomb," he said. "You say he worked as an oil broker?"

"Yes," Neeley said. "There's a large black market for oil that can't go through normal channels, for example that coming out of Iraq despite the embargo. Jean-Philippe would put together the deals. He worked with a loose-knit group of men who did this."

Gant had nodded. "The shadow world. There's one for every niche and they all touch each other at some point."

Gant left her alone that day as he searched Berlin for her old associates. The business house was empty and wiped clean. The small group had completely disappeared, leaving no tracks of itself behind. Gant did as much as he could without arousing suspicion but he said little to Neeley about how his days were spent. She had enough awareness to realize that his place here was a cover; that he was beyond the Army, even beyond the classified Special Forces unit he was apparently assigned to in Berlin. A cover within a cover. There had been whispers among Jean-Philippe's friends of a special American unit hidden in Berlin, but nothing specific.

After a few days, Neeley questioned Gant about his work. They were watching the news and there was more coverage of the crisis in Mogadishu, the failed raid, and the attempts to get back the pilot.

"I had instructions to get the hell away for a while," he told her.

Neeley looked over from the television and President Clinton's haggard face as he discussed what had gone wrong in Africa. "What does that mean?"

Gant pointed to the television. "That. That cluster-fuck. They just want me to disappear for a while. I think I might make it longer than just a while. I've got a strong suspicion they may not want me back at all."

As if sensing her surprise, Gant continued, "Look, Neeley, we've been thrown together and it's going to take us some time to figure out what we're doing. I've been thinking about some things and I want to talk to you about them. In the meantime, just understand that I did some work for the U.S. government that those who gave the orders want to hide. I left what you would call the normal military a long time ago and I've been in the dark for so long it's hard to get used to talking at all. Another reason this house is empty.

"I've got only one real talent and it's the one my bosses needed the most. It's patience. I can sit in the same spot and wait. For days, weeks, even months if I have to. Then I can do what I'm told to do in an efficient manner. You're going to have to develop some patience. We have to sit quietly and come up with a plan. A good plan because we both have enemies out there in the world and we need to keep them off our backs. I'm not sure what exactly is going on and I don't know if I ever will figure it all out, but my priority right now is our safety so I'm going to see what kind of deal I can get for us."

That night, she slipped out of the little bunk bed and tiptoed to the other bedroom. She put her hand on the knob and slowly turned. The door silently opened onto more darkness. She felt in the dark for the furniture and, finding the bed, moved around to climb under the covers. Gant was a still form lying on his back. She started to slide her hand down his stomach but he stopped her with a firm grasp of her wrist. Holding her hand in his, he pulled her until his warm body was spooned behind her. "Why are you here?" he whispered in her ear.

"Because you've been so good to me. Taken care of me."

"I don't take barter, Neeley."

She started to answer and he hushed her. "We'll call this rule number two. Never use your body when you can use your brain. And Neeley, next time you sneak up on someone in the dark, remember it's more than likely they have a gun pointed at your face. I'll let it slide tonight because that's how you learn. Now, get some sleep. Big day tomorrow."

Neeley heard the soft click of the pistol hammer being lowered, then Gant's other hand was wrapped around her, holding her tight.

The day after she had snuck into Gant's room, her life changed forever. Gant told her that both her and his old lives were over. To try and go back would mean death.

A new identity would just be a way for her enemies to find her one day. Gant offered her a different life. A life in the shadows with him with no identity. She wouldn't need all the names and numbers that held the normal people to their place on the planet.

They disappeared together and started as teacher and pupil. They each had so much the other needed. Neeley remembered those years as physically exhausting yet intensely fulfilling. She traveled the world with Gant, learning the backdoors of most of the world's cities.

Gant kept his business to himself, and she didn't pry, but she knew he received money each month. He told her he was retired, but she wondered at that. She knew the less he told her, the more he was protecting her in the perverse way of the covert world where black was white and white was black and things only made sense to those who could think very differently from the average person in the street. He didn't tell her much about the Cellar, the organization he had worked for, just enough to let her know it existed.

The only constant was that Neeley learned and worked and sweated and every time she thought she couldn't possibly run another mile, do another pull-up, or strip down another weapon, Gant would be there, whispering encouragement sometimes, but always reminding her that she had to do it, she had no other choice. She had to be ready. It was strange, but Neeley had never pinned him down on what it was exactly she was supposed to be ready for. It just seemed a natural part of their strange life together to do all these things. It made the here and now important and deflected reflection on the past or concern about the future.

Now, driving through southern Connecticut, she still had no choice. She and Gant had been one. His legacy was all she had left. And it wasn't a legacy he could have just handed her. She would have to earn it as she had in the

Bronx. She knew that as instinctively as she had known it was a bomb on her lap on that plane so many years ago.

Gant may have died, but she would go on. She would have to pick up all that he had once held and make it her own in order to protect herself. The money was the first part. John Masterson was the second.

HANNAH WANDERED THE HOUSE. Only the main floor. Not the upstairs. That reminded her too much of her earlier major failure. The room she had spent months on readying for the baby. And then the miscarriage that had stopped those plans and that work abruptly.

That brought another choked sob to her lips. If they'd had a child would John have stayed?

She stopped in front of the large mirror in the foyer, staring at herself. She didn't have a clue why he had left; how could she know what would have made him stay? Her eyes shifted over her own shoulder to the wall behind her, the only one not coved in books. The photographs in the large frame. All of her and John. No one else. Not only no children, but no family for either of them.

She'd had no blood relations and neither had he. Another lock to chain them together. Two orphans against the world. John had never talked about his past before he met her and she had had no desire to talk about hers either. It was as if by being together they could start with a fresh slate.

Hannah reached forward and placed her hands against the mirror, staring at the reflected palms that met her own. Another sob forced its way out her throat and she slid down to the floor, until she was sitting in the foyer, her head against the glass, her palms still meeting the one of the crying woman the mirror showed.

After a few moments, she pushed herself away from the glass. She went into John's home office, where he had spent many nights working late. She'd never gone through his stuff, an implicit agreement between them that his space was

totally his own. What she had learned in Howard Brumley's
office removed that agreement. If John wasn't coming back,
then he had no rights in this house.

Hannah worked methodically, going drawer by drawer,
file by file.

Nothing. No sign of a mistress, a girlfriend, a boyfriend,
trouble at work, blackmail. Nothing that would explain his
sudden departure.

There were a couple of odd things, though, that Hannah
couldn't figure out. One was a folder labeled *H* that held a
thick sheaf of papers stapled together. On each page books
were listed by title, author, and publisher. Hannah recognized every title—they were the books that John had
brought home to her over the years. Each one had a little
check mark in pencil next to it. Where had he gotten such a
list, she wondered? There was nothing else in the file other
than the book list.

She shrugged it off, realizing it wasn't important at this
point.

She also found an old map, stuffed in the back of the bottom drawer of the filing cabinet. She took it out and opened
it. It showed southern Asia. There were two red lines drawn
on it, both originating in Turkmenistan. One went south and
west, crossing Afghanistan and terminating at the Arabian
Sea. The other went south and east across Afghanistan and
ending in Pakistan.

Hannah frowned. John's work at Tyro involved pipelines
so she assumed that's what these lines represented but she
had never heard of any such lines being built. The map was
old so she had to assume these were proposals that had never
come to fruition. She folded the map up and put it back in
the rear of the drawer.

The thing that was curious to her was that there was nothing in John's office that predated the time they met. No
school records, photos, army records—nothing. John had always kept a veil around his past, but it had never bothered
Hannah because she felt the same way about her past. The
last thing she had wanted to do with John was discuss her

childhood. They'd met in college and for her all that had occurred since then had been enough. Apparently not, she thought as she slammed shut his file drawer.

She looked at his computer. She pushed the on button and waited. It booted, but instead of getting a desktop, it stopped loading and a flashing box appeared, asking for a password. Hannah knew John worked with classified material at his job, so she figured this was just an extension of that. She tried his birth date, their anniversary, every name or number combination that came to mind. None worked.

Hannah sighed and leaned back in the chair. She was no closer to understanding why John had done what he did.

How could she have been so ignorant?

C H A P T E R

5

THE MAN HAD BEEN in the tree line for four hours, since well before dawn. It was cold in Vermont, especially at this elevation, but he wore heavy clothing underneath his white camouflaged Gore-Tex pants and parka. There had been no sign of life in the cabin. The information he'd received had listed a pickup truck as current mode of transportation for the owner of the cabin, but there was nothing parked outside.

There were tire tracks. As near as the man could tell from his position, they had been made before last night's light snowfall.

He scanned the cabin with the thermal scope one more time, picking up no heat sources. Still, he took no chances as he moved forward. He kept his silenced submachine gun at the ready as he crept to the cabin. It took him forty minutes of stealthy crawling to make it to the back wall. He waited there another fifteen, listening. Nothing.

He entered via a window, watching carefully for trip wires. He hated jobs like this, checking on another professional.

But there were no traps. The interior was empty except for

an old double bed. There wasn't even any food in the cabinets. He began his search, top to bottom, in a clockwise direction as he'd been taught and as he'd taught others. If there was anything hidden in the cabin, he knew he'd find it. After several hours he came to the conclusion that the place had been swept, and, most interestingly, swept by a professional.

Finally he paused at the small window and looked at the small mound of frozen dirt. He walked outside. Sighing, he pulled the head of a pick out of the backpack he wore and slid it onto the wooden handle that had been tied on the side of the pack.

Leaning the pick against his leg, he pulled out a pack of gum. Methodically, he unwrapped one stick, rolled it into a tight log and popped it into his mouth. He was careful to push the wrapper deep into his pocket and seal the Velcro flap before retrieving the pick.

He took off the parka. He was in good shape despite being in his mid-fifties. He had sandy hair, lightly tinged with gray and a bland face, one that would never be noticed in a crowd.

He began digging, eventually stripping down to his T-shirt as the work progressed. The dirt was like concrete for the first two feet, grudgingly chipping away. Then the going got easier. Eventually he got to the frozen body. He carefully brushed dirt away from the corpse. It was wrapped in a camouflage poncho liner. He peeled the liner away and looked at the face. The cold had preserved it. He stared at it for a minute, remembering other times he had seen that face, alive.

With great difficulty, he checked the corpse's clothes, going through the pockets. The only thing he found were a few strands of dark hair on the man's clothes. He peeled one loose and put it in a plastic bag, inside his backpack.

Satisfied, the man stood in the grave, straddling the corpse. He pulled a specially modified satellite phone out of his backpack and punched in a number. The signal was uplinked to a military MILSTAR satellite, frequency hopped and scrambled and then broadcast on a tight beam down to a receiver at the National Security Agency at Fort Meade, and then relayed to the bunker below ground.

"Yes?" a strangely mechanical voice asked.

"Anthony Gant is buried here, Mr. Nero." The man's accent was English, filtered by years of living in the States.

"You've confirmed this?"

"I'm standing on top of his body."

"How long has he been dead, Mr. Bailey?"

Bailey looked at the body. "Hard to tell. He's been in the ground for a while, but it's cold up here."

Even through the cipher scrambling Bailey picked up the sarcasm in the voice that rasped at him—no one else might have, but Bailey had known Nero for many decades. "More than a day? Less than a week? A month? A year? Since the Second World War?"

"I'd say about a week."

"Cause of death?"

What am I, Bailey thought, a pathologist? But he kept his tongue. "I can't tell."

There was a spate of coughing, and then the voice came back. "Is there a bullet hole in his forehead? Did he die violently?"

Bailey clenched his teeth, more from the cold than his superior's harsh words. The corpse looked gaunt, as if it had suffered a terrible disease. Bailey knelt down, tucking the phone under his chin. He lifted the body up, ignoring the cracking noise it made as it broke contact with the ground underneath. "No sign of violence. Looks like he was sick. He's wasted away. I'd say he weighed less than one-twenty pounds when he died."

There was a pause as Nero digested that information, then his rough voice came back. "Did you find the videotape?"

"No."

"You searched thoroughly?"

"Yes."

"Then we will have to assume whoever buried him has the object in question or at least knows where Mr. Gant hid it. Any clue as to that person's identity?"

"I would assume it is the woman from Berlin—Neeley."

"All right. That's all."

"What do you want me to do with the body?" Bailey asked.

"Rebury him. We will let Mr. Gant go in peace. We owe him that at least and his brother would expect us to." The phone crackled with what sounded like coughing before the voice came back. "Miss Neeley is another matter."

Bailey looked at the large pile of earth and shrugged. "Anything else?"

"Rebury him and return here." The phone went dead.

Bailey folded the phone, put it away, and returned to his work.

OVER SIX HUNDRED miles away, three hundred feet underground at Fort Meade, a wrinkled hand cut off the speakerphone that had been connected to Bailey. The hand then retrieved a burning cigarette and brought it to his lips.

The other man in the room watched as filaments of smoke escaped through the permanent tracheotomy in Mr. Nero's throat. The fingers that reached up to cover the hole were gnarled with age and tinged with nicotine. The face was hidden in the shadows, the three lights tilted toward the visitor. The tracheotomy was something that had gone into place when Nero had been out of action for several critical months prior to the 9-11 disasters.

When the cigarette was done, Mr. Nero capped the hole in his throat and reached for the hand-held voice box that substituted for his larynx. Nero's voice through the wand was harsh and crackly.

"As we suspected, Mr. Anthony Gant is no longer with us. There is no sign of the object you are concerned with and we do have to assume that someone was with Gant at his death due to the fact that he was given a proper burial."

The other man finally spoke. "Then we must act."

Nero placed the fingers of his free hand along the side of his face. "Senator, I understand you are concerned, but premature action might upset the balance we have so delicately maintained all these years and bring about that which you most fear. Gant did nothing to upset things all these years; I do believe the chances are his legacy will do nothing either."

The most powerful man on Capitol Hill shifted in his seat, trying to restrain his anger and concern. "I wouldn't have to be afraid of the past if we had terminated everyone who was involved in the incident and collected all their various objects of blackmail."

"Does everyone include you?" Nero asked.

"Don't get smart with me, Nero. I'm going to be nominated by the party. This couldn't have come at a worse time. I've got all sorts of congressional staffers from the other party sniffing around, looking for dirt."

"Nothing has happened," Nero noted, "other than Mr. Gant expiring, for which you should be grateful. If you wait long enough, this will most likely go away as the others die natural deaths also and their secrets die with them."

"Including you?" Collins snapped.

"Including me," Nero acknowledged. "Everyone has their time. I've been living on borrowed time for decades. The difference between me and you is that I am aware of it."

"What does that mean?" Collins demanded.

"You know so little," Nero said.

Collins didn't take the bait. "We don't know where Gant's videotape or the plans and contracts are. We don't know how the others are going to react to his death. I can't afford to sit around and have this hanging over my head. And remember, there are others besides me who were involved in this. A lot of powerful people who never agreed with the way you handled this."

"The way I've handled it has been successful so far," Nero said. "Every action has a reaction, even if it takes decades for that reaction to occur. The CIA has a term—blowback. I assume since you're on the Select Intelligence Committee, you've heard of it."

"When weapons we've sold end up getting used against us," Collins said.

Nero nodded. "I like to think in larger terms than simply weapons. The world is changing. As is apparent now that our enemies take different forms. Therefore we must take different forms."

"What the hell are you talking about?" Collins demanded, confused by the change in directions.

Nero ignored the questions. "I recommend we do nothing until something happens to force our hand."

Collins stood. "I'm not going with your recommendation. I want the others terminated and I want everything collected like it should have been years ago."

"Are you ordering me to do this?" Nero asked.

"Yes."

"You don't quite have that power."

"I speak for those who do and you know who they are," Collins hissed.

"You also understand my mandate," Nero said. "I am to do as ordered as long as it is in the best interests of the country."

"We—" Collins thumped his chest—"the politicians are elected to determine exactly that."

"In most cases that is true," Nero said, "which is why the Cellar takes action only infrequently. However, political squabbling between the parties might not be in the best interests of the country."

"You went along with the initial mission," Collins noted.

"The mission was recovery of damaging material," Nero said.

"The recovery turned out to be a disaster," Collins said.

"Everyone knows what happened in Mogadishu," Nero said. "They even made a movie about it."

"But people don't know the real reason it happened."

"The fake reason was real enough," Nero said. "Or else I would not have allowed the mission. The failure had nothing to do with the fake or real mission. That was the vagaries of battle."

"Damn you Nero." Collins fought to get under control. "At the time the material recovered wasn't that big of a deal," Collins said. "Recent events have changed that. Regardless, you're involved."

Nero's wand made a scratching noise that might have been laughter. "I am always involved."

"Just do what I told you to," Collins snapped.

Nero regarded the other man, dressed in his finely cut suit for several moments.

"If you don't act, I'll get the Agency involved," the Senator threatened.

A gargling sound came out of the wand. It took the Senator a few moments before he realized it was indeed laughter. Nero inclined his head. "As you wish."

Collins stalked out of the office. It was only when he was in the elevator heading toward the surface that he realized Nero had never really answered him.

CHAPTER

6

IT WAS A SIMPLE SHOT. Just a few feet to the hole, but Hannah watched as her putt veered to the left and threatened to leave the green. She turned and gave her partners a feeble grin. "I guess I'm not having a good day."

"No kidding," Sara muttered as she marked the scorecard, then selected her club and moved forward.

Rita and Amelia were with their own cart, about thirty feet away. It was a windy day and Hannah could catch snatches of their conversation.

"Michael said there's a lot of trouble at John's firm," Rita was saying. "He said everyone's in a tizzy. I also heard that there's another woman involved."

"Another woman?" Amelia asked, her voice rising, then just as quickly going down. "Who?"

"I don't know. Some secretary at one of those firms they contract with."

Amelia frowned. Hannah was watching her out of the corner of her eye. For all Hannah knew, there was another woman, but she was pretty sure that was just a juicy tidbit someone had added for interest's sake. Hannah had watched the gossip hotline for years, never participating. She couldn't claim ethical responsibility, rather it was a case of not giving a damn. She had never anticipated having the spotlight thrown on her.

"I talked to Celia Brumley," Amelia added her own inside scoop. "She didn't say anything about another woman, but she did say John took everything. There's some question of criminal acts."

"My God!" Sara exclaimed. She looked over at Hannah, who raised her eyes and met the gaze. Sara's face twisted in what must have been an attempt at a smile but looked more like a grimace.

Hannah wasn't surprised. She knew the story would make the rounds quickly. She wished she could gripe to John that their lawyer had a big mouth. She walked toward her cart, causing the women to quickly cease their conversation. Hannah wondered how much longer she could pretend. Yesterday afternoon she had called Dr. Jenkins. She'd been going crazy and she knew she needed help. She'd made an appointment and asked him if there was anything she could do in the meantime. "Keep to your routine," had been his sage advice, so she had kept this engagement even though it was the last thing she wanted to do.

She only played twice a year when the Junior League held its tournament. Hannah wondered why she should be worried about questions right now when the ship was going down with all hands, but she felt she had to trust the psychiatrist somewhat. He was a professional after all.

Now, after six holes of questioning looks and catching bits of their muttered confabs behind the carts whenever she putted, she decided that other's advice should be given less consideration than her own instincts.

Amelia and Rita climbed into their cart without a backward glance and that left Hannah with Sara who had been probing Hannah at every opportunity. Sara had displayed enough disbelief when Hannah mentioned that John was on a business trip to alert her that the cover story was wearing thin. People were whispering and Hannah had lived in Cedar Creek long enough to know how quickly the winds of gossip fanned a rumored whisper into a bonfire of truth. She had been hoping to keep things quiet until she had a plan, but that option was fading fast. She wished she had known this before driving to the country club. She could have saved the money on the cart.

The change was coming, Hannah could feel it. The gulf separating her from the other women was opening at her feet and they were on the other side. They had been acquaintances for years, going to each other's parties, listening to troubles, dishing out sympathy and compliments with equal abandon.

Hannah slid into the passenger side of the cart and glanced at her partner. Sara was a lovely woman who lived her life as if there was going to be a quiz at the end. She was always asking questions. Her current silence meant that she'd gleaned enough information to have answered all the necessary questions and graded the test. Hannah knew she'd failed. She was no longer a player in Sara's eyes. She had lost her glove so nobody was going stand around and pitch to her any more. If only they knew the entire truth, Hannah thought.

Looking at the cart ahead of them, Hannah was more surprised by Amelia. Theirs was a relationship she had thought was based on a little bit more than my wife-life is better than your wife-life. Today, Amelia acted as if she were disappointed in Hannah. She had the perturbed look of a woman whose guest list has just dropped to an odd number. Amelia had her head bowed toward Rita as their cart sailed along the smooth expanse of concrete that slithered the course like some obscene tapeworm. Hannah wondered what the two were saying now.

They were both married to doctors, or as they said: physicians. Left alone so much by the almighty beeper they had naturally gravitated together. Their empty hours were spent sucking each other in with a ferociousness that left them both overwhelmed but justified. They had seven children between them and were always on the verge of a teenage, teething, bedwetting crisis. In that particular area, Hannah had been an outsider so she had never really fit in.

Sara finally broke the silence and was starting to talk in general terms about the museum fund-raiser. With a start, Hannah realized her friend's real unspoken quandary: What to do about the fund-raiser? Was it appropriate to leave Hannah in the position of chairing the publicity committee or should they replace her? If they replaced her, how would she respond? If they didn't, how would the thing turn out? If Hannah went by herself would their husbands ask her to dance?

Hannah could have walked away right then and there. Maybe she should tell them she didn't have the money for a ticket. Waking up this morning there had been a slim hope she would find some help among her three acquaintances. That hope had died as she'd sensed their growing coldness, as if she had a sickness that they could catch. Sara's musings about the fund-raiser had struck to the heart of the matter. The priority here was appearance first; substance if you could spare the effort.

Hannah also realized that much of this was her own fault. She had never gone out of her way to cultivate any special friendships. She was in this cart because of the position she filled in their social circle, not because of who she was. She was a piece that could easily be replaced if broken and with John gone, there was no doubt she was broken.

Hannah took the easiest way out for all involved. As the cart pulled to a halt, she briefly touched Sara's arm. "Sara, I know it's late to bring this up, but I don't think I'm going to be able to attend the fund-raiser. The publicity is almost all wrapped up and, since I can't attend, maybe you could take over for me?"

Sara put her hand to her chest. "Oh, I really don't know, Hannah." She turned to the other two women waiting for them. "Hannah doesn't think she can make the fund-raiser and wants to know if I can finish the publicity."

Hannah realized the tone indicated Sarah wasn't phrasing it as a question.

"What?" At least Amelia had the grace to appear surprised and a little bit worried.

"Oh, come now." Rita had a strange look on her face. "We've been working on that for months now. Certainly you can make it."

"I don't think John will be back from his conference by then," Hannah lied, knowing, even as she said it, that it was foolish to pretend anymore.

Amelia's eyes drew together. "Well, that's not a problem. Come by yourself then."

"I don't think—"

"I can understand if you didn't want to come," Sara said quickly.

Hannah felt a sharp irritation. Sara was always worried that someone wanted to steal her short, fat doctor from her. Hannah imagined Sara's biggest concern at the moment was that Hannah was the dreaded "unattached" woman. If only I was unattached, Hannah thought, rather than locked to a man who had skipped out after breaking several laws.

"Hannah, if you want to talk . . ." Amelia began. The other two women looked exceedingly uncomfortable. They wanted the scoop but they didn't want the emotions, not here on the country club golf course.

Hannah didn't even bother to muster up a reply. She looked away, so angry that she worried she couldn't control it. Anger at John was just the tip of the iceberg. She knew the unseen bulk of the anger was toward herself and that was a bitter realization to accept. She blinked rapidly. On a hill near the tree line she thought she saw someone, a tall, dark figure in a long coat.

"Hannah?" Amelia said, cutting into her thoughts. Amelia pointed to the tee. "Your turn, dear."

Hannah turned to look again for the odd figure; there was only the shadow of the trees.

*   *   *

THE CONVERSATIONS among Hannah Masterson and her golf partners intrigued Neeley. She could hear almost everything from her position at the top of the hill overlooking the course. The small directional mike hooked to the earpiece worked quite well. Definitely worth the exorbitant fee Gant had paid for it. Even more intriguing were the whispered discussions among Hannah's golfing part-ners when she was out of earshot. Hannah was a woman with a large problem and that meant Neeley had a problem. It was John she needed to find according to the information she had and he was gone.

The last few hours of watching Hannah had left the rather frustrating impression that the woman had no clue of her husband's activities or whereabouts. It appeared that not only had John Masterson gone under, but he had also left his wife high and dry. Of course, it was also very possible that all this was a smokescreen left behind by John to confuse his trail and Hannah knew where he was. Regardless, Neeley recognized this was more than coincidence.

Neeley knew time was of the essence. The Cellar had to know that Gant was dead by now. Which meant that whatever ace he had held up his sleeve to protect both of them from the Cellar now had to be up her sleeve. But John Masterson held part of that unknown card.

Gant had told her, and she had known from her own experience, that a person never truly retired from the covert world, no matter what part you played or who you worked for: government spy, contract worker, terrorist, hit man, it didn't matter. Once you were in the only way out was death. Or having a lot of money to be able to cover one's trail, which was why Gant had kept a line into his Uncle Joe in New York City for so many years. Even the money though, wouldn't be enough. You needed "leverage" as Gant called it and he'd had it. He'd never shared it with her because that was part of his provision with the Cellar to keep his end of the deal in balance.

Neeley didn't know much about the Cellar because Gant hadn't known everything and he'd been reluctant to talk much about it with her. He understood that knowledge could be a very dangerous thing in the covert world. He had told her that he'd been contacted by the Cellar while he was still in the army, working in the Special Forces, well before he met her in Berlin. He'd done occasional, outside the line of military duty, jobs for the Cellar.

When they'd disappeared out of Berlin, Gant had left the army behind. And Gant's leverage had bought them not only that freedom but a monthly paycheck from the Cellar in return for his silence.

And now she was on her own and she needed to know what Gant and John Masterson had shared. Neeley felt foolish on the hill, directional mike in the briefcase at her side, earplug in, standing in the shadows. Worse than foolish, she felt vulnerable. She didn't have a very good cover story for her presence.

Neeley stiffened. Hannah Masterson looked straight up the hill at her. Neeley felt a shiver as they made distant eye contact. Neeley turned and walked away, out of sight. Returning to her truck, Neeley drove it to a point where she could wait, unobserved, for Hannah to leave the country club.

After forty-five minutes, her wait was rewarded as the black BMW pulled out. Neeley followed at a discreet distance and, when she was sure Hannah was returning home, she drove in another direction. She parked the truck over three kilometers away from Hannah's house.

Hannah lived in Manchester, a wealthy suburb to the west of St. Louis. The neighborhood was a juxtaposition of forest and development. Neeley had parked just off the main strip, Manchester Road, in the lot of a small shopping center where the truck would not stand out. The forest started right behind the stores.

Neeley turned on her hand-held Global Positioning Receiver. A flashing question mark appeared in the center of the screen for about ten seconds, then the receiver triangulated on the closest three global positioning satellites and locked in her position. Neeley entered Hannah's address in the hand-held GPR. Then she punched the "go-to" button.

An arrow went from her position toward the house. Using the GPR Neeley moved unerringly through the woods to come out right behind Hannah's house.

The street Hannah lived on, Cedar Creek, was a dead end. Hulking, brick houses lined the way, evenly spaced apart, separated by the price of a lot of land. On Neeley's side, behind the Masterson house, the backyards ended in a tree line that extended back to a creek almost half a kilometer away from the shopping center. Neeley had followed that creek most of the way coming here. She'd climbed up over the bank and moved forward until she could see the back of the house.

Neeley had gotten the address from the phonebook. She'd checked it the previous night with a drive-by. That exercise had been dangerous, dead end street and exclusive neighborhood, but she was from out of town, and as such could have easily explained her presence to being lost. A weak cover but one she had felt would be sufficient.

Neeley pulled out a pair of field glasses and focused on the back of the house. She scanned the facade and frowned. No sign of life, but she was surprised, and pleased, that all the windows were basically uncovered except for a frame of drapes. She flicked left to the neighboring house and checked it out. Same setup. Neeley thought about that for a second. Why have curtains back here anyway? No one should be looking in except woodland creatures. Still, she couldn't imagine living inside such an open structure—it practically invited a sniper to take a shot.

Neeley checked each window, cataloging the room beyond according to function. Bedrooms and bath on the top floor. The ground level was oddly shaped. The center of the back bulged out and a large window, slightly to the left of that center bulge, revealed what she supposed was the master bath. Neeley grinned as she compared the size of this one room to the entire inside of Gant's cabin and realized his wooden palace was several square feet short. To the left of the bath were the only windows with heavy curtains interdicting the view. To the right, on the ground floor, was the kitchen.

A light caused Neeley to shift left. She watched as Hannah walked into the bathroom. Her hair was disheveled and she wore a floor-length robe. She stood in front of the mirror for almost thirty seconds without moving. Hannah's position was directly in front of the huge window that must have been above a proportionally large tub that Neeley could just make out the far edge of.

Neeley twisted the focus knob, straining to see what thoughts were reflected on Hannah's face as she tugged the robe off her shoulders. After a few moments Hannah turned toward the window and then disappeared from view as she stepped into the tub. Neeley lowered the glasses and relaxed for a few moments.

Neeley looked back at the bathroom window. She could still see in despite the gathering steam. Hannah stood so quickly the water sloshed over the edge of the tub. Neeley followed window to window as Hannah wandered, naked, into the kitchen, picking up a drink.

Hannah strolled back to the bathroom and settled back into the tub, drink on the edge. Neeley watched as Hannah finished her drink. Neeley didn't know if Hannah knew anything about her husband's past activities or present location, but the bottom line was that she was the only link Neeley had to John Masterson.

HANNAH SLID into the hot water and pondered the recent developments in her life in a distant reflective manner. When her own parents had died, Hannah had gone to live with the first of a succession of foster families. Although she had been only six, Hannah had felt very separate from the members of her new family. She had tried hard, but she had never again felt like part of a family. Even with John she had sometimes wondered if she was forever meant to be an outsider. He had always been so secretive about his life before he met her and rarely ever talked about his work at Tyro Oil.

Hannah realized that John's leaving had taken something very important from her life. She wasn't exactly a soon-to-

be-divorced woman; she was a gardener without a garden, a
shepherd without a flock. John had been her excuse not to
think, not to dwell on her life by itself. His life had required
lots of support and Hannah had allowed his daily existence
to become her focus. Had that been love? Hannah uncon-
sciously pushed her wet hair from her face and forced her
thoughts elsewhere.

She looked down at her submerged body. It was a good
one, not perfect but good. Slim with full breasts and a nice
feminine flair at the hips. John had loved her breasts, especially braless under those silk blouses he bought her.

Eyes tightly closed, body completely still, she allowed the
water to envelop her with its heavy weight. Hannah suddenly
started, realizing she had briefly fallen asleep. A person
could drown like this, she realized. Using a towel, she wiped
some steam from the mirrored wall across from her. The
woman in the mirror appeared to be alive. She crossed her
slim legs yoga-style under the water and leaned forward to
stare directly into her pupils. After her parents died, she had
spent hours staring in mirrors, accepting that because there
was a reflection she was alive, that she did have substance.

She reached toward the towels piled on the tub edge next
to the wall. Her hand slid under the pile and her fingers
curled around the handle of a knife. She pulled it out and
stared at it in the mirror, holding it between her and the
glass. She turned the point toward herself and placed it between her breasts. Her breathing grew shallow.

She felt the pressure of the point as if it were happening to
someone else.

Hannah suddenly stood and grabbed a towel. She dried
off and put her robe on, then made her way to the kitchen,
glass in hand. She poured herself another drink and turned
on the TV mounted on the kitchen counter. She blindly
grabbed a book and took it with her to the couch. She went
over to the couch, the noise of the TV a comforting distraction behind her and began reading until her head nodded forward and she fell asleep.

* * *

DEEP IN THE SHADOWS, Neeley hadn't moved. She considered options, but then realized there weren't many courses open to her.

Neeley took one final look at Hannah asleep on the couch. Neeley felt reasonably confident Hannah wouldn't be doing anything else tonight. There was no guarantee of that, but she couldn't stay here forever just watching. She doubted very much that John Masterson would show up in the middle of the night. She could think while she moved.

Neeley slid the field glasses into the backpack and threw it over her shoulders. She moved through the darkened woods, heading back for the truck, not needing the GPR to find her way back. After fifteen minutes, Neeley came to the parking lot. Before leaving the shadows, she scanned the street and the other lots. There were no other vehicles that looked like surveillance. There was no reason why there should be, but Neeley never took chances.

Neeley drove without thinking. She pulled the pickup into the underground garage at the hotel and parked. She took the elevator up to the second floor and went into her room, leaving the lights off. Always the second floor—low enough to be able to get out the window, but not the first floor where it would be easy for someone to get in the window.

Pushing the bed aside, Neeley stripped and stood in front of the large mirror that topped the dresser. Slowly she started stretching, working from her neck down. After years of intense work, she could finally do a complete split of her legs to the sides and, after a few minutes, she got down all the way. There, spread on the floor, she bent over and pushed her hamstrings even farther, touching her forehead to her knees. The strain on the muscles felt good.

Satisfied she was loose, Neeley stood back up, faced the mirror and began the first kata. Low block left. Sliding step combined with middle punch. Reverse. Low block right. Sliding step with middle punch. Ninety degrees left. Middle block left flowing into a snap kick to the face. Middle punch. The first kata was forty-eight movements and took her almost a minute.

Neeley liked the discipline of the katas, the formalized movements required of martial arts students. She enjoyed watching herself in the mirror. Her muscles rippled and flowed as she blocked, punched, chopped, and kicked. The only thing lacking was an opponent. She moved without a noise. Even the required jump kicks were deadly silent on the room's carpet.

Katas one through eight, those required of the level one black belt, took almost ten minutes. Neeley repeated the cycle ten times: eighty complex minidances. By the end, the sweat was pouring off her. As Neeley finished the tenth number eight she drew her fists together in front of her eyes and slowly brought them down together in front to her waist. Feet shoulder width apart, she stood that way for a long minute, arm and chest muscles vibrating from the pressure she was exerting on the fists.

A vision of Gant passed across her eyes and was reflected in the mirror. The discipline of the art slid away. In one fluid movement she slid her right leg back, reached across her chest with her left fist and then pulled back with that same fist toward her side as her right fist flashed forward toward the mirror, push-pull, the essence of power. Some remnant of sanity stopped her fist a scant inch from the flat surface of the mirror and the projected image of Gant.

Neeley shivered as she realized what she had almost done. The ridges of muscle across her stomach and chest relaxed as she took a deep breath. Neeley turned to the bed and collapsed across it.

CHAPTER

7

HANNAH GROGGILY PUT HER ARM over her eyes to shield them from the bright morning sun. She rolled away from the huge palladium windows that allowed the unfiltered light to blaze through their high arches. John's windows, she thought. Those two windows had probably cost more than the first house she was sent to in Kansas. She raised her head from the pillow to check the time and was hit with a tremendous wracking pain that told her she had once again drank too much.

She tried to think of a good reason to get off the sofa and had just about decided there wasn't one when the phone rang. She reached across and grabbed the phone. "Hello," she croaked in a voice husky enough to cause concern.

"Hannah Masterson?" a female voice tentatively inquired.

"Yes?"

"I'm just confirming your appointment today with Doctor Jenkins."

"Jenkins," Hannah repeated. "Oh, yeah, right. I'll be there."

"See you at eleven." The phone went dead. Jenkins. Hannah had been seeing him intermittently for about five years. She'd gone the first time at John's insistence after the miscarriage. She wasn't sure the psychiatrist was doing her much good but Howard's urging had spurred her to make the appointment and she figured now that she was locked in, she might as well go, considering she'd be charged whether she were there or not.

Hannah put her feet on the ground. She looked around the room, remembering the time she had painted the walls, when her greatest concern had been making sure the paint color matched the curtains.

The doorbell echoed through the empty house. Hannah threw on a robe and staggered to the front door.

Amelia Lewis looked surprised for only a moment, and then she walked through the open door and set down a folder on the foyer table. Hannah searched her muddled mind for the proper role.

"I have the information you need for the fund-raiser," Amelia said.

Hannah looked at the folder. "I'm sorry Amelia but I thought—"

Amelia held up a hand. "Listen, Hannah, I know something's going on. But there's no need for you to bury your head in the sand. If you don't want to talk about it, that's your business, but remember, I am here for you. I don't think you should just chuck everything."

Hannah bit back the insane laughter that welled in her chest. "*I* didn't chuck everything, Amelia."

Hannah could almost hear the synapses connecting in the other woman's head. Amelia fidgeted, looking very uncomfortable and concerned.

"Well, come in," Hannah said, more to get her out of the foyer and view of the street than anything else. She led Amelia to the kitchen. "Care for a drink?"

There was a part of her that took pleasure from the shocked look on Amelia's face.

"Hannah, what's going on?"

"Oh, come off it," Hannah said as she poured herself a glass full of scotch. "I'm sure Celia has filled everyone in."

Amelia's face tightened slightly. "John really left you?"

" 'Left me'?" Hannah repeated.

"You shouldn't blame yourself for what happened, Hannah."

"Oh, that's good," Hannah said. "I'm not blaming me for John. I'm blaming me for me." She saw the lack of comprehension on Amelia's face and knew they were so far apart now, in just a few short days, that they could never really talk again. There was no common ground for understanding.

Hannah knew deep in her heart that there had never been any to start with. She was here because of John. None of these other women had been raised as wards of the state, moving from foster home to foster home, seen the things she'd seen at such a young age. She had tried so hard to pretend but ultimately she had failed at this life. She didn't know yet how she had, but there was no doubting now that she had. Staring at Amelia, Hannah felt something shift inside of herself. The pretend Hannah was dead—the thing she wasn't sure of was who was the real Hannah?

"Hannah—" Amelia began. "Well, you know, I mean, there—" she sputtered to a halt, out of gas in uncharted territory.

Hannah took another drink. "Sure you don't want some?"

"Hannah! You need to pull yourself together!"

"Why?" Hannah asked. "I *was* together. I got abandoned, so being together that way, your way, this way—" Hannah waved her hands, taking in the house—"didn't work too well. Don't I get to fall apart first before I have to be *together* again?" Hannah felt something rise in her chest. "Don't I get to be upset for a little while? I got screwed, Amelia! More than screwed. Don't I get to be angry? Pissed off? Just for a little while?"

Amelia was backpedaling. "I have to go."

Hannah didn't follow her to the door as she finished her drink.

*   *   *

NEELEY PULLED her backpack from under the bed. Grabbing the locked trunk from the hotel room's closet, Neeley dialed the combination and swung up the lid. There were several small plastic cases inside and Neeley sorted through. She'd planned all this last night as she lay in bed after her workout. She knew that Gant probably would have kicked in the door last night at Hannah's house and forced her into giving up John's location; if she knew it. Neeley preferred a less direct approach.

Gant had lectured endlessly about women having the same violent capabilities as men, but he had usually been discussing terrorists or criminals. Neeley had argued vainly that while women were just as susceptible as men to emotional inducements to violence, women on the whole required those inducements and seldom resorted to violence for the act itself whereas men would maim and kill without much reason. Neeley had often wondered which gender was the more realistic. She also knew that despite her observations, it was dangerous to classify people into groups. Gant had always said that you could never really tell about a person's true character until you saw how they acted in a crisis.

All the previous night she had pondered the problem and her only solution seemed to be to carefully monitor Hannah Masterson while she tracked husband John through other means. A very important question that nagged at Neeley from the moment she found out John had gone under was *why* had he done that? Had he heard of Gant's death? Or was something else going on? Had the Cellar already moved on John Masterson? But if that was so, why had the Cellar left Hannah dangling? The biggest issue to be resolved was what was the connection between Gant and John Masterson?

Neeley transferred the needed items from trunk to backpack and then relocked the former. She wore a pair of faded blue jeans and a black windbreaker over a T-shirt. Throwing the backpack on her shoulder she headed out, locking the door behind her.

She looped around the city, melding with the flow of the early morning rush hour, careful to observe all traffic rules. Neeley didn't need to consult the GPR to get to Manchester. Once she navigated somewhere she could always get there again.

Soon after parking the pickup truck in the same spot, she was at her perch behind the log. She pulled out the glasses and scanned.

Hannah was at the kitchen putting some dishes in the sink. Then she turned and headed for the bedroom.

IN HER CLOSET, Hannah scanned the racks for something appropriate. It was hard to concentrate. She could hardly decide what to wear to see her shrink, much less how she was going to handle the meeting. A part of her wondered if he'd still see her given that John's insurance was probably going to disappear soon. She'd never particularly felt that Jenkins had much empathy for her. Hannah had found the dialogue once a month since she started seeing him to be intellectually stimulating but of little use otherwise. But John has insisted she keep going and she had no real reason not to, so she'd continued.

She turned on the shower and, as the steam flowed over the top of the glass door, pulled off her nightclothes. She stepped into the hot spray and let the water pound some of the tension from her back and shoulders. She put both of her hands against the tile and leaned forward until she felt a comfortable stretch in her legs.

She stood in the shower a long time thinking of how she had let herself be led into this gilded cage of a marriage. There was a truth somewhere, a reason she had settled for so little while foolishly believing she had so much.

She towel-dried her hair. When her hair was reasonably dry, she quickly applied her makeup using extra concealer to cover the dark smudges under her eyes. When she finished her face, she started back on her hair, throwing her head down and brushing it so hard she could feel the tugs at the roots. Done, she took one last look in the mirror and then pivoted out of the room.

Forgetting the earlier quandary of what to wear, she grabbed the first dress off the rack and slipped it on. She stepped back to look at herself in the mirror. The Ann Klein dress fit perfectly and the warm peach color was good with her hair and eyes. That made her feel slightly better.

She walked to the kitchen, grabbed her keys and purse and went out the front door.

NEELEY CHECKED LEFT AND RIGHT. No sign of life. She was glad that the houses were spaced well apart. Neeley jogged downhill and was at the back of the house in less than twenty seconds. She knelt at the patio doors and pulled out a specially made tool. It looked like a set of extremely thin needle nose pliers. The name of the security company on the warning signs posted on all the windows of the Masterson residence had alerted her to what she would need.

She slid the thin edges of the tool between the door and frame and pushed it down toward the floor. Four inches from the ground she felt an obstruction. Neeley slid the tool back slightly and opened the jaws, then reclamped them on the mechanical sensor that was pressed against the inside of the door. She locked the jaws in place and folded the handle over, hooking the adjustable catch on it over the edge of the molding on the outside of the door. All set.

Neeley picked the lock and entered. The pliers held the alarm sensor in place as the door opened. From kneeling to entry had taken ten seconds.

Closing the French door, Neeley paused, scanning the immediate surroundings. She worked top to bottom, left to right, in steady arcs. Smoke detectors in the ceiling corners. No sign of any internal alarm system. No rug on the floor, which precluded ground sensors unless the Masterson's had put some extremely sensitive—and expensive—ones under the tiles. Neeley doubted that.

Her eyes went back to the bookcases that lined almost

every wall. She'd never seen this many books outside of a library. And she could tell they weren't for show as there were numerous well-thumbed paperbacks nestled among leather-bound hard covers. Titles were jammed horizontally on top of rows, filling every available space. Who had that much time to read all this, Neeley wondered?

She had planned out her movements the night before based on the observations of the interior that she was able to make from the outside. Her first move was to the portable phone in the kitchen. She opened the battery case on the backside of the handset, pulled out the rechargeable battery and replaced it with one she had brought with her. The phone would still work, but now it would also simultaneously transmit on a second frequency.

She moved to the stove hood and unclamped the filter. Reaching up as far as her arm would go; she attached a tiny magnetic transmitter to the metal. Backup if the portable phone was taken out of the room.

Neeley turned. Dining room next. She paused in the entranceway and checked it out. Looked clean. She moved along the wall and used a Swiss army knife to unscrew the grating over the air vent. The third bug was in place.

Next the foyer. Neeley stepped into the large open area at the bottom of the double staircase and froze. Her eyes were riveted on a small plastic box in the far corner of the ceiling, pointed at the front door. She slowly looked up and saw a similar box in the corner above her, pointing in the same direction as the other. Neeley slid her feet back and reentered the dining room. Infrared sensors. That wasn't good, but not unexpected. She was prepared for the possibility. Neeley considered and made a tactical decision. The foyer wasn't that important and the mikes she had planned for the den ought to pick up conversation there unless they were masked by a TV or other noise emitter in a closer location.

Neeley turned and went around the back of the dual staircase to the den. She checked that out. No sensors there. If there were more IRs than those two out front they would logically be near the master bedroom. On the way across the den, Neeley pressed another bug into the flue of the fireplace.

She paused at the short hall leading between the master bath and a room off to the right. The main bedroom was ahead. Lurking above the door to that room was another IR sensor. Unlike the foyer, this one would have to be dealt with. The master bedroom couldn't be ignored.

Neeley slid her backpack off and pulled out something that looked like a small hand-held searchlight. She plugged it into a wall socket and flipped the switch to on. Nothing apparent happened, but Neeley knew that the bulb was throwing out intense infrared light, enough to blanket any movement she might make. She'd been half-afraid that simply turning on the emitter would trip the alarm, but had taken the chance. The sensor worked off of movement and variation. The solid beam from her light changed the level of IR to one that allowed her to move freely. The electronic engineer in desperate need of money who had sold it to Gant had assured him that it would work on most home IR alarm systems.

All this gear was Gant's. He had taught her how to use it and it was part of his legacy to her. Some men left insurance policies and mutual funds, Gant had left her the tools of breaking and entering along with assorted weapons. More importantly, Gant had left her with knowledge and experience.

Leaving the light in place, she crossed the hall and entered the master bedroom. This was the only room she had not been able to see from the outside. Neeley stared at the massive four poster bed against the far wall for a minute. The bed was made perfectly. Neeley bet that if she checked, the top sheet was upside down so the flowers would be right side up at the blanket fold. Her grandmother in France had taught her to make a bed like that and she imagined that Hannah had been taught the same.

Neeley moved to the nightstand and bugged the phone. That one would be good for both the phone and the room. All the bugs were voice activated so their batteries ought to work for at least two weeks given Hannah was alone. Neeley sincerely hoped it would take less than that to find John Masterson. Neeley had gloves on and the bugs were all sterile, so even if one was found, they couldn't be traced to her. Not that anyone could make anything sensible out of her fingerprints, Neeley thought with a bitter smile. That would certainly cause the police some consternation if they ever got a good print from her and ran it through their computers. Better not to ever have that little situation come up at all had been Gant's advice.

Neeley pulled a Polaroid out of her backpack and took a picture of the room. She tossed the developing film onto the bed. She then began to search. Every drawer she opened, she checked first to make sure there were no telltales to indicate it had been opened, such as a piece of hair taped across the bottom. She also took a picture of each as soon as it was open so that everything could be put back into place exactly as it had been left. The bedroom yielded no information about where John might possibly have gone. Using the Polaroids she returned the room and drawers to their original state.

Neeley retraced her steps out of the bedroom, down the hall and recovered the IR light. She had decided last night not to do the upstairs. She'd yet to see Hannah go up there.

Neeley went into the room that had obviously been John's den. She found the map in the back of the file drawer with the two red lines on it, but knew, as Hannah had, that no such pipelines had been built. Still she slid it into her backpack. The computer refused to allow her access as she didn't have the password. Neeley decided her time was up.

Neeley scanned the rear of the house to the wood line before stepping out. All clear. She closed the door, relocked it, and retrieved the special pliers. She quickly sprinted across the backyard and disappeared into the wood line about twenty feet in, near a tree she had scouted earlier. She pulled a square box, about six inches cubed, from the backpack.

Neeley climbed the tree until she was twenty feet above the ground. She taped the box in the crux of a branch, making sure it was secure. Then she pulled a spool of very thin wire from the top of the box and pinned the end to another branch about six feet above, leaving the exposed antenna hanging free. She flicked the box on and shimmied back down the tree. She knew it was chancy to leave it unattended, but she had no choice. There were too many things to do. She felt it was reasonably secure above the ground. The odds that someone would look up in that particular tree were slim.

Hannah's house taken care of, Neeley headed back to the truck.

HANNAH FOUND a parking space despite it being Westport's busiest time of the day. The complex consisted of various groupings of buildings—shops, office buildings, and two Sheraton Hotels. As she made her way toward the building that housed Jenkins, Hannah suddenly realized she'd been here to see another doctor once—to have her wisdom teeth removed. That had been a bad experience; she remembered as she entered the lobby and walked to the elevator.

For some reason that memory brought to mind another one: her miscarriage, an ordeal she had believed at the time she would never recover from, if she ever had.

Standing alone in the elevator, Hannah was overwhelmed with the urge to cry. She held it in until she was afraid the pain in her chest would explode, sending fragments of her helter-skelter in the confined space. Finally, despite her efforts, it escaped.

That was the way Hannah entered Dr. Jenkins office, sobbing silently for a life lived uselessly and, more importantly, the one never lived at all.

The receptionist didn't seem to think Hannah's state unusual at all and simply waved her through to a partially opened door like a flagman on the highway trying to prevent a pileup on her section of the road.

Hannah came to a stop just inside the door. She remembered being surprised the first time she'd met Jenkins that he didn't look a thing like she had imagined from his voice. Jenkins was young and small, very inoffensive looking. The only immediate acknowledgment he made of her presence was to hand her a Kleenex and shut the door behind her.

As soon as they were both seated, he spoke. "You mentioned something about having problems with John?"

Right to the point. Hannah liked that. It almost made up for his brief advice to follow her routine, which had not worked well. She closed her eyes and thought for a moment how easy it would be to just sit here and have that voice explain everything. To tell all her secrets and then have them interpreted and fed back in a way she could handle. She'd told Jenkins a lot about herself over the last several years, but his feedback had been minimal. Since her life had been on a reasonably pleasant cruise control, Hannah had had no desire to press him for anything.

"He's gone. I assume I drove him away."

"You forced him to do what he did?"

"I know what you're doing," Hannah countered. "If I had been more aware I would have been able to do something prior to his leaving. Made things better somehow."

"How do you know he wouldn't have left no matter what you did?"

She looked at him and thought briefly about what he had just said. "Doctor Jenkins, I know you want to help me but I don't think I can do this. I—"

"Did your husband say or do anything to you that indicated he was getting ready to leave you?"

She thought shrinks weren't supposed to interrupt. "No."

"Did he tell you he was unhappy?"

"No."

Jenkins was matter of fact about it. "Sounds as if your husband made a conscious decision to leave and it might well have nothing to do with you. Why do you feel responsible?"

"He wouldn't have left if he had been happy with me."

"Were you happy with him?"

Touché, Hannah thought, but didn't respond.

Jenkins shifted his angle of approach. "Tell me exactly what has happened since we last met."

Hannah relayed the events, completely, for the first time to another person starting with waving bye to John as he headed off to golf. She wound up with the meeting with Brumley. It took her most of the allotted time for the session.

Jenkins had his hands folded neatly in his lap as he finally spoke, but through her own fog of emotions, Hannah was surprised to sense that Jenkins seemed nervous.

"Do you feel suicidal?"

"No." Hannah remembered the knife and the tub. "Yes."

A single eyebrow went up and Jenkins waited.

"I play with a knife sometimes."

"Is this something new?"

"No."

Jenkins waited, probably wondering why she'd never mentioned this. Finally he gave in. "Ever cut yourself when you play with the knife?"

"No."

"Why do you do it?"

Finally the open-ended question, Hannah thought. She'd been a bit disappointed with Jenkins for a few moments there. "I think there's a part of me that I want to get rid of."

"And what part is that?"

Hannah shrugged. "The bad part."

Jenkins was probably remembering that silence didn't work well with her. "What do you think is the bad part of you?"

"The part that allowed me to end up in the situation I'm in right now. I should have known better."

"Known better than what?"

"To entrust my life to someone else. It never worked as a child, I don't know why I thought it would as an adult. I suppose I took the easy way and it's turned out to be the hard way."

"Other than that bad part, though, do you have a desire to hurt yourself?"

"No."

"And if you get rid of that part of you?" Jenkins asked.

"Then I can control me."

"And?"

Hannah's eyes flashed with anger as she looked at Jenkins. "You don't think I can control myself?"

Jenkins spread his hands wide, a giving up gesture. "That's not my province. I think you have great untapped potential."

She laughed bitterly. "Like a newly discovered oil field? That's the area John worked in. Oil. They were always looking for the untapped potential."

"You're a person, not oil."

Hannah narrowed her eyes and stared at Jenkins without saying anything. For the first time she really focused on him.

Jenkins shifted in his seat uncomfortably. "Okay. Listen, Hannah. You've got to understand that you are under stress. There's a lot going on in your head and in your gut right now. You're feeling anger, guilt, relief, fear—every emotion in the book. And all within minutes of each other. Each emotion brings a new one on its coattails.

"There's even a small part of you, and you don't have to admit it to me if you don't want to, that's happy your husband is gone. Even the best marriage has its bad times."

Hannah didn't protest although she supposed it would have been normal to do so.

"The problem is that the feeling of relief probably immediately triggers a feeling of guilt," Jenkins continued. "Guilt is the baggage women carry, while men wield anger."

Not all women, Hannah immediately thought, but didn't say. She didn't feel guilty. She was shocked to suddenly realize it. Not in the slightest.

"Maybe—" Jenkins drew the word out—"the part you've really wanted to cut out was your marriage. The life you were leading."

That surprised Hannah. In all the years she'd been seeing him he'd never talked this much and had most certainly never taken a stand on anything. Jenkins eyes slid past her and she realized he was checking the time. "We can get together next week if you like."

Hannah felt like there was a hole in her chest with cold air rushing through. Jenkins had said a lot in a very short period of time. The interesting thing was that none of it had particularly surprised her.

Jenkins slowly stood and walked over to the side of her chair, placing his hand on the back of it. She realized he was indicating that the time was up. She stood. "Thank you, Doctor."

CHAPTER

8

THE SECRETARY'S NAMETAG identified her as Lois Smith. She looked like the woman who sat behind the window at the DMV and administered those quick eye tests rather than Nero's gatekeeper. She had a thick gray bun, reading glasses held around her neck by a thin black cord when not in use, and a bulky sweater of muted color covering the shapeless form of her body.

At the moment, Lois Smith was finding it difficult to maintain the mild indifference her job required. As Mr. Nero's personal secretary for over twenty-five years she was familiar with and personable to all his "employees" and "contractors." The exception was the man in front of her. He made her skin crawl. He could have been handsome but at some point he had let his inherent nature control his facial muscles to produce a haunting, feral quality. His head was completely bald, the lights gleaming off the white skin. He was tall and slender, but walked with a slight hunch, as if always protecting the front of his body from some undetermined blow.

Ms. Smith smiled with her lips tightly clenched. "Mr. Nero is on the phone. Could you please take a seat, Mr. Racine?"

Racine never did what a woman asked unless there was something to be gained from it. He remained standing, staring at her, enjoying her discomfort.

NERO HUNG UP the phone. The report from Dr. Jenkins in St. Louis was encouraging but he didn't feel any excitement. It was as he had predicted. It would have surprised him if he'd been wrong at this stage. More pieces needed to be moved into place and then set in motion. One such piece was waiting outside his office right now. Reluctantly, Nero buzzed his secretary.

Ms. SMITH NODDED to the steel door behind her. "Mr. Racine, Mr. Nero will see you now."

Racine puckered his lips. To Ms. Smith's credit there was no outward reaction on her part. Accepting there would be none, Racine moved to the door and entered some numbers on the eye-level keypad, while Ms. Smith kept her finger pressed on the positive access button under her desktop that activated the keypad.

The door swung open and automatically shut behind him. Racine stood in a narrow hallway and started to walk to the door ahead. His footsteps activated the floor sensor and a somewhat female metallic voice filled the small enclosure.

"Identify please. Name, number, and code. You have ten seconds." The voice went twenty decibels lower as it began the countdown.

Racine was in a hurry and the voice stopped at six. Racine didn't even bother to glance at the small portals that held the incapacitating gas should he fail to make the ten-second countdown. He found it quite an irritating routine to go through.

A drawer slid open from the wall. "Deposit all weapons please."

Racine slid the pistol out of his shoulder holster and dropped it in the drawer. He carried a Desert Eagle, a massive gun made by the Israelis and chambered for .44 magnum cartridges. It made a solid thump as it hit the bottom of the drawer. He did the same with three knives from various hidden spots in his clothing along with the garrote secreted on the inside of his belt. He pushed and the drawer slid shut. A red light flashed and he knew a magnetic sensor was being activated. The light flashed green, then went red again, as a puff of wind from the grating below blew up and explosive, chemical, and biological sensors in the ceiling sniffed the air. The light turned green and stayed that color.

"Proceed, please."

The far door slid apart and Racine entered Nero's office. He took the chair in front of the desk and waited. As long as he'd been coming here, the room had not changed, nor had Nero's discourteous manner of greeting. The damn lights were pointed right at the seat and Racine took a pair of cheap plastic sunglasses from his pocket and slipped them on.

Nero pulled a pack of cigarettes from his inside breast pocket and made a gesture of offering it to Racine. The pack was withdrawn before Racine had time to say no and Nero was inhaling before Racine could completely wipe the distaste from his face.

Racine waited and watched the old man smoke. When the ritual had ended, Nero capped the hole in his throat and reached for the voice box.

Nero's voice through the wand made the computerized one in the hallway sound like Greta Garbo. Racine took no notice of how the old man sounded. He was interested in only one thing: Why had he been ordered here?

"I'm so pleased that you could make this appointment on such short notice, Mr. Racine."

Racine felt a bead of sweat on the back of his neck slowly roll down. This place was always warm. Or was it the lights?

"I understand you visited Baltimore last week," Nero said, his empty, scarred eye sockets staring over the desktop as if he could see into Racine's soul.

Racine finally spoke and his voice was more tense and more rushed than he would have liked. "Look, Mr. Nero, I'm sorry about what happened in Baltimore. Trust me. It was just bad luck. No harm, no foul, right?"

Nero straightened and continued turning the smoldering butt of his cigarette against the glass edge of his ashtray with his free hand. "Mr. Racine, surely you can imagine my dilemma in trusting anyone, least of all you. It causes me concern when a government contractor does freelance work. It causes me to consider a possible conflict of interest."

"But there's no conflict, I—" Racine shut up after only five words.

"Interesting," Nero said. He shifted in his seat ever so slightly. "But we're not here to discuss the unfortunate incident in Baltimore."

Racine smiled with relief. "Mr. Nero, it won't happen again."

Mr. Nero returned the wand to his throat. "Let's not push, Mr. Racine. Let's agree that you have made your mistake for this year."

The younger man didn't bother to respond. He could see the fog of smoke wafting through the beams of light directed at him.

The metallic voice continued. "I've asked you here today because I have a new and delicate assignment that requires a man with your special talents."

Racine leaned forward. He waited through a thirty-second tortuous coughing spasm until Nero could continue. "It seems we can no longer rely on the stability of Mr. Anthony Gant's position. As a matter of fact, Mr. Gant has truly retired. He's dead."

Racine couldn't hide his surprise. His immediate frustration at the display of emotion made him clench the arms of his chair. Even though Nero couldn't see, Racine knew the man had an extraordinary ability to discern things in other ways.

"I know," Nero continued, "we are all shocked and saddened by Mr. Gant's untimely demise, especially the circumstances. It appears he died a natural death, quite ironic if one takes into account the shocking rate of violence in his chosen profession."

"How do you know he's dead?"

"Let's just ignore your impertinent question. Chalk it up to grief, yes? More importantly you should ask why you are here. I'm well aware of the animosity between you and the late Mr. Gant, and even more so with his brother."

"I'm sorry, sir, you're right. I must be overcome." Racine was making an extraordinary effort, for him at least, to control his voice and words.

Nero nodded his acceptance of the apology, ignoring the sarcasm of the second sentence. "Mr. Gant's death potentially upsets a rather delicate balance of secrecy that has been maintained over the years. I myself feel the balance can be maintained but there are others, people in positions of importance, who feel that this should not be left to chance. They want what Gant has held all these years to maintain his end of the balance. We looked for the object in question. Mr. Bailey paid a call and found a sterile cabin and a dead Mr. Gant." Nero's voice broke and he took a long pause.

Racine was having a hard time taking it all in. He was still trying to accept that Gant was dead. After all these years, to have it end like this. He had never imagined such a thing. He decided to cut to the chase and work through it all when he was alone.

"What about this thing Gant had?"

"We must assume that Gant gave it to someone or if it is hidden, as is most likely, gave someone the means to find it." Nero coughed. "After all, someone had to bury him. And sterilize his place."

"Who? His brother, Jack?"

"Not his brother. It has been many, many years since the two have spoken. Let's call this person Gant's ghost for the moment." Nero slid a picture across the desktop. "There was someone else who held part of the balance. Another old player who retired long ago. Gant's piece works in concert with his piece. That is John Masterson."

Racine stiffened and didn't look at the picture right away. "Who is he?"

Nero was perfectly still, head cocked as if staring at Racine. Finally he spoke. "Mr. Masterson only ran one mission for us years ago. A mission with Gant. He's been a civilian for over a decade with a new life."

"There's no such thing as a new life," Racine said.

"There is if the old one wasn't real," Nero said, almost to himself rather than Racine.

Racine frowned. "So what does Gant have? Or had?"

"Mr. Gant's piece of the puzzle is a videotape."

"What is the tape of?"

"Of a meeting we would prefer not become public."

"I'll get it," Racine promised.

"Don't forget Masterson and his piece," Nero said. He slid a picture across the desk. "This is Masterson's wife."

Racine took the picture. He looked at it and was careful to control his reaction to the woman. Very nice. "I'll take care of the Mastersons. What does John Masterson have?" he asked. "Do I need to get that too?"

"No. His piece of the puzzle is relatively unimportant without the other two parts."

"Other *two* parts?" Racine's tongue snaked over his lip nervously.

"Focus on your job," Nero ordered. "We must assume Gant passed on his piece of the secret to whoever buried him; after all, even our redoubtable Mr. Gant couldn't hop in a grave and cover himself up after he is dead, no? So, whoever has Gant's piece will most likely also go to John Masterson to try to reconstruct their balance and therefore you can do the proverbial killing of two birds with one stone by going to St. Louis where the Mastersons reside."

"And the third piece?"

Nero shook his head. "Not your concern at the moment."

"It would help if I knew—"

Nero's voice was sharp and brooked no argument. "No, it would not."

Racine stood. "I'll take care of it."

Mr. Nero allowed himself a smile. "Gant's ghost is not to die before that tape is on this desk. And Mrs. Masterson, I would like to talk to her to see what her husband told her."

Racine blinked. "But—"

"Allow an old man his curiosity," Nero said, cutting Racine off.

Racine frowned. "But I thought—"

"Ah, thinking," Nero interrupted once more. "That's my job, Mr. Racine, and I've already thought about this situation. No need for you to waste what little talent you have in that area on this. I have to assume Mr. Gant would have played his cards close to his vest but he certainly wouldn't have wanted those cards to be buried with him. After all there is his wife, Jessie, and his son, Bobbie, to consider."

Racine bit the inside of his lip, waiting on Nero's words.

"From a hair sample we found at Gant's cabin we think his ghost is a woman."

Racine assimilated that startling piece of information. "The woman from Berlin?"

"Her name is Neeley," Nero said.

"She's been with Gant all these years?" The concept was quite strange to Racine.

"I believe she has," Nero said. "Now you understand why I chose you for this."

Racine bridled at the reference. It was well known in the Cellar that Racine had no problem taking contracts on women. Not all of the specialists in the Cellar shared Racine's attitude. Racine said, to those who cared to listen, that if women wanted equality, he was happy to oblige.

Nero slid a piece of paper across the desk. "That's an Agency number in Operations. Someone with quite a bit of pull has gotten support from our friends in Langley. If you need help, you may call upon them."

Racine took the paper, knowing this was strange. Implicit

in Nero's comment was that he couldn't call the Cellar for backup. That wasn't totally bad, considering the Agency had a lot of resources, but the quality of those resources was a different story. Racine had to assume this was his punishment for Baltimore.

"You are dismissed."

Racine left. As soon as the door closed behind him, a panel on the wall behind Nero opened and Bailey walked in, jaws working as he chewed his ever-present gum.

"Baltimore?" Bailey asked, taking the seat Racine had occupied.

"Racine did a freelance job. Made a bloody mess of it. Killed a couple of nonplayers. A woman and her husband."

"For who?" Bailey asked.

"For Senator Collins."

Bailey frowned.

Nero nodded as if he saw the frown. "Yes. Raises all sorts of questions, doesn't it?"

"Wheels turning within wheels," Bailey said.

Nero grunted. "Aren't there always?"

"Why the kill?"

"The good Senator was having an affair with the woman. Her husband had learned of it and was threatening divorce. It would have gotten ugly. The good Senator is in a precarious position as he tries to move upward in the world."

"The woman—Neeley. What do you think she will do?"

"Most likely go to Masterson," Nero said. "That's what Gant would have told her to do."

"You mentioned a third piece?" Bailey asked. "A third person?"

Nero nodded. "I'm not sure everything was as we thought it was so long ago. I was fishing with Racine."

"What do you mean?"

"I've been rearranging the facts. They're vague and distant sometimes, but they are there. Sudan. Mogadishu. The Embassy bombings. Nine-eleven. Afghanistan. Action—reaction. Shortsightedness. Even before then. We never quite tied up the loose ends on Pan Am one-o-seven."

Bailey's eyebrows lifted at Nero's tone. He'd never heard the old man so angry.

Nero could tell from the heavy silence that Bailey didn't quite believe he was telling him everything, but implicit in their relationship from the beginning had been that Nero was the one who controlled all the pieces, and knowledge of both the players and the moves were only given when needed.

"Why did you put Racine on this?" Bailey finally asked.

"Because Senator Collins wants the issue resolved but I have yet to decide exactly how that resolution will develop and I want to keep my options open. Since Senator Collins was involved on the front end and appears to be involved in something currently with Racine, we might as well involve Racine in this. I think I need to take a harder look at Mr. Racine and the past. You never know what might come out of the forest if a fire burns through it."

CHAPTER

9

NEELEY MADE HER WAY through the darkened woods, another night creature foraging in the dark. It had been a frustrating day. John Masterson had vanished and left no trail that she could find.

Her investigation had yielded no connection yet between John and Gant. John Masterson had been here in St. Louis for almost ten years working for the same oil technology company. He worked on some classified projects connected with the Pentagon but Neeley didn't think that had anything to do with the current situation. Before coming to St. Louis his past was hidden and Neeley had to assume it was behind that distant curtain she couldn't penetrate that Gant and John had known each other.

It took Neeley a few minutes to find the right tree behind Hannah's house. She climbed and opened the box by feel. She pulled out the four microcassettes on the revolving cartridge and replaced them with blank ones. She slipped the tapes into her coat pocket.

Neeley wanted to get back to the hotel and listen to the tapes, but first she took the time to move to the tree line and pull out the field glasses, searching the windows for Hannah. She was seated in the den, wearing a robe and drinking. Reading.

Neeley still didn't know how she would get to John but she hoped the tapes would give her the hook. She had a feeling she wouldn't have much more time. The Cellar would move as soon as they knew Gant was dead, of that Gant had been certain.

It was a long shot, but who knew? Maybe John had been foolish enough to call his wife and the tapes had caught it.

As Neeley watched Hannah guzzle down her drink and pour herself another, she felt an odd sense of urgency press on her. Her normally cool mission mode gave way to a feeling of utter loneliness. Gant was gone. Hannah was just sitting and staring, lost in her aloneness and vulnerability. Neeley saw herself. This whole thing was bringing back specters she didn't want to deal with. Neeley tried to shake the feeling off and stood. She turned and headed back.

The gloomy forest pressed in on Neeley's already dark mood as she negotiated her way. Neeley's walk through the woods shifted into a jog and then into an all out run.

Branches slapped at her face, but she didn't even feel them. At one point, Neeley tripped over a fallen tree and landed face first. She was on her feet in a flash and continued. Neeley kept it up until she reached the back of the stores where her truck was parked. She broke out of the woods and finally halted, breathing hard, her clothes covered with dirt and leaves.

With tremendous effort, Neeley reined in the panicky feeling that had overwhelmed her. She was momentarily confused. What the hell had happened? She wasn't sure if it was simply reacting to stress of the last several months watching Gant die, or if it was Hannah and the current situation.

That last idea gave Neeley pause. Why was she so concerned about a woman stupid enough to tie herself to a man like John Masterson who would keep her in the dark and leave her hanging? A man who would do such a thing— Neeley shook her head. She couldn't judge Hannah. Not given her own history.

Neeley forced herself to walk calmly to the truck. She started it and drove back to her hotel. She negotiated the roads with her characteristic safety, but her mind was swirling with thoughts that she had kept at bay for years.

Finally, she pulled into the underground garage. She locked the truck and went to her room, throwing the backpack onto the bed. Before she took out the recorder and reviewed the tapes, Neeley knew she needed to regain positive control. Sitting in the lotus position on the floor, she slowed her breathing down and focused her eyes on a spot she picked on the wall. After fifteen minutes, Neeley's pulse settled down and she felt confident she could recommence the mission in a competent manner.

Neeley stood up and took the four tapes and machine with her to the balcony. She opened the sliding doors and sat on the uncomfortable metal chair at the small table. The chill night air pricked at her skin as she slid the first tape in. She wasn't even sure if there would be anything on this first tape, never mind the other three.

She hoped that Hannah had not had the TV or stereo on the whole time. That would have activated the nearest bug and kept the tapes running. Then even if Hannah had talked on the phone, the two bugs activated would have overlapped their respective sounds. Neeley didn't feel like trying to sort through that kind of mess. Each microcassette was good for two hours on slow speed.

She slipped the first tape in and pressed the earphone into her left ear. She put a notepad on her knees and clicked out the lead point on a mechanical pencil so she was ready to make notes. Neeley pushed the on button and waited. The slight hiss of the tape running was broken as a phone rang. Neeley heard Hannah's voice close up for the first time:

"Hello?"

"Hannah? This is Howard Brumley. How are you holding up?"

Neeley scratched the name onto the pad.

"I'm fine Howard, thank you for calling. What do you need?"

"Did you see Jenkins?"

"Yes."

There was a pause, and then Brumley spoke again. "We need to set up some time for a talk. I know you weren't ready to deal with the other day, but we do need to discuss the MDA."

"Marital dissolution agreement."

Lawyer, Neeley thought. But who was Jenkins?

"I'm sorry, Howard. I didn't know there was more to talk about. I don't see why I should give John what he wants. Why the hell does he want a divorce anyway, if he's in the South Seas?"

"I don't know why he wants it," Howard said, "but it's in your best interests to finish it quickly."

Neeley frowned. That was odd. Why was John trying to put such distance between himself and Hannah and why was the lawyer so interested in it? The only evidence that John was in the South Seas was John's card to Hannah and her lawyer. Which made Neeley doubt very much that that was where the man was. Misdirection was one the most basics tenets of covert operations.

"Doesn't John have to sign papers too?" Hannah asked.

"I told you the other day that John sent them to me already filled out," Howard replied.

"Who did them for him?" Hannah asked. "You're his lawyer too."

"Not anymore," Howard quickly said.

"So who filled out his papers?" Hannah asked again.

"He did them himself, the way they look," Howard replied. "It's all boilerplate anyway. John just had to fill in the blanks."

"Do you have a way to get in contact with him, to send him the paperwork back?" Hannah asked.

"No," Howard said. "We can file it here in town without him. Listen, how about we discuss it over lunch?" the lawyer asked. "Say tomorrow at one?"

A pause. "That will be fine, Howard. Where do you want to meet?"

"How about Al Baker's?"

"Fine. See you tomorrow. Good-bye."

Neeley made a new heading on the right side of the pad, labeling it with the next day's date. She penciled in the appointment, restaurant, and the lawyer's name on her pad.

Neeley shut the tape down for a second. She thought about the conversation and felt a pinprick of excitement. Perhaps she'd just been given a clue.

Neeley turned the machine back on. There were about ten minutes of assorted tape time consisting of the voice activated device being triggered by the noises of Hannah moving around the house; making drinks for herself, moving a bar stool, running the water. Neeley patiently waited these out. Then the phone rang again.

"Hello."

"Hannah?"

"Yes. This is Hannah Masterson."

"This is Sam. Sam Evans."

Another name was added to Neeley's list.

"Oh." Pause. "Oh, hello Sam. I'm sorry I didn't recognize your voice. I guess I'm sort of out of it."

"I'm returning your call. Don't tell me you and John are thinking of relocating already?"

"I need to put the house on the market."

There was a pause. "Has John been transferred?"

"You could say that," Hannah replied.

Sam sounded confused. "Won't the company be buying your house? That's the way it usually works."

Hannah's voice was tight. "It's my house, Sam. I want to sell it. All right?"

The voice was syrupy at the thought of the commission.

"Certainly, Hannah. I just thought you ought to know that the market isn't very good right now, but I think I can drum something up for you. I have quite a few buyers who are interested in your area and I think your house would go very quickly."

Neeley labeled Sam on the paper: real estate agent.

"Great. Let me know what you come up with."

The oily voice was persistent. "That's fine, Hannah. But listen. Would it cause you any problems if I brought some people by in the next day or so. Just so I can get a feel for the market and also so I can give you an accurate idea of what you can get?"

Hannah's voice was weary. "Fine. Whatever."

"Good. That's good."

"Thank you for your time, Sam." The phone went dead.

The first tape played out with normal house noises. Neeley grimaced five minutes into the second one. Hannah had turned on the TV. Neeley fast-forwarded, stopping every twenty counts on the machine to check. The rest of the second tape was filled with the noise of the TV with no apparent interruptions.

Neeley popped the third tape in. More of the same. Neeley fast-forwarded and zoomed through the rest of the tape. Normal house noises. She loaded the last one. Ten minutes in, another phone call.

"Hello?"

"Hannah, is that you?"

"Yes, Amelia, it's me. What do you need?"

"I just realized that I forget to tell you what I came by this morning to talk to you about."

"What's that?"

"You probably don't remember, but tomorrow is the hospital auxiliary board meeting.

"You're right, I didn't remember."

"I just want you know that I would be happy to take over your duties as president tomorrow until you're able to resume them."

"I have a great idea, Amelia. Why don't you just keep

those duties and any others that might interest you forever?"

"Well, I was just trying to help. I know no one would expect you to be there, but it is the monthly meeting."

Hannah's reply was clipped. "Is that all?"

"Well, there is the question of the Museum Guild and . . ."

"Amelia, I want you to listen very carefully. Don't bother me with this shit. Do you understand what I'm saying? I can't deal with this now. Just do it."

"All right, Hannah, please don't get upset with me. I'm just trying to help"

"You can't help. No one can help. If everybody would realize that one simple fact I could maybe get my life back together."

"Hannah, I think of what you're going through and I wonder what I would do if something were to happen to Ralph. My God, it just terrifies me!"

"Right. Good-bye Amelia." The tape clicked off.

Neeley pushed the forward and scanned the rest of the tape. There was nothing. The fourth tape came to an end and Neeley pulled the earpiece out and leaned back in the chair, contemplating the stars overhead. There was no indication that Hannah had a clue where John was or what he had been doing.

Neeley looked down at the notepad. But someone else might.

DESPITE THE INTRUSIONS of the phone, Hannah realized she was happy to be home. She sipped on her third drink and pondered her day. She hadn't said much to Dr. Jenkins, but by the time he had finished the brief session, she had felt good enough to make another appointment. She had done so knowing she could cancel, but as long as John's company health policy would cover the costs of the visits she figured she'd use it. She sensed there was more to Jenkins than he had let on and she was curious.

The afternoon stretching on into evening had been a series of idiotic phone calls and futile attempts at distraction. Even her books hadn't worked well in that field. Hannah settled back onto the cushions. That jerk Howard. How could John have had a lawyer like that, better yet how could Celia stay married to a man like that? Granted he made enough money to get away with just about anything, but for crying out loud the man had no chin. Why was he pushing this divorce? There was nothing in it for her. There was nothing in anything for her. And why did he care if she had seen Jenkins or not?

Hannah had a pretty good idea what lunch would be like tomorrow. Howard was going to be patronizing. It irritated her that Howard presumed she knew nothing of John's finances. It irritated her even more to know that Howard was correct. The meeting the other day had been a shock. The only thing she had to look forward to was her next appointment with Jenkins but even that carried a negative edge. As soon as the company found out about John, if they hadn't already, and got the paperwork rolling, the insurance would be cut off. She didn't see herself being able to pay a hundred and forty-five an hour to feel better for very long. And feeling better wasn't going to change the circumstances of her situation.

Hannah felt vulnerable because she knew that soon the scavengers would be nipping at her heels. She was beginning to feel that before it was over everyone would want a little piece of Hannah Masterson. The phone calls today had only been a taste of what was coming. She was going to have to level with Sam Evans about the urgency of the house sale unless of course he picked up the story from his wife this evening.

Lifting the glass to her lips, Hannah had a sudden moment of resolve and insight. The bottom line was that she was going to have to protect herself. There was nobody else.

She set the glass down and tried to gauge her level of drunkenness. She hadn't had enough to pass out, but certainly enough to induce a somewhat stuporous sleep. She had never drunk like this before, but she'd never been in this situation before. She knew it couldn't go on, but she needed some sleep and it seemed like the only way. She had promised herself this morning—after running Amelia off—to back off, but it was all just too much. John was sitting on some island with all their money; the least she could get to do was finish their liquor cabinet off. John hadn't taken that with him.

Hannah was a little unsteady as she rose to her feet and began her nightly ritual to shut down the big house. First, she checked the alarm. The steady red light on the master console mounted in the wall of the foyer comforted her.

Walking through the quiet house, checking the doors and turning off the lights, it occurred to her that in a way it was a good thing that Sam had returned her call. At the time she had been put off by his greed-induced tactics, but she now realized that she had to be rid of this millstone. She just wanted a little place, something that was really hers. Not a house that fairly screamed out loneliness and isolation. Even with John here, the sheer size was sometimes overwhelming. Especially the upstairs with its empty bedrooms. Hannah made it a practice to go up there as rarely as possible.

By the time Hannah had completed her circuit and was at the edge of her bed, she was beginning to wonder if maybe she wouldn't pass out after all. She looked at the bed and thought of how soft it looked. She wanted to fall across it, but forced herself to take off her robe and crawl in correctly, covers up, everything neat and secure.

Lifting her head from the pillow to turn off the light set the room into a slow spin. Damn, she hated that. Hannah extended her leg from out of the covers so that her foot on the floor would stop the room from moving.

As she slid into unconsciousness, she felt a yearning need for the same simple solution in her life. She needed somehow to stop her whole world from spinning. She needed to put her foot down and control her situation. Her last conscious thought was about Dr. Jenkins. Her session today had barely opened the door to her past but it was enough. What she had tried so hard to bury and ignore was returning. She fell asleep hearing the tortured screams of the small child she had once been.

C H A P T E R

10

NEELEY WAS CRAMPED and uncomfortable. She'd assumed that a successful attorney would have a bigger car. Maybe Howard Brumley wasn't so successful. Neeley wondered if Hannah suspected that Howard knew more about John's disappearance than he should. Neeley didn't know the answer to that question. She only knew that Howard's eagerness to put distance between John and Hannah was very suspicious. One thing she had learned traveling in the shadow world with Gant was to question every word, every action. Something was wrong about the way Brumley was acting toward Hannah and it didn't take a rocket scientist in Neeley's opinion to figure the person behind that something was John Masterson.

The time to be discreet was past. Neeley knew the clock was ticking and time was not on her side.

Neeley tried to straighten her shoulders but it was impossible. Her hope was that Howard would not work overly late. However, it seemed like he was in no rush to get home to his loving wife.

Howard's arrival at the car in the back of the practically empty underground garage was hours after most of the other workers had left. He unlocked the door which had taken Neeley less than five seconds to open without a key. Not looking into the shadowy backseat, he slid onto the black leather. Before he could completely insert the key, Neeley reached around and pushed the barrel of her Glock pistol against the side of his head.

"Let's make this easy. Where is John Masterson?"

"I don't—"

Neeley pressed the tip of the muzzle against the skin, a persuasive argument to the uninitiated.

"Where is John Masterson? Answer or you die in three seconds," Neeley said in a flat voice. "Have you ever seen what a bullet to the head does?"

Howard may have been a foolish man in certain business associations, but he tended to be practical when the stakes moved from money to survival. "Across the river. The Cloverleaf Motel. Room twenty-seven."

"Does Hannah Masterson know where he is?"

"No."

"Does she know anything about this thing John has set up?"

"No."

"Why is John doing this?"

"I don't know. He didn't tell me."

"Why is he disappearing?"

"I don't know."

"Bullshit," Neeley hissed.

"I really don't know. Please! I'd tell you if I did."

She believed that. "Why are you helping John?"

"He's paying me."

Neeley was impressed how quickly the answers came. Howard wasn't very loyal. Which triggered her next question.

"What else?"

The momentary silence told her there was indeed more. Neeley waited, noting the drip of sweat from his temple around the tip of the gun. She'd have to clean it after this. There were oils in sweat that were not good for gun steel.

"I was told to tell her to see her psychiatrist."

Neeley frowned. "Dr. Jenkins?"

"Yes."

"Who told you to make sure she saw Jenkins?"

"I don't know. I got an envelope with a thousand in cash and a note with Jenkins's card attached. The note said make sure Hannah Masterson made an appointment with Jenkins right away."

"Was it John, her husband?"

"I don't think so—I mean, why would he do it that way?"

Good question, Neeley thought. Maybe Howard wasn't totally stupid. "You know, Howard, if you tell anyone about this little chat, I will have to drop everything in my life and spend the remainder of my days hunting you down. You don't seem to be hard to find so I'm not reluctant to commit the time because I don't think it will take me more than a day or two. Do we understand each other?"

The lawyer's whisper was hardly audible. "Yes."

Neeley rapped the barrel hard against Howard's temple. "Good," she said to the unconscious body.

Walking out of the garage into the night, Neeley looked like any of the other late-fleeing secretaries of the downtown business district. Her simple knit dress was neither stylish nor well-fitted and the loose jacket did little for her figure except to hide the shoulder holster. Even her tennis shoes on stockinged feet drew no notice since pumps had become passé. Neeley remained alert to her environment but allowed the majority of her thoughts to formulate the next step.

THE CLOVERLEAF MOTEL was in Alton. It was on the east side of the Mississippi River, north of the Gateway Arch. Neeley drove her truck across the Eades Bridge and pulled over at the first gas station. She got the key and unlocked the door to the filthiest toilet she had ever seen. Neeley hadn't been this repulsed in Morocco when she'd gone there with Gant.

She quickly pulled some more practical clothes from her backpack and put them on the cleanest spot on the counter she could find. She only kept the sneakers on, putting the Glock and its holster on top of the clothes. After stashing the other clothes in a zippered pocket of the pack, she reached into the pack's main compartment.

She retrieved a second gun, this one a Model 59 Smith & Wesson semiautomatic pistol with a MOD O silencer attached. She slid a magazine of Gant's specially made 9mm, subsonic rounds into the handle and pulled back on the slide, chambering a round. She let the slide go forward, and then locked it down so when she fired it wouldn't jump back and make noise. She would only be able to fire one shot at a time like this but the gun would be almost perfectly quiet when she did so. She put the pistol on top of the new clothes.

She strapped a thin, double-bladed Fairburn knife to her right calf. Another, even smaller knife, went in the exact center of her back, clipped to the top of her panties, a spot Gant had told her police often miss in searches.

She slipped on a pair of comfortable jeans, then made sure the thin wire garrote was still in place on the inside waist, held there by single loops of thread along its length. She pulled on a loose fitting T-shirt and then the shoulder holster for the Glock. On top of that went a sports jacket with large pockets. She slipped the Model 59 into the right pocket.

When she was done, she looked in the mirror. The woman staring back was calm and determined. Satisfied, Neeley returned to her truck.

The motel was in a dingy industrial area. Not exactly top of the line and a long way from the South Seas. She drove around the block once until she knew what the area was like.

Room 27 was on the second floor. It opened onto a walkway and was about twenty feet from the outside stairs. The parking lot was nearly empty but there were two cars next to the stairwell. One was a rental and the other was a heap.

She drove to the payphone across the street and checked the page she had torn from the phonebook at the gas station. She punched the numbers and was put through to room 27. There was no answer, but that didn't mean anything.

Neeley moved her truck as far away from the motel office as possible while keeping in sight the door to room 27. Darkness had slid over east St. Louis and the area looked even more forlorn. Neeley sat in the shadows and waited. After a few minutes she could see the glow of a light come through the fabric on the inside of the window in 27.

Neeley quickly got out of the truck and moved up the stairwell, her hand on the grip of the Model 59 in the coat pocket. She stood to the side of the door and knocked. She mimicked the voice as well as she could, hoping the door provided a muffler. "John, it's me, Hannah. Let me in! Hurry, please, John!"

She heard rapid footsteps and the locks clicking. She had the silenced gun in his chest, pushing him back into the room before he could say a word. She kicked the door shut behind her.

John Masterson looked haggard, as if the despair of the room had broken his spirit. "Where's Hannah?" he choked, barely registering the gun.

Neeley shoved him back to a chair and he fell into it with an audible plop. He was at least twenty pounds overweight and had that soft, pinkish exterior that Neeley had always associated with weak men. She couldn't believe he had ever known Gant. When she didn't say anything, he began to stammer.

"Who are you?"

"Gant sent me," Neeley said.

"How do I know you're not from the Cellar?" John asked.

"You don't," Neeley said.

"Where's Gant?"

"He's dead."

John nodded. "He called me fifteen days ago and told me he was dying. He told me someone would be coming from him."

"Is that why you ran?" Neeley asked.

John gave a strangled laugh. "Hell, yeah. Who knows what Nero's going to do now? And how did I know I could trust whoever Gant sent?" John cocked his head and looked at her more closely. "If you're from Gant, then you have the videotape," John said. "Let me see it."

Neeley paused at this unexpected development. "I didn't bring the tape with me," she said. "That would have been stupid." As she said these words she caught the shift of John's eyes to a metal briefcase lying on the cheap wooden table.

"But you know where it is?" John was growing nervous again.

"Of course," Neeley answered.

John licked his lips. "Maybe we can get things back to normal then. Maybe Nero will deal."

"What do *you* have to deal with?" Neeley asked. She regretted the question as soon as she asked it.

"Gant didn't tell you shit did he?" John didn't wait for a reply. "No, that son-of-a-bitch wouldn't. He always played everything close to the vest and didn't trust anyone. And he *couldn't* tell you. We promised Nero we would never tell anyone. And Gant, oh boy, he sure was one for doing exactly what he was supposed to do."

"I've got the tape," Neeley said, trying to keep him talking.

"Maybe," John said. "But then again, maybe not. I shouldn't have hung around. I should have left town right after Gant called. God damn Nero, pulling strings. God damn it."

"Who is Nero?"

"The head of the Cellar," John said.

"Why did you leave your wife like you did?" Neeley asked, her head spinning from John's words, trying to make sense of it all.

John now focused on the gun. "Look, my wife is out of it, okay?"

"Out of it?" Neeley felt the sliver of metal under her finger and she forced herself to ease off the trigger. "You leave her high and dry and she's out of it? Because you say so?"

"I wish you'd quit pointing that gun at me. Those damn things are dangerous. Hannah knows *nothing,*" John insisted.

"Why did you have Brumley send her to that shrink right away then?"

The confusion on his face was real. "What are you talking about? Jenkins?" His face crumpled as if hit. "Oh shit."

Neeley felt the floor almost shift under her feet as she realized there was another layer to all this, but she knew she didn't have the time to get into it right now. "Why did you run if Gant told you I was coming?"

John was trying to regroup. "Did Gant tell you about 'dead time'? About living with knowledge that others want buried? Always being afraid that someone is going to show up in the middle of the night and kill you and everyone you love if something changes, or if someone gets a bug up their ass and just decided to tie up a few loose ends?

"When Gant told me he was dying, I knew I had to get out of sight. I'd tried to make a new life but I always knew it was hanging by a thread and his phone call brought everything crashing down around me. Hell, I knew Nero didn't give a damn about me. It was Gant that kept the peace. Gant and his brother, Jack. Without Gant, I was nothing. I've been trying to close everything out."

She wondered how the brother fit in, but she didn't ask that right now. "Why did you stay here?"

John shrugged. "I guess there was a part of me hoping you would show up from Gant and have the videotape and maybe we could deal with Nero and get things back like they were."

"So you decided to take all your money and leave your wife dangling without a clue?" Neeley asked.

John lowered his eyes. "I had to. I had to convince whoever came from the Cellar—if they got here first—that Hannah knew nothing. That she was out of it."

"Do you think the Cellar and Nero will buy off on that?"

Neeley asked. Gant had never mentioned Nero. She already knew more now in five minutes with Masterson than she had in a decade with Gant. The cowering man in front of her was right about one very important thing—Gant had to have been the one holding things in balance.

"Not really, but it's her best chance," John said. "That is until you showed up here," he added. "Like I said, maybe we can make a deal now with Nero and reestablish the status quo."

Neeley shrugged. "Maybe." She wanted to know what was in the briefcase and more about this videotape Gant had supposedly left her. The only thing she could think of was Gant's second request: that she climb the route in Eldorado Canyon. She waved the gun. "Let's go back to your house and talk this over with Hannah."

"Hannah's out of it," John said.

"Jesus Christ!" Neeley exclaimed. "She's your wife. That means she's involved. She has the right to know what is going on and to make her own decisions." The muzzle of the weapon allowed for no argument. John reluctantly stood and picked up the briefcase.

HOWARD BRUMLEY COULDN'T SLEEP. It was 1:30 in the morning and not only was he wide awake, but he had enough adrenaline going to finish an Ironman competition. It had been hours since the gun was pressed to his head but it seemed like fifteen seconds.

Lying in the dark next to his gently snoring wife, he kept lifting his hand to his head and feeling the spot. There was a bruise on his temple that was already darkening. He'd had to tell Celia that he hit a door. She didn't believe him but she also didn't seem to care.

He noticed a drip in the master bath and fought to ignore it. He wrapped his pillow around his head, praying that sleep would end this terrible day.

Howard took shallow breaths hoping to lessen his anxiety

because if he wasn't going to sleep a wink at least he could
be spared the racing heart. He kept replaying it in his head
and it always played out the same way. He was a stupid man.
Always letting Celia buy whatever the hell she wanted and
the boys, too. Just to keep some peace, because he didn't
want the endless confrontations. That was a laugh. He almost got killed today because he needed the money John
Masterson had offered. That was a whole new level to con-
frontation. What the hell had John done to him? And who
the hell had left the envelope and card about Jenkins? But
what was he supposed to do with a thousand in cash? Keep it
and not do what the card said? There was no way to return it.
Damn. And what was the big deal with Hannah going to see
her shrink. Hell, she'd looked like she needed it. Howard felt
a headache growing in concert with the throbbing in his
temple.

John must have heard he was having some trouble because
the son-of-a-bitch hadn't minced any words when he made
his offer nine days ago. He just needed some help covering
his tracks and the legal work that went with skipping out on
his life. He had assured Howard that Hannah had plenty of
money in her own name from some family trust. But it
hadn't seemed that way when Hannah stood in his office.

Howard was beginning to believe that his friend John had
told him a pack of lies. It made him feel better to think that
since he had given John up so easily. He was willing to
break some ethical laws, even a few civil ones, but by God,
he'd never have gotten mixed up in this mess if he'd had any
idea that it involved guns. What exactly had John gotten him
into?

Howard looked at the glowing numbers on the clock:
1:45. The night was never going to end. He continued staring at the ceiling and resenting the hell out of Celia for forcing him into this even though she didn't know a thing about
it. He could hear the damn drip in the master bathroom and
it irritated him even more.

Finally, he slid back the covers and walked confidently
through the dark room. At his age a man knew well the trip

from his bed to the bathroom. As he stepped across the tiled expanse to the sink faucet he felt rather than saw the presence.

Before his sensory system had time for any reaction he felt two awful and rapid movements. A hand wearing a rubber glove covered his mouth and the cold feel of steel once again pressed to the side of his neck. The whisper was deadly: "Where's John Masterson?"

Howard started to talk through the hand. Two fingers slid apart to give him working room. In the few seconds it took to give John up for the second time in less than twelve hours, Howard deduced something very important. The steel wasn't the barrel of a gun, it was the edge of a knife. When it suddenly moved across the front of his neck he was surprised that there was no pain. The hand was firmly pressed against his mouth as he felt an explosion of warm liquid on his chest. The dark went black.

RACINE QUIETLY DROPPED the lawyer's body onto the big bathroom rug. He reached over and pushed the faucet knob completely shut, stopping the drip. He stood still, not even his breathing audible until he was sure no one in the house was moving. He could feel the gentle blow of air from a vent across his naked body.

He slid his feet slowly across the tile and peered in the bedroom. He could see the sleeping form in the bed. He wondered what she looked like. Racine stood there for several minutes, taking shallow breaths. Finally he reluctantly turned back into the bathroom. He moved toward the big window over the Jacuzzi.

Once through, he grabbed the bag under the window and slipped behind the bushes to the side of the house. He loved these big new houses. Security systems that were junk, windows big enough to push an elephant's butt through and, of course, all the wonderful landscaping. Racine could have slaughtered an army next to the house and no one from the street would have been the wiser.

He pulled a small garbage bag from the rucksack leaning against the side of the house and deposited his latex gloves and the plastic wrap from his feet. It was all he had been wearing. He ran his hands over his smooth naked body and felt no sticky wetness. The lawyer had sprayed forward. He had given up so quickly that there had not been the struggle and messiness Racine had anticipated.

Racine's body was completely hairless and he knew he had left no trace of himself behind. He had shaved his entire body just two hours ago. He quickly dressed and put everything back in the bag. He still wasn't breathing hard as he bent and tied his sneakers. They were two sizes too large and clumsy, but he was careful as he retraced his steps to the street. Once there, he calmly walked the block and a half to his car.

He left the headlights off until he reached the first light. It was blinking yellow at this hour. He drove another five minutes and pulled the car over. He changed his shoes, then reached over the seat and retrieved the St. Louis *Yellow Pages* and the map. Within a few minutes he knew where he was going and how to get there.

Racine lifted an apple from the seat next to him and contentedly munched it as he carefully drove toward Alton. Once on the main Interstate, I-70, he set the cruise to three miles below the speed limit and allowed himself to think of Anthony Gant. He still couldn't believe the bastard was dead. He wondered how Gant's brother, Jack, was reacting. That was a dangerous man, not that Anthony hadn't been a hard-ass too. And Racine really couldn't believe that A. Gant had shared so much of his undercover life with another human being, much less a woman. Pussy. Racine shook his head. Too many men were ruled by it.

Racine wondered what had been in Gant's head. He had run into the other man several times on operations prior to Mogadishu and the two had come close to exchanging bullets more than once due to tactical disagreements.

It was a good thing the stupid fuck was dead. Racine would have killed him for free. As it was he could amuse himself with Gant's alter ego, Neeley. That thought was exciting enough to force him to push it away and focus on the Mastersons. After John he planned on going straight to Manchester and doing the bitch. The only catch was Nero's order to bring Mrs. Masterson in alive. Not only would that make it more difficult, but it zeroed out the possibility of immediate job satisfaction. And there was Senator Collins to consider. Fucking politician could fuck up anything.

Racine wasn't tired at all, even though he'd been up now for over twenty-four hours. The flight had been enjoyable due to the extra attention of a pretty young stewardess named LeAnn. Racine didn't even wonder anymore about the women who found him intriguing. All his life he'd only generated two responses in the fairer sex. Utter revulsion or a base sexual heat with the preponderance toward the former. He had long ago decided it was something in them and had very little to do with him. He simply ignored most women and the few that fell to him blindly, he usually took.

On the plane he had played it slow and easy with the girl but he had suspected it would take little effort to do her right there in the toilet. He regretted the expedient nature of this business prevented him from getting her phone number. His name for this op, even though it was an alias, was on the passenger roster. Someone could remember him and the last thing he needed was more crap from Nero. Thinking of the lost opportunity with the stewardess as he left the plane made him relish the idea of killing the old blind fart in the damn office of his. Bashing his brains out with that stupid phone or his voice wand. Or maybe just blocking off the hole in his throat.

Racine checked his watch as he drove by Masterson's dumpy motel. Racine parked his car at the end of the building, as far away from the office as possible. He put a fresh pair of gloves on, and then got out of the car.

He moved quietly through the darkness, avoiding the few lights. There was a light on in room 27 but he didn't care. He held his heavy Desert Eagle against the side of his leg and pressed against the cheap door. He didn't have to jam any of the locks and before the door was fully open, he knew why.

Masterson was gone. Racine locked the door with gloved fingers and spent a couple of minutes on a thorough search of the room and bathroom. There were clothes in the closet. A passport for John Masterson was inside a shoulder bag hanging on the bathroom door. That meant John was still in town. Racine smiled. He'd come back for John. There was someone else who could occupy his time this early morning. He left the room and headed for his car.

NEELEY HELD THE SILENCED PISTOL in her right hand, muzzle pointing across her lap at John Masterson's right leg as he drove her truck. She didn't expect any trouble from him, but it paid to be safe. John was grasping at the possibility of making a deal with Nero like a drowning man at a life preserver. He obviously assumed that Neeley had some way of contacting this man whose name she had just heard today.

"How did you know Gant?" Neeley asked.

"I was in the army," John said. "I met Gant on a mission."

"What kind of mission?"

John nervously laughed. "Lady, if Gant didn't tell you, then I sure as shit ain't telling you. Watch the tape." His eyes shifted over. "You'd better have it. You don't want to play games with Nero."

"I know where it is," Neeley said. "Gant said you had the 'what.' Is that 'what' in the briefcase?"

John nodded. "Yeah. But it's a lot less powerful without the videotape. That's why I was scared knowing Gant was going to die. I didn't trust that he'd send someone here. I was afraid the tape would be gone with him."

Neeley had been watching the road. She wished John would stop playing "I've got a secret" but she knew Gant had played it also. Whatever they were covering up had to be both very powerful and dangerous. She would get to the bottom of this when they got to the house and Hannah.

"If Gant called you, how come you didn't run right away?"

John's eyes shifted and Neeley knew whatever he was

about to say was going to be a lie. "There were things I had to do first."

"Turn here," Neeley ordered, while wondering what he was keeping back from her.

"The house is—" John began, but Neeley cut him off.

"We're not exactly going to walk in the front door," Neeley said. "That's not the smart way to do things."

CHAPTER

11

HANNAH HAD TOSSED and turned for hours with an occasional dozing off, but she was too angry to sleep. It would be light in a couple of hours and if she could just sleep now it would be enough.

She had just punched the feather pillow into a more pleasing shape when the shrill ringing of the phone ended all pretense of sleep. The voice on the other end was more of a shock than the timing of the call: John.

"Hannah, it's me. I have to see you right now. It's important. I'll come through the back. Just let me in the patio doors, okay?"

Hannah stared at the phone in disbelief, trying to think of something to say, but the phone had already gone dead. Hannah quickly pushed back her covers and shivered in the cool air. After belting her robe, she moved to the security alarm pad by the bedroom door. She punched in the code so she wouldn't set off the hall sensor.

By the time she got to the den, she could see John's form filling the partitions of the French door. She noticed a couple of things as she opened the locks: John's eyes were wide and frightened looking and there was someone behind him.

John seemed to propel himself through the doorway even as Hannah had the knob in her hand. He pushed her back until her legs hit an ottoman and she dropped into a seated position. John kept going and rolled onto the carpet, his hands behind him.

In the dimly lit gloom from the outside security lights, Hannah noticed something around his neck and wondered what it was. At that moment her eyes left John and she saw that the other person had followed John into the room.

The woman kicked the door shut and walked out of the shadows until she was standing in front of Hannah. Hannah looked down and saw what she had in her hand: a wicked-looking gun with a bulky barrel.

"John, what is going on?" Hannah demanded, feeling strangely calm in spite of the strange circumstances of his return.

The woman leaned forward. "My name's Neeley and yours is Hannah Masterson and I suggest you shut up and do what I tell you if you want to live."

Neeley then motioned to her two prisoners to move over to the couch. Hannah now noticed that John's hands were tied behind his back. There was a rope around his neck and Neeley had used that to move John through the woods.

When Hannah and John were seated on the couch, Neeley turned off the light and then sat on the edge of the coffee table, gun still pointed.

"I'm sorry, Hannah," John said.

"What is going on?" Hannah demanded once more.

"It's a long story," John said.

"One I want to hear also," Neeley said. "We've got a problem."

Hannah was still looking at her husband. "John, who is this woman? What is going on? Where did you go?"

Neeley leaned forward and spoke very clearly, biting the words off as if she were speaking to a wayward child. "If you want to live, shut up and listen." That caught Hannah's undivided attention. "We don't have much time. John has a story to tell us and once we hear it we need to make some decisions."

"Listen—" John began, but Neeley pulled the hammer back on the gun.

"I want to know what happened."

John's eyes shifted between the two women, and then he sighed in defeat. "All right. I was in the Army. In the Engineer Corps. A dumb second lieutenant. My area of expertise was oil pipelines. Pretty boring stuff. Putting in my time to pay off my ROTC scholarship."

Hannah's eyes were boring into her husband, as if she were trying to see beyond the words he was saying and was looking at someone she'd never seen before.

John continued. "Then I got a visit from this guy named Bailey in August of ninety-three. He had orders assigning me to him. He didn't say why. We flew overseas to Germany. I met Gant in Berlin. As soon as I met him I knew I was in over my head. Like Bailey, he wasn't wearing a uniform, but he sure had a lot of weapons. They told me that he would take care of me."

"Who was Gant?" Hannah ignored Neeley's look and concentrated on her husband.

"The man who was in charge of the mission," John said. He pointed at Neeley. "She knows—knew—him."

"Keep going," Neeley ordered.

"They told me that they wanted me to listen in on a meeting and judge the viability of what I heard. I didn't have a fucking clue what they were talking about and no one busted their butt to inform me of anything else.

"We flew out of Berlin aboard military transport. To a staging base in Saudi Arabia. There, in the middle of the night, Gant wakes me, makes me grab my gear, and drags me to a waiting Combat Talon—a modified C-130 cargo plane. There was some sort of all-terrain vehicle with big tires strapped down in the cargo bay. An army version of a dune buggy with lots of cans and stuff tied off on it.

"We got on and the Talon took off. We were in the air a long time. They were flying low level, below the radar. I knew we were over Africa, but had no clue exactly where. The plane was jerking around so much I got sick, puking my guts out into the barf bags the crew gave me. Gant, hell, he slept most of the flight.

"Then the plane slows down and descends even further as the back ramp opens. Gant cuts the straps holding the all-terrain vehicle and tells me to get in the passenger seat. As soon as I was in he told me to buckle up. I strapped in just in time. The 130 touched down on the desert floor, rolling. Gant cranks the engine as the ramp lowers even farther, until it's just about a foot above the sand. It was night and there was sand blowing everywhere and I couldn't see a damn thing. Gant had on night-vision goggles and his hands were on the wheel.

"We're still moving and Gant throws the thing into gear. Scared the shit out of me as he hits the gas and we literally fly out of the back of the plane, hit the desert floor, bounce, and then he's tearing ass away, even as the plane accelerates and lifts off. Whole thing took less than thirty seconds from the plane touching down to it was back up and we were driving away.

"I had no idea where the hell we were."

John came to a halt, beads of sweat on his forehead. Neeley glanced at Hannah. She was surprisingly calm, still simply staring at her husband.

"And then?" Neeley prodded.

"Gant drove for about an hour, then parked in a wadi. I helped him throw a camo net over the all-terrain. All he was doing was issuing orders, not explaining a damn thing. We grabbed our rucksacks and climbed out of the wadi toward a ridge about a mile away.

"It took us about two hours to get a spot just below the top of the ridge. We maintained listening silence after radioing in that we were on the ground in position. We broke that silence only twice in the ten days we were on the ground." John's voice was flat now, his sentences clipped as he recited his story.

"It took us two nights to dig the hide site. We hid under camouflage netting during the day. God, the sun was hot. And that hole—" he shook his head. "It was six feet wide by four feet front to rear and five feet vertical from the small slit that we looked out to the bottom. The overhead cover was made of small metal rods with canvas on top. Gant covered the whole thing with sand before sliding in. The site was set on a ridge looking toward the compound."

"What compound?" Neeley asked.

"I saw it the first day as we hid. A cluster of buildings in the middle of nowhere. Pickup trucks with machine guns in the cargo bed coming and going. A chopper flew in that first day. Russian design, but that didn't mean dick in Africa." He looked up at Neeley, backtracking slightly. "Gant finally told me after we had begun digging that we were in the Sudan, about fifty kilometers south of Khartoum. That a meeting was supposed to take place in the compound soon—he wasn't sure quite when—and we were going to listen in."

Neeley felt the sweat on her hand, between the flesh and the plastic of the pistol grip. Gant had never told her he'd even been in the Sudan, but she had a good idea who they were trying to listen to. During the early nineties the Sudan was a hotbed for terrorists.

John continued. "With our backpacks, radio, and water cans crammed in that hole, it was almost impossible to move more than a few inches in any direction. The smell was the worst part. We urinated in a small cup and carefully dumped it out the left front into the sand. We collected our feces in small plastic sandwich bags and buried it in a narrow trench Gant dug in the rear bottom." John gave a short laugh. "There wasn't much shit because we only brought enough food for one cold meal every day. Hell, we'd both lost ten to fifteen pounds by that last day, maybe more. I'd never done anything even remotely like it. But, Gant, it was like he was on vacation. He was so calm about it all."

Neeley remembered how gaunt Gant had looked when she

met him in Templehoff. Masterson was repeating the story he told at his mission debriefing.

Hannah cut in. "All this—" she waved her hands indicating Neeley and John, "is about something you did before you met me? That's why you ran away?"

John nodded.

"It has nothing to do with me?" Hannah pressed.

"I'm sorry," John said. "I thought—"

"Finish the story," Neeley said, checking the glowing clock in the kitchen.

"Gant—" John Masterson shook his head as he remembered. "He could handle doing that. Sitting in that fucking hole, shitting in a bag. It drove me nuts." John nodded, thinking back. "Gant's biggest concern going in had been water. He'd tied down four ten-gallon cans on the all-terrain. Every three days he went and retrieved one. By that last day only one still held a little bit of water. I was getting nervous but Gant didn't seem worried. He'd check the satellite radio twice a day, just listening.

"So we sat and waited.

"Then the activity in the compound picked up. A convoy came from the north, from Khartoum. Ten pickups with machine guns and two Land Rovers with tinted windows. Around a dozen people got out of the Land Rovers and moved into the main building while the ones on the pickups took security positions all around.

"Then the helicopter came and a half-dozen people offloaded, including several Westerners. They went into the same buildings. Gant pulled out this device—some sort of laser. He aimed it at the building, at one of the windows. They'd painted them all black, so you couldn't see inside, but this laser could pick up sound vibrations off the glass. He hooked it up to a laptop computer. Then he plugged in two headsets, handing me one.

"I put it on. We could hear what they were saying in there." John barked a bitter laugh. "They were negotiating. About a couple of oil pipelines."

"From Turkmenistan to the Arabian Sea and to Pakistan," Neeley said.

John nodded, surprised. "Yeah."

"Across Afghanistan," Neeley added.

John nodded once more. "Which at the time the Taliban ruled. That was one of the groups there at the meeting. There were also a couple of Pakistanis. For their end of the one pipeline. And some Saudis about their end."

"And the Americans?" Neeley prompted.

"The head of Cintgo, who was supposed to build the pipelines along with a couple of his people. And to broker the deal, Senator Collins."

"Shit," Neeley muttered.

Hannah spoke up. "Was bin Laden there?"

The other two turned to her in surprise, so she quickly explained. "It was in the papers and magazines. He hung out in Sudan in the early nineties. He—his construction company—even built a highway there. Before they kicked him out and he went back to Afghanistan. Everyone knows that."

"No," Neeley said, "everyone doesn't know that." She turned to John. "Well?"

John's eyes took on a distant look. "Yes, he was there. Brokering for the Taliban. Cintgo was worried about security for the pipelines in Afghanistan. The Russians had tried to build one in the country when they occupied it and the mujahaideen, led by bin Laden, had cut it so many times it failed.

"Gant was on the radio with someone. Telling them what he knew so far. Someone named Nero."

"Who's Nero?" Hannah cut in.

"The guy who runs the Cellar," John said. "The organization Gant worked for."

John looked at Neeley. "I could hear them through the headphones. And I figured out pretty quick that Gant was there for more than just listening. The laser device also could paint the target."

" 'Paint'?" Hannah asked.

"Designate whatever it's pointed out as a target," John explained to his wife.

"But Collins was there," Hannah said.

"No shit," John said. "I've thought about it over the years, then one time I was watching the Godfather and it came to me—Collins was like that police captain that those mob guys brought to that meeting in the Bronx. To ensure safety."

"Except in the movie they killed the cop," Hannah pointed out.

Neeley was surprised at the other woman's comments. She'd gotten over her surprise about her husband rather quickly.

"Well, Nero wasn't going to kill a senator, apparently," John said. "Nero told the Navy jets that were on station to head back to their carrier."

"Did Gant tape this?" Neeley asked.

"No."

Neeley was surprised again.

"They all reached a basic agreement to build the two pipes," John Masterson continued. "Then the meeting broke up. Collins and the Cintgo guys got on the chopper and flew away. The Pakistanis drove away. But we were still listening. That's when we learned then that the Taliban had made a secret videotape of the meeting. It was in the possession of a guy named Sheik Hassan al-Turabi."

John fell silent. Neeley gestured with the Mod-59 to Hannah. "Go make us some drinks." Neeley went to John and untied him.

Hannah walked to the wet bar and fixed three drinks. Her hands were still, her head clear. She came back and handed one to the other two and sat on the other end of the couch from John with her own drink. For some reason learning that this wasn't at all about her, but came from something before her time with John outweighed the betrayal of his leaving and his lies. She felt strangely free of responsibility.

"And?" Neeley pressed.

"At the time it wasn't that big of a deal," John said. "The proposed Afghan pipelines. Dealing with the Taliban. Hell, even I'd heard Cintgo was trying to do this. You could read it in the trades. And we'd been supporting bin Laden for years against the Russians."

"But Collins being there—" Neeley let that hang.

"Still not that big of a deal," John said. "Gant radioed in a final report of the meeting and requested pick up. While we were packing up we got new orders. Someone wanted that videotape."

"Collins," Neeley said.

John shrugged. "I guess. Or Nero to use as leverage against Collins. So we hung around a little longer. Listened. Found out that al-Turabi was to keep the videotape. He was going back to Afghanistan via Somalia. Give some support to in-country brothers there."

"So you went to Somalia," Neeley said.

"Yeah," John said. "We pulled out of the hide sight, went back to the all-terrain, and loaded up. Gant drove us into the desert and we waited. The Talon came back, landed, and we drove on board. Took us to the airfield in Mogadishu where all the special operations people were stationed—the Rangers, Delta Force, and the Task Force 160 helicopters."

John fell silent for a few moments and Neeley didn't feel the inclination to prod him forward anymore. She wasn't sure she wanted to hear what he was going to say. Hannah was sitting, drink in hand, watching her husband. Neeley noticed the other woman had yet to take a sip of her drink.

"We saw the special ops guys running their missions. The humanitarian part, then the snatch raids when things changed. The place was getting hairy. Gant disappeared into town a couple of times, searching for al-Turabi. I guess he found him."

John's voice went flat once more as he recited, just as he had probably done years ago at a debriefing. "The third of October. There was going to be a raid later that day. Gant was talking with Nero and he was pissed, the first time I saw him get really emotional. I was just an engineer and wasn't sure what he was talking about, but he laid it out for me—the Ranger and Delta Force guys had no armor support and they were running their missions in daylight, negating their night-vision technological advantage. And, what really ticked Gant off, was that they were using the same tactics over and over again. And Nero wanted him to use the raid that day as cover for taking out al-Turabi and getting the fucking video.

"The first wave of choppers lifted. I heard Gant ask: 'Is this thing a go or no go, Mr. Nero?' I don't know what Nero said, but Gant didn't act like he appreciated the answer."

Neeley could hear the sound of a clock chiming in another room as John Masterson continued.

"We saw the raid go into downtown. Everything seemed to be going all right. Then Gant and I loaded onto one of the Little Birds, an OH-6, to run our own little op in the middle of this. We flew downtown, to where the raid was. We landed on the roof. Delta guys had secured the building and snatched a bunch of their targets, including al-Turabi.

"Gant found the tape and some documents on al-Turabi, taped around his waist. Gant gave me the documents and stuck the tape in his pack. Then we shoved al-Turabi onboard one of the Blackhawks. Things were beginning to get a little hairy. We were getting incoming fire. Gant and I were supposed to go out on the Blackhawk with al-Turabi but Gant decided against it. He felt the Delta guys could use our firepower as the ground column was caught up in some trouble and hadn't arrived yet.

"I was pissed at him," John said. "I wanted to get the hell out of there as fast as possible. But he saved my life by doing that. Cause that chopper lifted, and started to move away, when it got hit by rocket fire from an adjoining building and went down. Al-Turabi and several others on board were killed."

John sighed and became quiet. Neeley was trying to sort through what he had already told her. She wanted to know everything about the past very badly, but she also wanted to know what John was lying about concerning the present. "You didn't leave Hannah the day Gant called."

John stared at her and finally reluctantly nodded. "I was scared when Gant called, but he told me I was covered. That someone—he must have meant you—would come by and everything would stay the same. I was going off to golf when Nero called me on my cell phone. He told me it was time for me to go."

"That's why I didn't sense it," Hannah sounded relieved, as if a great mystery had been solved.

"I don't get it," Neeley said. "What did he mean by that."

John looked at his wife. "I am so sorry. I never really thought Nero would come for you."

Hannah was surprised. "For me?"

John shook his head, rubbing his hands across weary eyes. "This has all been a nightmare. Ever since that day in Mogadishu."

Hannah was about to say something, but Neeley cut her off. "I don't understand. If you were working for Nero, why did you and Gant keep the video and documents?"

John looked up at her. "Because Gant had seen who had fired the missile that downed the helicopter we were supposed to be on, killing everyone on board."

Two things happened very quickly. There was a sharp crack as if someone had thrown a rock at the big window and Neeley reached over, grabbed Hannah's head and smashed her face down onto the carpet.

Hannah heard another loud pop and then Neeley was on top of her and whispering. "Keep down. Crawl into the hallway."

Hannah started to move and only then noticed the weight of John on her legs. Hannah gasped and struggled to free her feet. She felt something warm and wet soak her back. "Get off me, John!"

Neeley's voice was insistent and level. "He can't, Hannah. He's dead."

Hannah pulled her feet loose with a jerk. She started a low

crawl toward the hall all the while hearing the shots and the crashes that followed them. Whoever was firing was using a damn large caliber gun. As she got close to the hallway, a glass frame above her shattered, raining splinters of glass on and around her.

Hannah paused and turned to look for Neeley. Another well-placed shot caused her to roll into the hall, regardless of the glass.

Suddenly Neeley was at her side, John's briefcase in her hand. "Crawl into your room. Get dressed, fast. We've gotta get out of here."

Hannah looked at the strange woman. "John is dead?"

"Yes."

Hannah closed her eyes. A hand pinched her arm. "You don't move, we're both gonna be dead too."

"Why should I listen to you? You were going to kill John and me a few minutes ago."

Neeley pushed her. "I wasn't going to kill you. I came to help. Now go get dressed!"

Hannah shook her head. "What do you mean you weren't going to kill us? You had a gun pointed at us! That's certainly—"

Neeley brought the pistol back up, cutting her off. "Okay, I will kill you if you don't get dressed right now. Whoever's out there is an expert. We only have a few minutes to get out of here so do what I say now!"

Whether the words or the tone worked wasn't clear, but Hannah crawled to the big bedroom. Neeley followed and darted around Hannah, making her way to the bathroom. By squatting in the tub she could see most of the backyard. With the light off, she knew she couldn't be seen from the outside. It was still dark out there but the promise of daylight was not far away.

Neeley couldn't see a thing and regretted leaving her pack in the truck. Whoever the Cellar had sent had been amazingly fast. The firing had stopped once they got out of the den. She had been surprised at the number of bullets the firer had put into the house. He couldn't have seen them once Neeley shoved Hannah down, but he had continued to fire as if he knew where they were. And he should have come into the house by now. How did he know they hadn't run out the front door or garage, or called the cops?

Neeley had it then. This guy was smart. He had access to the same equipment Gant had had and would operate in the same way. Neeley braced her forearms on the edge of the tub, the barrel of her pistol pointing into the backyard. She took a chance. "Hannah, get away from the kitchen window!" she yelled.

She saw the bright muzzle flash right where she expected it. By the old tree. She heard the kitchen window shatter. Hannah was calling out but Neeley ignored her as she fired rapidly. First shot to blow out the plane of glass between her and the target, then three rounds as fast as she could pull the trigger at the muzzle flash even though she knew the firer would have relocated as soon as he fired.

"What are you doing?" Hannah was yelling, the sound of the gun echoing off the tiles.

Neeley ran to the bedroom, staying low just in case and grabbed Hannah's arm with a fierce grip. She hissed in Hannah's ear. "The house is bugged. The person outside can hear us. Do whatever I say if you want to make it out of here alive."

Neeley looked down and realized Hannah had on a silk dress buttoned wrong and had been trying to pull on pantyhose. "Jesus," Neeley muttered.

Neeley reached into the closet and felt around. Nothing felt like denim. "Socks, Hannah," Neeley whispered. "Socks and tennis shoes. Sneakers," she added. Neeley grabbed the nylon out of Hannah's hand.

In a minute she had Hannah reasonably well put together. She edged back to the door of the bathroom and looked out. Nothing moving. Neeley looked at Hannah, who was moving now, stuffing clothes and items into a large tote bag. "Call the cops," Neeley said loudly.

"What?" Hannah asked, confused.

"Call the cops. As soon as you get them on the phone, I'll be gone," Neeley said. She was watching the wood line. "Move!" Neeley snapped. "Call them now!"

Hannah crawled over to the nightstand and picked up the phone. Neeley saw something moving in the wood line and smiled. She turned and grabbed Hannah's arm. "Let's go," she whispered.

"But—"

Neeley clamped a hand over Hannah's mouth and dragged her toward the garage, the phone falling to the ground.

RACINE WAS RUNNING through the woods, heading back toward his car. He rubbed his hand down his left side as he moved. There was a little bit of blood. Splinters from the tree. The bitch was good with a pistol. It must have been sixty–seventy feet from his position to the window she'd fired out of. Contrary to the cop shows on TV it took a damn good shot to even get close with a pistol at that distance.

Racine pulled the small headphones off and tucked them into a pocket, sealing the Velcro cover to make sure they didn't fall out. The house had been wired, just as he'd expected. He'd picked up the conversation in the kitchen as he'd hit the right frequency. Jesus! Masterson had just been sitting there spilling his guts and that had forced Racine to act before he was ready.

He'd taken out John to shut him up, but the women had reacted faster then he had expected. He'd peppered the fucking house, tracking them by sound from the wire as best he could, trying to flush them out, until they'd mentioned the cops. That was a bit too much publicity for him, especially after Baltimore.

"Fuck!" Racine came to a halt. Neeley wouldn't call the cops! She'd tricked him. Just as she'd tricked him to shoot at the window. Racine half-turned back toward the house, and then realized it was too late for that.

He smiled, his teeth giving him a ferocious appearance in the dark. It didn't matter. He knew exactly how to meet up with Hannah and Gant's ghost. Racine began sprinting, heading back the way he had come.

CHAPTER

12

HANNAH GLANCED AT THE WOMAN behind the wheel. Neither of them had said a word since they had switched to Neeley's pickup and made the on-ramp for Interstate 70. They were going toward Kansas City and Neeley, if she had a plan, wasn't sharing it.

Hannah was surprised at her own calmness. She had no idea what was going on or who this seemingly dangerous woman was other than her name, yet she felt a detachment that seemed to insulate her from even curiosity. Though John had apparently been a stranger to her, his death still mattered to her on some level. She had spent most of her adult life with this man and to her there still remained the John of her reality. That John was dead too and despite the lies, the John she knew deserved to be mourned. Maybe that mourning would come later. The last week had angered her beyond her imaginings. Now it was as if the events of the past hour had shifted her into the eye of the hurricane, taking her out of the turmoil she was in. She didn't know what was coming, but she was sure it would also be bad. Most impor-

tant though, was the realization that had seeped into her as
John told his story that his leaving had had nothing at all to
do with her. She felt as if the past ten years of her life had
been wiped clean.

She watched the endless businesses, strip malls, and
larger shopping centers that constituted northern St. Louis
zip by her window. She thought of the stores she had fre-
quented and was reminded of the meager supplies in her
current possession. She had her purse with its few cosmet-
ics and useless credit cards, the tote bag with the stuff she
had crammed in it in the dark, and was wearing sweats that
Neeley had grabbed for her with a nylon windbreaker, socks
and sneakers. That was it.

Hannah felt certain she wouldn't be going home anytime
soon, or even ever. In the space of less than two weeks, she
had effectively lost her husband and the whole of her possessions. A couple of hours ago she had almost lost her
life.

Hannah pushed memories of the shooting from her mind.
Neeley seemed intent on her own thoughts and just driving
the truck. Hannah could appreciate the distance they were
putting between them and whoever had made Swiss cheese
of her den. When Neeley spoke, the suddenness of it caused
Hannah to jump.

"Aren't you going to say something?"

"No."

Neeley turned to the woman huddled in the passenger
seat. "Are you in shock or something? Aren't you interested
in what's going on?"

"I don't want to talk right now, okay?" Hannah said.

"This isn't going away, Hannah. You can't draw into yourself and pretend you're on a Sunday afternoon outing."

"Where are we going?" Hannah finally asked.

"Right now I'm just trying to get out of town."

"And then? What are we supposed to do once we get out
of town?"

"I figure first we just get away from the guy trying to kill us. I agree, we'll have to figure something out though, because he'll find us soon enough."

"What? How can he find us? And who is he anyway? What is going on? Who exactly are you?"

"He found your house." Neeley recited the facts in logical order. "He found the frequency on the bugs that I placed in your house. He—"

"Bugs in my house?" Hannah cut in. "That you placed?"

"I needed to find John," Neeley said.

"You bugged my house? You listened to me?"

"I was doing a job," Neeley said.

Hannah turned away and silence again reigned inside the truck.

Neeley glanced in the rearview mirror. As far as she could tell they had not been followed. She had not liked going back to her pickup truck, given that the shooter had probably come from the same direction, but there was too much irreplaceable gear in the truck-bed under the camper shell. She couldn't leave it sitting there, waiting for the cops to find it. Her fingerprints were all over the truck and when John's body was found it wouldn't take the cops long to put something together.

She realized she had not done well. The fact that the shooter, whoever it was, had not done particularly well either, taking John out first instead of the person with the gun, did little to console her.

"Whoever it was heard what we were saying?" Hannah asked.

Neeley nodded, trying to figure out a plan.

"Why was John shot first?" Hannah asked. "You had the gun."

Neeley was surprised that this housewife was asking the same thing that had just occurred to her. "He screwed up."

"Whoever it was is a professional, right?"

"Yeah."

"Then he didn't screw up, did he?"

Neeley frowned, but Hannah continued.

"He shot John to shut him up."

Neeley realized Hannah was right. She replayed the scene, trying to focus on what John had been talking about just before getting killed. Hannah's observations disturbed her, even though they were pretty much the same as her own. Neeley pointed to the generic restaurant at the next exit. "We'll stop for some coffee. We can talk there."

They rolled into the lot and Neeley parked the truck. They walked in and took a booth where Neeley could watch outside.

FOUR MILES BACK, Racine had a small metal suitcase open on the passenger seat. A power cord ran from it to the cigarette lighter. He watched the dot that represented Neeley's truck come to a halt. He smiled at the thought that the bitch's training would be her downfall. He'd known exactly where to find her ride and the Vermont plates had just been icing. She had by-the-book-Gant stamped all over her. Gant and his fucking rules. There were problems with rules and if the dip-shit have ever condescended enough to treat Racine like an equal, he would have been glad to explain some of them to Gant. Number one was if someone knew your rules, they could predict your actions and be one step ahead.

Racine saw the first sign for the exit the women had taken come up. The bitch had outsmarted him at the house. Time to push things, Racine decided as he flipped open a small black book. He thumbed through until he got to the page he wanted. Then he opened his cellular phone with his free hand. With difficulty, he punched in a phone number.

He grimaced when the other end was picked up, but he knew one had to make due with what was available. He didn't have much time to plan anything elaborate but all he needed was a few minutes of quiet time to kill Neeley and get the blonde into the trunk. He knew Nero was adamant about not killing her and he couldn't afford another mistake. At least not yet, as far as Nero was concerned.

* * *

HANNAH GLANCED at the other patrons in the restaurant and decided it was a place where no one would find her oddly dressed. Neeley was fussing with the coffee they had been brought by the middle-aged waitress. For the first time Hannah could clearly see the other woman's face and decided she was lovely. The dark hair and eyes highlighted the pale skin that seemed to glow with an athletic health and vigor. Hannah knew this was a dangerous, hard woman, but she had to admit she was also a pretty one.

Neeley reached over and clasped Hannah's free hand. It was not a gesture of comfort but rather one of restraint. Her voice had a steady quality that was more frightening than the information it conveyed.

"Listen closely, Hannah. If you want to survive this, you'll listen to me and do what I say. I don't know what kind of dreamworld you've been living in, but it's time to check in to reality. In the real world your life is worth spit about now. I'm not the bad guy, okay?"

Hannah stared at her. "You walk in with John all tied up and waving a gun and you're not the bad guy?"

Neeley shook her head. "No, no, that's not how it is. You see, your husband screwed you over. He not only took everything when he split, he left you hanging in the wind knowing that someone like me or the man who shot up your house would show up."

"John wasn't a bad man for God sakes. He was a little egotistical and overly involved with material possessions but that hardly damns him." The words sounded hollow to Hannah even as she said them. Just this evening she'd been damning John at the top of her lungs to the empty rooms of her house.

"Hannah, your husband just told you he was involved in something a long time ago that killed him earlier this morning. But he never told you a word about it, did he?"

"You're lying. John was making that up."

"There's the briefcase in my truck with something in it

that John has had all these years that says I'm not lying and that he wasn't making it up." Neeley squeezed tight on Hannah's wrist. "You were angry about John leaving you, but understand he betrayed you when he met you by not telling you the truth about his past. Use that anger, work with it, because you need something to get you through this."

The waitress appeared with the coffeepot.

Neeley let go of Hannah and pushed her hair from her face with impatience. Neeley waited until the waitress refilled their cups and was gone before continuing. "What we need is a plan, because everyone else is going to have one."

"Who is everyone else and just what's going on? For starters, who exactly are you?"

"First let's get you up to now," Neeley said. "You now know your husband was involved in something that forced his termination. The man that I spent the last ten years with was also involved and he sent me to John."

"This Gant fellow?" Hannah asked.

Neeley nodded.

"Where is Gant now?"

"He's dead."

"People seem to die around you a lot," Hannah said.

"Not just everyone around me. I'm dead too in a manner of speaking."

"Great. What did John mean?" Hannah pressed. "About Nero coming for me? Why would he come for me?"

Before Hannah could say anything else, Neeley interrupted. She had been looking past Hannah and now she shook her head. "See those two men who just pulled in to the parking lot?" Neeley inclined her head toward the glass.

Hannah could see two young men in dirty jeans and brown leather jackets climbing off large motorcycles. Both had beards and were not the type you wanted to run into in a dark alley or anywhere else for that matter. They were looking about. "Yes?"

"They're here for us," Neeley said.

"How do you know?"

Neeley smiled coldly. "Woman's intuition."

The two men sauntered to the door of the restaurant and walked in. One was tall, with long flowing dirty-blond hair. The other's skull was shaved. The tall one looked about, then his eyes settled on the booth Neeley and Hannah were in.

"Just stay calm," Neeley said. "Let me handle this."

The men walked over, then slid onto the seats, pinning the women against the window. Tall blond was next to Neeley and the shaved head was next to Hannah.

"Can I help you?" Neeley said. She glanced out into the parking lot. There was a car parked, facing their window. The glass was dark but she could tell the engine was running by the exhaust coming out the tailpipe. It had pulled in right after the two motorcycles. She couldn't see the driver, just the form of someone sitting there, waiting.

"I like my women big," Blondie said. "You like your men big?" He grabbed Neeley's left hand and pushed it into his crotch.

Neeley turned her attention back to the booth. Hannah was scrunched up as far as she could against the glass. The man next to her had his hands under the table. Hannah gasped and jerked farther away as the man did something.

Neeley curled the fingers of her left hand and squeezed. "Not big enough, buddy boy."

Blondie gasped as he doubled over. "Ah shit!"

Neeley's Glock was out and pointing straight at Baldie. "You'd better have your hands on the table right now," Neeley said.

Blondie swung with his right arm and Neeley ducked the blow. She twisted her left hand and he screamed as his balls did a 180. The muzzle of the pistol hadn't wavered from between Baldie's eyes. "Put your hands on the table," Neeley ordered again.

Baldie did what he was told, a strange-looking knife with a notched point in his right hand. There was blood on the tip. Neeley rapped the muzzle of the gun against the side of Blondie's head and it thumped down on the tabletop.

Neeley could see the waitress on the phone. The cops would be here in a couple of minutes. She brought the gun back to bear on Baldie. "Who hired you?"

"Some guy."

"Bad description," she said, slamming the barrel down on top of his right hand. He screamed as bones broke. She looked at the parking lot. The car was pulling out.

"That him?"

Baldie was holding his wounded hand. "Yeah, some guy. That's all I know. He had a lot of cash. Crazy dude with crazy eyes. You broke my hand, you bitch!"

"Get out of the seat," Neeley said as she pivoted and used both her legs to push Blondie onto the floor. Baldie did as he was told.

"Let's go," Neeley said to Hannah who had remained frozen throughout the entire proceeding.

Hannah stirred. "I'm bleeding," she said, looking down at her left leg where blood was dripping down from a cut in her thigh, just above the knee.

Neeley tossed some napkins. "Use those." She stood. "On your face," Neeley ordered Baldie. He did as he was told and Neeley grabbed Hannah's arm, dragging her out of the restaurant. The other patrons fearing the worst at the sudden outbreak of violence and remembering more than one restaurant shooter were huddled under tables and chairs seeking invisibility.

They hustled to the truck and Neeley quickly drove out of the restaurant and onto the Interstate, heading back toward St. Louis.

Hannah finally spoke as they merged into traffic. "Who were they?"

"Some shitheads the man who shot up the house hired."

"Why?"

Neeley just stared. "Why do you think? To grab us, drag us some place quiet, and blow our brains out. Evidently he doesn't want a public spectacle that he's involved in."

Hannah was holding the now red-soaked napkin to her

thigh. "What about the gun battle at my house? That was pretty public."

Neeley shook her head and pointed behind them. "Not like that. And I think you were right—John talking forced the play at the house. Unless the Cellar called in a disposal unit and cleaned up your house, we're going to be fugitives soon. I can't go to the police but you still could. I don't know how much they'd believe and I can't guarantee someone from the Cellar won't show up with the proper papers and identification to take you away and nobody would ever see you again. We've stepped into some deep shit here, Hannah."

Hannah was starting to shake her head. So much for the eye of the storm. "I don't know who you are but don't leave me, okay? Let's just get out of here. There's got to be someplace we can hide. Right now I feel like a bullet's going to punch me right between the eyes any second."

Neeley was trying to think. She hadn't thought they had been followed after picking up the truck, but obviously they had.

"That guy was a creep," Hannah said. "He was grabbing my leg. He jabbed me with his knife."

Neeley glanced over. There was definitely blood seeping through the napkins that Hannah was pressing against her skin. The wound was deeper than she had initially thought. Hannah was now wrapping a kerchief around the wound.

"Is it bad?" Neeley asked.

"Not too bad," Hannah replied as she tied off the cloth.

"We have to get rid of this truck," Neeley said. "There's got to be a bug in it somewhere and if we don't get rid of it, neither of us will live."

She saw what she was looking for. She slammed on the brakes and spun the wheel, turning onto the crossover. Tires squealing, she quickly drove up onto the westbound lanes.

Hannah made no comment on the move. Indeed, she didn't react at all, other than to grip the door handle to keep steady during the turn. Her stillness was a bit disconcerting to Neeley, who, although she preferred it over panic, wasn't sure what to make of the other woman. Neeley checked the mirror. No other car imitated the maneuver, but that wasn't much consolation.

CHAPTER

13

"JOHN MASTERSON IS DEAD," Nero's metallic voicebox grated the words out.

"Do you have his package?" Senator Collins asked. He hadn't bothered to sit down since entering the room a minute ago. One of the lights over Nero's head was out; making it look like a pair of headlights was over the old man. Collins wondered if the effect was deliberate or simply that no one had mentioned to the old man that the lightbulb had burned out.

"No."

"Damn it!" Collins exclaimed.

"His package isn't as important as Gant's," Nero said.

"What about the woman?" Collins asked.

"Masterson's wife?" Nero was puzzled for the moment.

"No. Gant's girlfriend. I assume she has his package."

"Ah, Neeley," Nero said. "She made it to John Masterson before we could."

Collins grimaced. "Then she has Masterson's papers now. She has to."

Nero shrugged. "And she probably either has Gant's tape or knows where it is. When Gant was alive they had them also. I still believe nothing has changed and by acting we are forcing a dangerous situation."

"Do you realize the repercussion if this becomes public?" Collins asked. He didn't wait for an answer. "This will make Iran-Contra look like a parking violation! A lot of heads will roll, yours among them."

Nero did not appear to be particularly worried about that possibility. "It is curious you mention Iran-Contra. I was never briefed on that action, never mind sign off on it."

"Remember your place," Collins threatened.

Nero abruptly shifted the subject. "I understand you had Mr. Racine perform a task for you in Baltimore not long ago."

Collins frowned. "So? It was a minor matter."

"Racine works for the government under specific contracts, not for you," Nero said.

"I am the government," Collins said. He caught the look Nero gave him and quickly amended: "All right, not exactly, but I have input. I'm on the Oversight Committee for Christ's sake."

"Input?" Nero repeated the word, as if considering it. "The action in Baltimore was not sanctioned by the Committee. Has Mr. Racine worked for you in the past?"

"No."

Nero was running his fingers over a piece of paper. Collins looked at it, but all he could see were the raised Braille bumps. "I have the official report from when you were in the Sudan in August 1993. You were helping Cintgo negotiate pipeline rights across Afghanistan. I had surveillance on the meeting. When I found out you were there, I contacted you about the tape. You asked me to send my people to recover it. I did.

"But what exactly happened there? Racine seems to have disappeared during that time period also," Nero continued. "It was of no great concern at the time because Racine often took extended, how shall we call them, jaunts. But I've done some checking and it turns out, of all things, that he was in

Africa also at that time. An interesting coincidence considering you say he never worked for you before."

Collins face went pale, unnoticed of course by Nero. But the change in his breathing pattern was obvious to the old man. Collins remained quiet.

"Also what's curious about the Sudan at that time was that the FBI had a counterterrorist cell there. And certain notorious terrorist figures were also concurrently in-country. And shortly after your visit, the FBI's team was pulled out." Nero tossed that piece of paper to the side and picked up another one. "You know the Cellar rarely takes action, don't you Senator?"

Collins nodded, realized Nero couldn't see him, and spoke. "Yes." The word came out drier that he wished.

"Mainly the Cellar's job is to gather information. Information unbiased by political, religious, moral—any slant. Just the facts. Even if they don't, how should I say, shine a favorable light on our own country. After all, we do bad things in the name of freedom, do we not? For the greater good?"

Collins remained silent.

"The problem though is who determines the greater good? All the information is useless unless someone is able to do something with it. Do you know what a Bodyguard of Lies is?"

Collins still didn't answer.

"Winston Churchill said that 'in wartime, the truth is so precious that she should always be attended by a Bodyguard of Lies.'" Nero put the paper down and Collins's shoulders relaxed slightly. Nero held his hands up and then pointed at his face. "Do you know what happened to my eyes?"

Collins tongue snaked across his lips. "No."

"Someone put a red-hot steel reinforcing rod into each eye socket and burned them out."

Beads of sweat were on Collins's forehead. "Listen, I—"

"That someone was a Gestapo interrogator," Nero continued as if he hadn't heard the Senator speak at all. "History. It's very, very important. There's the famous saying that those who don't learn from it are doomed to repeat it. I think it's much simpler—those who don't know history are stupid. Ignorant. I've made history in this room. And you've made history, too, haven't you, Senator? Of course, much of it will never be written down in the books. Only the effects. Some good. Some bad.

"Do you know what a Jedbergh team was?" Nero asked. He waited a second. "Speak up man."

The powerful Senator had not been spoken to like this in many years. "No."

"The OSS?"

"No."

"SOE?"

"No."

Nero shook his head sadly. "The SOE was the Special Operations Executive. British. Their military spies in World War Two. The OSS was the Office of Strategic Services. The forerunner of the CIA and our spy service in World War Two. A Jedbergh team consisted of three men. One SOE—Brit; one American—OSS; and one Free French agent. Teams jumped into France, linked up with the Resistance, and carried on the guerrilla war against the Germans.

"Sounds pretty straightforward, doesn't it?" Nero didn't wait for a response this time. "But of course it wasn't. Did you ever hear of Ultra or Enigma?"

"Yes," Collins said. "Ultra was the British machine that decoded German messages sent via Enigma."

"Very good. Every time Ultra decoded a German signal, Churchill had to decide whether to take action. This was much more difficult than it might initially appear. Because the primary consideration at all times was that he had to keep Ultra a secret from the Germans so they wouldn't stop using Enigma. Quite a quandary wouldn't you say?

"For example, the Ultra operators decode a German message from a U-Boat giving its location. It's sitting right in the path of a convoy. So you go sink the U-Boat, correct? Wrong. Because the Germans will begin to wonder how you knew where the U-boat was if it just suddenly disappears without reporting being spotted. So, if you were going to attack it, you must send out a reconnaissance plane to that area, with the crew, of course, not knowing there was a U-Boat there. And when the plane reported seeing a U-Boat, why then you could attack it. But if the recon plane got shot down looking for a U-Boat whose location you already knew, not only was it tough luck for the crew of the plane, but tough also on the convoy because you couldn't attack it. Also, if the plane didn't spot the U-boat, which was likely, then again, tough luck on the convoy. This happened many times.

"Churchill allowed the city of Coventry to be bombed, even though he had adequate warning from Ultra to protect it. Which brings me to the Jedberghs. And things I didn't know in 1943. We were young and full of piss, ready to fight and die. And our bosses knew that. So when they learned from Ultra that a Resistance network had been compromised by the Gestapo they were in a quandary. After all, they had already radioed the Resistance group that a Jedbergh team would be jumping in to join them within the fortnight. If they canceled the team coming, the Gestapo would know something was up.

"So some really smart chap, as the Brits were wont to say, thought, well let's make the best of this, how shall we say, awkward situation. So they took me and my two teammates and they briefed us on various things." A strange noise came out of the wand—Nero chuckling. "All lies—disinformation is the proper term. Except we believed it. Why shouldn't we?

"So we jumped into France into a network our superiors knew had been compromised. We were quite disconcerted, to put it lightly, to be picked up by the Gestapo before we could even gather in our parachutes. The Frenchman was the smartest. He went down shooting on the drop zone rather than be captured. The Brit and I were taken prisoner."

Almost perfect silence reigned in the dark room for several moments. The only slight sound was Collins's breathing.

"I talked," Nero finally said. "After the first eye I talked. I never quite understood why they took out the second considering they were going to execute me the next day. A touch of sadism I suspect. The Brit talked too. And the Germans believed us. I would have believed too. Because *we* believed what we were saying under torture. Which were, of course, lies fed to us. Quite a brilliant scheme, if you think about. Which I have, of course. Often over the years.

"I don't regret it. In retrospect, my little team of three helped—along with many other lies—convince the Germans the invasion was coming in Calais, not Normandy. Do you know how many lives that saved in the long run? And I lived. The only one. These—" he waved his hand in front of his face—"what are the loss of these compared to death?

"Do you know how I survived? The Resistance attacked the Gestapo building where I was being held. One of the fighters got me out of my cell. But we were trapped on the third floor. There was only one way out. Through a window and sliding down a radio transmission wire extended across the street to the next roof." Nero held up his hands, showing the scars. "My hands were sliced to the bone sliding down that wire, but I didn't let go until I got to the other side. The Resistance gathered me in and eventually got me back to England.

"I later found out that someone here in Washington had approved of the mission I was sent on. My predecessor here in the Cellar. He'd heard about me and he had me brought here. He wanted to know how I felt about what had happened. I told him the truth." Nero paused for a couple of seconds. "That if I were him, I would have done the same thing."

Senator Collins wiped his forehead with a handkerchief.

"From that moment on he began grooming me to be his replacement. I took over from him in 1947 and have been here ever since. I also learned later that he had ordered that Resistance unit to rescue me. Most interesting and foresightful, don't you think?" Nero frowned, an obscene gesture with eyebrows furrowing over empty sockets. "Do you understand what I am saying to you, Senator?"

"Yes."

"No, you don't, I fear."

"Is this matter going to be taken care of?" Collins demanded as he checked his watch.

"Oh, yes, indeed, it will be taken care of," Nero assured the Senator, the nature of his artificial voice making it impossible for Collins to determine anything of meaning in the comment beyond the words themselves. "That's my job, taking care of things."

CHAPTER

14

RACINE SLOWLY DROVE by the abandoned truck. The two women had left it eighty miles west of the exit at which Racine had sent the two motorcycle thugs after them. He had been impressed with Neeley for the second time. She had handled herself well. Perhaps Gant had had more than pussy on his mind when he'd hooked up with her.

He could have taken them himself, but the restaurant was too public. Some dumb shit would call the cops as they had. The two motorcycle goons had been gathered up but they had no clue who Racine was other than a man who had their phone number and had given them each a thousand in cash.

Better to flush the game and set it running and catch up some place more private. From the way Neeley had handled the Glock back at the Masterson's house and her actions in the restaurant, he decided that Gant's woman could prove difficult. She'd obviously fight like hell to keep the blonde bitch alive. The situation was unraveling. Much as he hated to admit it, a more direct approach and some backup were needed. He'd already called the Agency number about the latter requirement and forces were moving.

He looked at the glowing dot on the screen of his tracking computer. It was sitting still in the middle; the bug that he had placed on the truck. He switched frequencies. "Come to papa," he muttered. A new, moving dot lit up on the screen to the west near Kansas City and Racine drove to the on-ramp in pursuit.

IT WAS NEARING NOON as Neeley and Hannah approached the eastern suburbs of Kansas City. Hannah had fallen asleep a couple of hours ago. It was more of a collapse from complete exhaustion than a pleasant nap. Neeley was grateful for the quiet as she tried to make plans for the immediate future.

They'd dumped the truck in exchange for a four door, white sedan that would be hard for police to spot. Another felony to add to her growing list of crimes. It didn't bother Neeley. If she was ever caught, and the authorities found out who she really was, she had a lot more to worry about than grand theft auto. She'd quickly loaded everything from the truck into the trunk and backseat of the car.

They were going to Boulder, Colorado, as Gant had instructed. Gant had another house there. She had no clue what to do with Hannah now that she seemed to have adopted the woman like a stray cat. For better or worse, they were joined together.

Glancing at the briefcases in the backseat, she consoled herself with the knowledge that they had money, and one could do just about anything with the right amount of cash. She also had John's briefcase and the material that was in it.

She was disturbed with the thought of Hannah as her companion in flight. Neeley preferred to work alone as did any true professional. Gant had spent years training her out of the everyday incompetence that ruled most people's lives. Adding another person to a mission doubled your chance of screwing up but it did not double your chance of succeeding. Another of Gant's rules.

How Neeley was supposed to deal with this bleached blonde was a mystery to her. Neeley was tired, though, and she knew they needed a good night's sleep before attempting the long haul across Kansas. She hoped they had some space from the Cellar.

As Hannah's slow regular breathing filled the interior of the sedan, Neeley began to warm to the idea of Boulder. As far as she knew, Gant's house there was an unknown to the Cellar. It was managed by one of the many accounts that had funded Gant's secret world. They had used it mainly as a base for their yearly rock climbing expeditions to nearby Eldorado Canyon.

Climbing was the one physical skill she had brought into the relationship with Gant. Jean-Philippe had introduced her to the sport when they were teenagers. She allowed herself a moment of emotion and remembered the childish excitement she felt every summer when she returned to Strasbourg, her grandmother, and Jean-Philippe.

Hannah stirred. "Where are we going?"

"To Boulder, Colorado."

"By car? Don't you know someone who will swoop down and rescue some damsels in distress?"

Neeley wrinkled her nose at the thought of being a damsel but she did get an idea. "I know someone who will swoop down and help us for money."

It was Hannah's turn to feign disgust. "My, what charming friends you have."

Neeley snorted. "Hey, I wouldn't talk. I heard you and the bitch brigade playing golf."

"You were the person on the hill!" Hannah exclaimed. "Did you hear everything? What were they saying?"

"Let's get into that when we're not running for our lives," Neeley said.

"I have a feeling that you're always running for your life," Hannah said.

"Better than running from it," Neeley said sharply.

Hannah changed the subject. "So what about our mercenary savior?"

Neeley explained that he was a pilot who could be persuaded to fly anywhere if the price was right. "I'll call him."

Hannah nodded. "Better than driving." Her eyes narrowed. "Why are we going to Boulder?"

Neeley figured she needed to take things one step at a time and not overload Hannah. "I have a safe house in Colorado. We'll go there and figure out a plan." She paused. "Do you know what a safe house is?"

"I've read a book or two," Hannah said.

"What was with all those books?" Neeley asked.

Hannah shrugged. "It beats living in the real world as you noted earlier."

Neeley spotted a truck stop and decided it was a good time to change cars again. Neeley took an exit and parked in the lot. After transferring the load to a new car, she wiped the old car down, removing their prints. She left the windows open and the keys in the ignition. With any luck it would get stolen again. She found a pay phone near the truck stop and left the motor idling while she talked.

"Hello?" a man's voice answered.

"Kent, this is Neeley."

"Hey, lady, how you doing? Been a long time since I heard from you. How's your Gant?"

"Gant's dead, Kent."

"Shit. What happened?"

"Cancer."

"Damn. Sorry to hear that. He was a good man. You could count on him."

"I need a flight."

"I only do domestic service now," Kent said. "Flat fee ten grand anywhere in the continental United States. One way. No hanging around waiting."

Kent was an old acquaintance of Gant's. He was the one who had flown them up into the mountains for the winter training a few years back. Gant and she had gone to his place in Wyoming twice more to do some skiing over the years.

"I've got the money," Neeley said.

"Where to where and when?" Kent succinctly asked.

"As soon as possible. I'll be in Lawrence, Kansas. I need to get to Boulder, Colorado."

"Hold on a second. Let me check the weather."

While she waited the operator demanded more money and Neeley slid the quarters in.

Kent was back on in two minutes. "I can leave tonight and do IFR. I'll be there in the morning. There's a small airfield outside Lawrence. No tower." He gave her the directions.

"I'll have one person with me," Neeley said.

"Just double the fee."

"All right."

"See you in the morning."

The phone went dead.

A car pulled into the lot and slowly drove along the front of the restaurant. Neeley recognized the make. The same as the one that had been in the parking lot of the restaurant outside St. Louis. Hannah watched it too.

"Goddamn," Neeley muttered as she hung up the phone. The car rolled through the end of the parking lot and disappeared but Neeley knew it wouldn't go far.

"He knows where we are all the time," Hannah said.

Neeley headed back toward the Interstate. She glanced at her companion and returned her attention to the speedometer. "You just figured that out? We've got to make it to Lawrence and that plane."

Hannah nodded. "But how do we keep that guy from climbing right onboard? He doesn't seem to have any trouble following us and this is a new car. He can't have bugged it."

Neeley banged her hand on the steering wheel with frustration, causing Hannah to jump. "We're going to have to make a run for it."

Hannah nodded in slow agreement and reached back for her tote in the backseat. She pulled out a brush and began brushing her sleep-matted hair.

"What are you doing?"

"What's it look like? Besides, it helps me think."

Neeley gripped the wheel tighter. "What you need is about fifty more IQ points to help you think."

Hannah tossed the brush back in the bag. She pushed the bag on the floorboard and reached for a metal case in the backseat. "And your stuff's perfect, right? Let's see what John had that was so damn important." Popping it open, she murmured, "Oh." Hannah didn't recognize the contents of the case in her lap. "What's this?"

"Wrong case," Neeley said. "That's mine and it's a receiver." Neeley glanced in her rearview mirror. No sign of the trailing car but she knew it was back there. Could he have had observation on them all this time? Neeley had been careful but she supposed it was possible.

Hannah reached along the side of the flat green screen and she pushed the small button that was there. There was a brief hum, the screen glowed, and a bright dot showed up square in the center accompanied by a low beeping noise.

"Damn," Neeley whispered as she heard the sound and glanced over.

"What?" Hannah asked. "Did I do something wrong?"

"You didn't do anything wrong." Neeley lifted a hand off the wheel and pointed. "That dot. It represents a tracking bug. We've got one in the car. That's how this guy is following us."

"How can we have one in the car?" Hannah demanded. "We switched cars."

"It's not in the car," Neeley said. "Well, it is, but not on the car."

"What do you mean?" Hannah asked.

"Your thigh," Neeley said. "It's in your thigh. That's why that guy stuck you with the knife. He was putting a bug in you." She should have focused on the fact that the knife had looked strange, but it had been one detail in the middle of a lot of things happening.

Hannah stared at the spot on her thigh with her first sign of emotion in quite a while. "Get it out."

Neeley switched out of the fast lane and headed for the nearest downtown exit. "Hold your horses, Hannah, I'm driving."

Hannah spoke in short clipped words. "I don't care. Get it out! Get it out now!"

"Well, at least we know how he's tracking us. We need to set up a trap and get rid of this guy."

RACINE KNEW they had spotted him. He didn't want them to become complacent. He always found it best to keep the quarry off-balance.

He stopped at the booth the tall one had been in. He called the operator for the company that serviced the phone. Using his FBI badge number, another perk from the Cellar, he had her give him the last number called from that phone.

After he hung up, Racine looked at the number for a few seconds. The area code was Montana. The shadow world covered the entire planet but the population that dwelled inside the borders of that world was a small one. Racine closed his eyes and his mind flashed through names and faces until it clicked.

"Damn," Racine muttered as he got back in the car. The bitches were going to fly. He couldn't allow that. Then Nero would get involved further and it would be out of his hands. He would have to stop them before they got on that plane.

Racine stood still for several seconds, thinking, coming up with his plans. Plan A was to stop them himself. But he knew he needed a plan B, just in case.

NEELEY WAS SLOWLY NAVIGATING through the crowded business district and looking for a place to park. They left the car and headed for a nearly empty restaurant, Neeley carrying a small black kit and John's briefcase. In the bathroom, Hannah looked down at the hole in her thigh as Neeley dabbed away the blood. "They can really make one that small?"

"They can make transmitters extremely small," Neeley said. "The problem is the battery. That's what takes up most of the space." Neeley looked about. "But I don't think he was worrying about it having to last very long. Just long enough to catch us."

Neeley felt with her fingers in the cut and Hannah took a sharp breath, but didn't make any other noise. "I can't feel anything in there."

Neeley reached into the kit. She pulled a small scalpel and tweezers out. "I'm going to have to dig. It'll hurt."

Hannah nodded and looked at the wall over Neeley's shoulder. "How did you end up like this?"

Neeley turned the faucet on hot, letting the water run until it started steaming the glass over the sink. Then she put the blade under the water and held it there.

Neeley turned to look at Hannah. It was a question she had only answered for Gant. She thought about it for a few moments, and then spoke. "My earliest memories are of my mother locked up in her room whenever my dad was gone. He was some kind of low-level Department of Defense spook and he was gone a lot. That's the way it was; dinner would stop, she would stop, our lives would come to a standstill while she waited for him to come home. He was gone for months at a time.

"I swore I'd never be like that, so dependent on another human being, but I followed in her footsteps like I'd been in training my whole life. His name was Jean-Philippe.

"He was a boy I knew in Strasbourg. My mother was French—my father met her when he was stationed in Germany—and every summer I went to my grandparents. You had John, I had my Jean-Philippe. I'd spend those weeks exploring the city with him and bettering my French. Every year he was taller and more beautiful and every year it was harder for me to leave."

Someone knocked on the locked door. "Cleaning," Neeley yelled. The person went away and Neeley resumed her story as she heated the blade. "Finally, after high school, I moved there to go to college and Jean-Philippe and I became lovers.

By then he was involved in a lot of weird businesses I barely understood. I really didn't even pay attention. I just loved the image of it. Me and my handsome French lover with his friends in a smoky café. Jean-Philippe was making money, a lot of money, and hanging with other people with a lot of money. For a nineteen-year-old it was pretty wild."

Neeley checked the blade, and put it back under the water.

"It was an exciting, wonderful time. My own studies were suffering, but that was all right because Jean-Philippe seemed to want me close all the time. As he was drawn further into his business, people appeared in our lives who should have frightened me.

"Today I know those people are the machine: they are the probes and tentacles that slither around from the main body and search for souls to feed it." She looked at the other woman. "They are not a particular cause, Hannah. They have no fixed values in their heart but just want to make money and don't care what they have to do in order to achieve that goal."

Neeley pulled the scalpel out of the water and came closer to Hannah. "Are you ready?"

Hannah nodded.

Neeley continued talking as she carefully pushed the blade into the cut. "I was so far in with Jean-Philippe, so dependent on him, that I didn't see the reality. Then some really dangerous people found us and nothing would ever be the same. They sensed our immaturity and used us. At the time it seemed like fate. Today I know you make your own fate. When you're empty and weak, other people give you your fate."

Hannah glanced at Neeley and seemed about to say something, but didn't.

"Jean-Philippe and I left France and spent the next two years working for those people in various places, particularly Berlin. I learned to worship values that weren't my own and in the end I lost the only thing I ever loved."

Hannah finally spoke. "You lost Jean-Philippe."

"No." Neeley looked up from the blood. "I lost myself.

"When the final betrayal came, I was little more than a robot, an emotionless thing following him. One day Jean-Philippe forgot his love for me because he was told to by someone who probably paid him a lot of money, which I know now was more important to him than any person. That was the end for me. I wasn't human anymore, just another tentacle of the machine."

Hannah leaned back against the bathroom wall, not looking at what Neeley's hands were doing. "And who was this Gant guy?"

Neeley smiled something that was a cross between pure pleasure and immeasurable grief. "He was the man who saved me." She reached with her free hand and pushed a finger into the wound she had widened. "There's something in here."

She pulled out fingers dripping blood and grabbed the tweezers. She pushed them into the cut flesh, ignoring Hannah's hiss of pain and clamped down. She pulled out a small piece of metal, half the size of the nail on her pinkie. "That's it."

Neeley placed it down on the countertop and took a small spray bottle of antiseptic out of the aid kit. "This will sting."

"Like what you just finished doing felt good," Hannah said.

Neeley squirted the wound, soaking it. Then she used gauze and tape to bind it. "You need to walk on it."

"Excuse me?" Hannah said.

"You need to keep the muscle from tightening up on you."

"I thought we were flying west, not walking," Hannah said as she carefully hopped down from the counter.

"We are, but you need to be ready."

"You sound like a Girl Scout troop leader," Hannah complained, but she was gingerly walking about, testing the thigh. "It's not too bad."

"That's the second time today you've impressed me," Neeley said.

Hannah paused. "Don't try to boost my ego with false flattery. You would probably be running a half-marathon with this injury. If you want me to believe you, then talk to me honestly, not like a child."

Neeley slowly nodded. "All right. *That's* the second time today you've impressed me." She looked at her watch. "We have to get rid of this guy who had you stuck with this."

Neeley dropped the bug in her pocket. Then she reached down and put John's briefcase on the counter. Hannah walked over and silently watched as Neeley flipped open the latches. She swung the lid up and both women stared at the contents.

A stack of papers and plans were inside. Neeley picked them and thumbed through. "Plans for two pipelines in Afghanistan like John said. Contracts."

Hannah took some of the papers and they spent several minutes reading.

"I don't get it," Neeley finally said. "Yeah, these papers implicate Senator Collins and Cintgo in a deal with the Taliban to build these pipelines but these are dated 1993."

Hannah ran a hand across her chin in thought. "According to John, Collins tried to tie up all loose ends on this deal back then in ninety-three. He failed and because Gant had the video and John these papers, they were able to hold things in a status quo. But something's missing."

"What do you mean?" Neeley asked.

"Didn't you say Gant told you there were three pieces?"

"Yes."

"What's the third?" Hannah didn't wait for an answer. "That's the critical thing. The video—if it shows Collins in the same screen with bin Laden will certainly be damaging, but at the time it wasn't. And these papers appear to be legitimate business documents. We're missing the critical piece."

"In his note Gant said I needed the who, what, and why," Neeley said. "We know who—Senator Collins and bin Laden; we know what—the Afghanistan pipelines; but we don't know why. We still haven't seen the video, so maybe that will give it to us. But I agree with you—I think the third piece, whatever it is, is critical."

Neeley took the papers and slid them back into the case and shut the lid. "We have to think fast before this guy chasing us is on top of us. Let's go." She didn't mention her surprise at Hannah's observations.

They were back on the sidewalk. Neeley fed more quarters into the parking meter and looked for Hannah. Hannah was staring at a store across the street and the beginning of a very slight smile was curling her pale lips. "I say we take the upper hand and use our advantages for a change."

Neeley looked at the store and grimaced. "No way."

Hannah pulled her arm. "Please, just this once let's do it my way. Bring the bug with you so our Prince Charming can find us."

Neeley did as she was told and followed Hannah across the street. "Okay, but we're not buying anything."

C H A P T E R

15

RACINE WAS FUMING. What had begun an hour and a half ago as a mild irritation had worked into a full-blown rage. He had traced the women to this street in downtown Kansas City. It hadn't taken long for him to discover their stolen car. He had watched it for a while until he saw one of them walk out of the damn store and feed the meter. They didn't realize he was still onto them. Probably thought they'd lost him leaving the parking lot. Still he had to be careful in such a public place and so he sat and waited.

He planned to nab them as soon as they hit the street. He had a serviceable shield in his wallet and handcuffs. He knew he'd have little trouble "arresting" the two women on the busy sidewalk. People hated to get involved nowadays.

He was getting cramped even though he had pushed the front seat back as far as it would go. Racine listened to the radio for a while, twiddled his thumbs, studied a map he found on the backseat, and read the airbag instructions a few hundred times. He couldn't stand waiting.

Racine had washed out of sniper school when he was in

the service because he couldn't wait. The instructor had told him if it was just about putting a round in someone's skull, everyone would be doing it. But they had exercises at Fort Bragg where you were supposed to sit still for two days just so you could put a single fifty-caliber round into a microwave relay tower to disable it. They called it Strategic Target Interdiction. Racine had called it a waste of time. Walk up to the damn tower, kill the guards, strap some C-4 on the sucker, and blast it, was his recommendation.

Racine had no idea how those stupid sons-of-a-bitches sat with those bushes on their head for days at a time. Gant could do that shit, but there had been lots of other things Gant had avoided that Racine could do with ease.

Watching the store, Racine felt a new surge of anger. Women were just plain different. They had things in their head they couldn't control—like the urge to buy stuff when they should be running for their lives. The women had been in that store going on two hours. What was left to buy? He glanced at the sign above the door. Give him ten minutes and a hammer and he'd know Victoria's damn secret.

He thought about the brunette, Gant's shadow. She didn't look bad if you forgot she was dead meat. Hannah Masterson wasn't too shabby either and it was a shame that Nero wanted her intact. Racine grew even more uncomfortable as he thought about the two women.

That was it. Racine decided to take out the store. Enough was enough. Who the hell did they think they were? He wasn't some schmuck waiting around while they modeled every God damn thing in the store.

He checked the gun in his jacket pocket, unfolded himself from the confines of the car and strode to the front of the store exuding purpose and barely suppressed rage. Three women in assorted stages of dress ran out onto the sidewalk as he reached the door.

His entrance was loud enough that the one remaining saleslady immediately stepped forward. She recognized Racine's state and without a word pointed to the back and then she, too, was gone. Racine nodded. Smart girl. Recog-

nized a man pushed to the edge. He looked around and figured it happened a lot in this snatch temple. As he walked in
the direction the clerk had pointed, he could hear them talking behind the closed door of the dressing room but he
couldn't make out the words.

Racine kicked his foot against the flimsy lock and walked
into the small room—and found himself staring at the
blonde. She was fully dressed and seated in a chair, one leg
resting on a stool.

What really caught his attention next though was the mirror behind her and the reflection of the brunette and most especially the gun she held and the red dot on his right temple.
He froze, recognizing the Glock 20 and knowing what the
bullet would do punching through his skull.

Neeley was in her jeans and jacket and she gestured with
the gun for him to move to the center of the room, out of
arm's reach, like a pro would. Hannah slowly got to her feet,
favoring her wounded leg slightly. She took a wide berth
around him and shut the door, locking it.

Racine almost tried to take Neeley, but he remembered
her shooting at the house and the fact that Gant had trained
her. The asshole had his faults but Racine had no doubt he'd
taught her to drop someone in this situation in a heartbeat.
And if she'd wanted to kill him, she'd have done so. She
wanted to talk so this wasn't a dead end scene. So like a
woman. Racine moved to the center of the room, hands
away from his sides so she wouldn't make a mistake.

Neeley nodded. "Well, it's nice to finally meet you face to
face. Do you have a name?"

Racine said nothing. She was going to pay. Pay hard. No
quick death for either of them, he decided right then and
there.

"Why don't you take off your clothes," Neeley said, no
hint of a question in it.

Racine started to protest but the combination of the muzzle of the Glock and the look in her eye pushed him toward
acquiescence. He warily watched the two women as he
stripped down to his shorts.

"The knives." Neeley gestured with the gun. Racine dropped the assorted weapons onto his pile of clothes. Hannah picked up the handcuffs. Racine sat in the chair Hannah had vacated. Hannah secured his hands behind the back with the cuffs, ratcheting them down tight on his wrists.

Neeley waited until Hannah was done before she spoke again. "Do you have a name?"

Racine remained quiet.

Hannah went through his wallet, pulling out a card. "This says he's FBI. Special Agent Harold Racine."

Neeley glanced at the massive Desert Eagle pistol deposited with the clothes. "No FBI agent would be carrying that thing. And the gun that shot up the house was big caliber like that, which isn't exactly what the FBI would do either. You work for the Cellar don't you, Harold?"

"Racine. No one uses my first name."

Neeley nodded. "Okay, Harold. Here's the thing. I want to make a deal."

Racine tried to maintain some control. "You're not playing nice for someone who wants to deal."

Hannah seemed about to say something but a glance from Neeley stopped her.

"Here's the deal," Neeley said. "I take Gant's place and Hannah takes John Masterson's. We keep things as they are with new people in the old places."

Racine shook his head. "You know the rules. Or you should know the rules from Gant. You can't beat the Cellar."

"I'm not trying to beat the Cellar, just you," Neeley said. "And I've already done that."

"You're stupid," Racine said. "I don't make the rules, I follow them. And the rules say you die and I take Mrs. Masterson back with me. There's no negotiating that."

"We're dealing with the wrong man," Hannah said. "We want to talk to your boss. Mr. Nero."

"Yeah, right." Racine's voice oozed sarcasm. "Mr. Nero doesn't deal with people like you."

"I think he will," Neeley said. "We have what John and Gant had. Nero knows that."

"What do you have?"

Neeley held up the briefcase. "John Masterson's piece of the puzzle."

Racine shook his head. "Whatever is in there isn't in my instructions so I don't care."

"Perhaps Mr. Nero does," Neeley said.

"What about Gant's piece of the puzzle?" Racine asked.

"I have that," Neeley said.

"And your piece?" Racine asked.

"I have that too," Neeley said, surprised at the question.

"Good," Racine said. "So before I kill you I can make you give both those pieces over to me. Real slow."

Neeley gestured and Hannah stepped forward with a nightie in her hands. "Open your mouth."

"Fuck you!" Racine yelled.

Neeley stepped forward and pressed the end of the gun against his lips. "Open or I blow it open."

Racine opened his mouth and Hannah stuffed the silky wad in. Then she tied another around his head.

When Hannah was done, Neeley looked down upon the helpless Racine. "Contact your boss. Tell him we want to talk."

Racine could only glare up at her.

"They'll find you soon, no harm done. We'll be long gone."

Neeley turned and walked out of the dressing room, Hannah following.

CHAPTER

16

"You DID WELL," Neeley told Hannah.

They had driven to the airfield outside Lawrence in a state of emotional collapse. They were waiting in the small metal hanger. There was no one else around this late in the day, just two small planes parked on the tarmac. They had a bench, a vending machine, four walls, a concrete floor, and a ceiling.

Hannah turned to Neeley. "I did well? What's that supposed to mean?"

Neeley now understood why Racine had been careful at the house and the restaurant. The idea that the Cellar wanted Hannah alive was more frightening than the fear of a quick, clean hit. And what had Racine meant about *her* piece? What did they think she had?

"He was going to kill you, wasn't he?" Hannah said in a level tone of voice.

"That's the basic idea," Neeley said.

"What do you have that they want?" Hannah asked.

Neeley shook her head. "I have no idea what Racine meant by that."

Hannah stared at her for several seconds.

"It's the truth," Neeley said.

"It's the third piece and he thought you had it," Hannah said. "Interesting."

Neeley said nothing.

"And why does Nero want me?" Hannah asked.

"I don't know," Neeley said. "Maybe to learn something about John."

Hannah changed the subject. "What are we going to do?"

Neeley knew she had to start letting Hannah in on some of what was going on. "I guess we have to find this video-tape. Knowing Gant, it's cached somewhere."

"If we get it, will he make the deal?"

"Racine can't make a deal. He doesn't have the power to. That's why we left him like that; besides the fact we didn't have the tape to deal with yet. But the man he works for can."

"And if Nero doesn't?"

"We're no worse off than we were before," Neeley said "Actually better off because we have Racine off our tail. Which reminds me," she added, taking Hannah by the arm.

"Which reminds you of what?" Hannah asked, standing and allowing herself to be led.

"Training time." She led Hannah to the car and opened the trunk. "We have to get this gear stowed quickly when the plane lands in the morning."

Hannah looked at the equipment. "What are those cases?"

"Guns."

"I've never handled a gun before."

Neeley put a hand on Hannah's arm. "Don't be afraid of these guns. They work the same for you as they do for any-one else. A bullet doesn't care if you're a man or a woman. Neither does the gun." She pulled two large rucksacks out. "Let's pack first, and then we can have your first lesson."

They quickly broke down the load from the footlocker, cases, and duffel bags. Neeley packed two rucksacks, and reloaded the duffel bags for the trip. Then she pulled out a pistol. "This is a Berretta 9mm pistol. It's the same thing the U.S. military uses and if a GI can use it, then you can too. It's a very safe gun."

"That sounds like a contradiction if ever I heard one," Hannah said.

Neeley picked up a magazine. "Fifteen rounds in the magazine, which is a lot of bullets." She slipped it into the butt of the weapon and slammed it home. "You can feel it lock in place." She pushed a button. "That's the magazine release." Neeley looked up. "Always, always, and always remember to make sure the chamber is empty also. Just because you take the magazine out, that doesn't mean the gun is unloaded. There can still be a round in the chamber."

"What's the chamber?" Hannah asked.

"Jeez," Neeley muttered. She pulled back on the slide. "Here, this is the chamber," she said, pointing into the small hole on the side of the receiver that was now exposed. "That's where the bullet that is to be fired sits."

Hannah chuckled. "I knew that. I was just pulling your leg."

Neeley stared at the other woman for a few moments, trying to figure out how she could be so relaxed in these circumstances. It was as if there was a disconnect in Hannah between reality and emotion.

Neeley put the magazine back in, and pulled back the slide. "There's a bullet in there now." She removed the magazine. "That bullet is still in there. Thus the gun, despite not having a magazine in it, is still loaded. With one round at least." Neeley moved her thumb. "This is the safety. I can set it either way. Are you right- or left-handed?"

"Right-handed," Hannah said,

"Fine, then it's ready for you."

Hannah took the gun. She slid the magazine in and chambered a round. Then she removed the magazine and pulled the slide back, taking the round out of the chamber.

"When you shoot, double-tap," Neeley said. "Always double-tap."

Hannah nodded. "Two shots, right?"

Neeley smiled. "All that reading was good for something, wasn't it?"

"And to the head." Hannah was looking down the barrel. "That's what the books say."

Neeley nodded. "To the head. A person can be wearing body armor. The head is always best. If you shoot, shoot to kill. None of that wounding crap on TV. A wounded person is a very dangerous person who is also now very angry at you."

Neeley kept the lessons going as they waited. The evening began to close in on the flat Kansas countryside and Neeley grew more nervous. Racine would be free by now. There was no reason to believe he would look for them here, but Neeley wanted to get as far away as quickly as possible.

They went out to the deserted airstrip and Neeley set up cans and let Hannah fire away. She was all right, but Neeley knew a lot more training would be needed to get her up to operational speed.

Neeley thought of the last time she had seen Kent. He was someone Gant had known from the service and then from the shadow world. Gant had hired him to fly them up into the Rockies from Vermont for extreme cold weather training. Kent had shown up at Montpelier Airport on time and taken Gant's cash, then immediately taken off and headed west. Flying somewhere over the Midwest Gant had produced rule number nine. "Never walk when you can ride. Never ride when you can fly."

She handed Hannah another weapon and started the wait for morning.

IT WAS QUIET except for the sound of the air system circulating. Nero had lived with that sound for so long, he would only be conscious of its absence. His living quarters were through a concealed door at the back of his office, a small room a monk would have been proud to call his own. Nero had not left the Cellar for eleven years. He'd even had his throat surgery done down here.

An eight-inch stack of paper was on the left corner of the desk, delivered there by Mrs. Smith, as she did every day. They were top secret intelligence summaries coded into Braille. Nero reached underneath the top of his desk and pressed a button turning on a hidden radio. The voice of the BBC news whispered through the room as he took the first piece of paper, rapidly running his forefinger across the raised dots.

A slight smile crossed Nero's lips as he read the report about Racine being bested in Kansas City. He knew what it must have cost the man to make that report. The smile was gone when he got to the section that detailed the support from the Agency that Racine had requested. The women must have upset Racine mightily. Nero could not recollect a time when Racine had asked for so much assistance.

Was it too much? Nero wondered briefly.

He closed the file and lit a cigarette, deep in thought. He had learned one of the most difficult things about running operations was to *not* do anything at critical junctures, to allow the pieces in place to continue their course. He realized his desire to intervene was based on hope, not a good motive. He had to let things play out and live with the results, even if it didn't turn out the way he wanted it to.

That didn't mean he would do nothing, though. A good chunk of the eight inches of paper Mrs. Smith had delivered were concerning events in the Sudan, Somalia, and elsewhere in the covert world in October 1993. Nero knew he'd missed something and he was determined to find it.

Nero lit another cigarette and continued reading the reports, the soothing sound of the BBC in the background.

C H A P T E R
17

NEELEY LOOKED UP from their meager vending machine breakfast when she heard the engine. As the plane approached, Neeley glanced at Hannah and smiled. "Never walk when you can ride, never ride when you can fly."

They had slept fitfully, but they'd be in Boulder before lunch. Hannah nudged the heavy rucksack with her foot. "That is so profound," she muttered. Sleeping on a bench was not her idea of a restful night.

The twin-engine propeller plane landed. Kent was a large, burly man and he didn't get out after he stopped the plane right in front of them, engines running. He pulled the cockpit window open.

"Got the money?" he shouted above the noise of the propellers.

Neeley walked up and handed him a stack of bills. Hannah watched the exchange without comment.

"Let's get loaded, ladies. Time's a wasting," Kent yelled.

After what seemed like forever the gear was aboard in the

lower hold and Hannah, sitting behind Kent now, seemed relaxed. Neeley climbed in the copilot's seat.

As they took off and started west, Neeley noted that Hannah was flirting with Kent and he seemed to be responding. Her memories of Kent were of his taciturn can-do gruffness. He had obviously respected Gant, but his attitude toward Neeley had been one of mere tolerance for her relationship with Gant. She had added him to the never-ending list of misogynists who seemed to populate Gant's world.

Yet here with Hannah he was acting like a fawning love-struck beau. Hannah's voice had assumed an almost girlish quality as she asked him questions about the plane. Hannah had him prattling on about fuel consumption, flying time, and the refueling stops between here and Jeffco Airport in Colorado, just outside of Boulder. Neeley found the change in persona strange and irritating.

Neeley wondered if she was going to have to shoot them both before they reached the Rockies. Kent was just beginning to explain the concept of wings when Neeley noticed the plane veering toward a flat open field. It was a very clear morning and despite the distance, Neeley could see two dark sedans parked at the far edge of the field in a tree line.

"Kent, what the hell is going on?"

"Hey, Neeley, no hard feelings, okay? They're not gonna hurt you, I swear. Racine just wants to talk to you. He says he wants to deal. Said you put an offer out and that Nero's accepted."

Neeley didn't believe that for a second. She slid her hand inside her jacket, grabbing the butt of her Glock. "You son of a bitch! You've killed us! Why?"

Kent didn't answer as he shoved the yoke forward and the nose of the plane dipped down toward the landing strip. Neeley knew it wasn't the brightest idea to shoot a pilot in the middle of landing, but she pulled her gun anyway. Kent, as she expected, ignored the weapon.

The wheels touched with a light bounce and they were down. Kent began doing all sorts of things with the controls, slowing them down, when Hannah suddenly leaned forward between the seats and slammed a heavy metal clipboard that she'd found in the back against the side of Kent's head.

Neeley grabbed the sagging pilot. "Jesus Christ, Hannah! Who's going to stop the plane?" They were rolling at fifty miles an hour and although there was another half mile of field, there was a row of trees at the end of that.

Hannah squirmed forward between the two seats, all signs of flirtation and innocence gone. "Here, come on, switch seats with me."

Neeley slithered between the seats over Hannah, who quickly claimed her place in the copilot's seat as half the distance to the end of the field went by. Hannah placed her hands on the controls.

Neeley leaned forward, looking over Hannah's shoulder. "You can handle this?"

Hannah kept her focus forward. "Look, I'm not great at this but I do know how the wings work, contrary to what your friend here thought." Hannah shook her head. "I'm not so stupid I would have knocked him out if I hadn't had a plan."

Hannah did something and the plane slowed further. Hannah jerked a thumb at Kent. "You don't want to take him with us, do you? I should be mad at him and we could just chuck him out now, but I thought we'd slow down a bit."

Neeley looked out the front windshield. There were several men standing around the two cars. They had that suit, sunglasses, blown dry hair look of guns for hire, government type. Average IQ was probably double digits but Neeley knew they could probably shoot quite well. They were watching as the plane rolled toward their position.

"Toss him!" Hannah yelled.

Neeley reached over, unbuckled Kent's shoulder harness, and then pushed down on the lever, opening his door. He fell, hit, and rolled and Hannah turned the plane and was accelerating as Neeley pulled the door shut. The men finally realized something was wrong and they were running toward the plane but Neeley knew they were already too late. She had no idea if Kent had broken his neck and she didn't really care. That was the price of betrayal.

Hannah pulled back and they were airborne as the goons began fruitlessly firing their pistols at the rapidly receding plane.

"My God," Neeley said, "you really can fly."

Hannah checked her gauges. "Ten lessons, thank you very much. I won them at the annual Spring Charity Bazaar." She was peering out the window. "I wish I'd gone to all of them now," she added in a lower tone of voice.

Neeley leaned forward and placed a hand on Hannah's shoulder. "Please tell me you went to the one on landing."

Hannah shook her head. "Sorry, that one conflicted with bridge club. As you can tell, I did go to the one on takeoffs. Landing can't be that hard. I watched the way Kent did it. I have it all figured out in my head. Really."

Neeley rubbed her chin nervously.

Hannah pointed with a free hand at the control panel. "Hey, the compass says we're heading in the right direction. West." She looked around. "There's Interstate 70 to the far left. The road below us parallels it. We can follow that." She smiled. "And the sun sets in the west. And we'll see the Rocky Mountains. And—" she paused. "Oh shit. There's a helicopter."

Neeley swung around and spotted a small black OH-6 helicopter heading straight for them from the north. Gant had called that type of chopper a Little Bird and told her it was extremely dangerous. It was the type of helicopter he'd flown into and out of Mogadishu on.

Hannah reached down and pulled the throttle out all the way. "I'll fly. You take care of the chopper."

"How the hell am I going to do that?" Neeley yelled. "I didn't exactly pack any air-to-air missiles."

"I don't know. Didn't Gant teach you to deal with a situation like this?"

"Damn," Neeley muttered. She opened the top of her backpack.

Hannah yelled something inarticulate and Neeley looked up. A line of tracers seared across the nose of the plane, and then the helicopter swooped by. Neeley could see the chain gun pod hung out the right door. "God is on the side of the superior firepower," she muttered as she reached into the bag. Another of Gant's rules.

"What?" Hannah asked.

"Nothing," Neeley said as she kept the chopper in sight. The pilot was maneuvering around behind them for another run.

Hannah was glancing back every so often at the helicopter chasing them. The plane had dropped close to the roadway. Neeley clearly saw a Coke can in the gravel they were so low.

"Too low," Neeley called out.

"Hold on," Hannah said.

The helicopter followed them, still firing, spraying bullets on the roadway right behind them. But not low enough. As Neeley was pulling an MP-5 submachine gun out of the pack she heard the explosion.

"What the hell happened?" Neeley exclaimed.

Hannah continued the turn to the right and they both looked as the burning fireball that had been the helicopter hit the road. Pieces cartwheeled through the air.

Neeley stared at the power lines stretching behind them, across the road. Two lines were down, snapping and crackling on the pavement.

"Jesus, Hannah, you flew *under* those power lines!"

"I did. He missed them. Tunnel vision in a sense." Hannah pulled back on the yoke and the plane gained some altitude. "I think Gant was maybe wrong on this one. Maybe sometimes it's better to walk."

Neeley nodded in agreement. "They know we're in a plane and they'll cover all the airfields. Find a smooth place to land, preferably close to a farm where we can get a car. This time we pay top dollar."

Hannah didn't say anything, concentrating on flying for a few minutes as she regained her equilibrium.

"Speaking of dollars," Hannah finally said as she peered

ahead, trying to find someplace to land, "I saw that stack you gave Kent. Exactly how much money do you have?"

"A million dollars. Well, a half now."

"You have a half million dollars in a duffel bag?"

"It's my nest egg."

"Big egg. You did better in that area with your man than I did with mine."

"*I* got the money," Neeley said, emphasizing the first word.

"But I bet Gant taught you how," Hannah noted. "John didn't teach me a damn thing worthwhile. Asshole."

A minute of silence went by. "You don't think Racine was going to make a deal as Kent said?" Hannah asked.

"Do you?"

"No."

As Hannah had predicted, she could land, she just didn't know how to come to a complete stop in less than four hundred yards, but fortunately the drainage ditch worked just fine and they had their seat belts on.

After piling their stuff at the edge of the field, Neeley made Hannah sit. "You've done great. Just stay here. I'll get us some wheels."

When Neeley returned an hour later, bumping across the field in a battered truck, Hannah had unloaded the plane. The bags and hard plastic containers were stacked neatly in a pile. She had broken down the Berretta and was cleaning it as Neeley had taught her. Neeley almost didn't recognize the woman from a couple of days ago.

RACINE LISTENED on his secure cell phone to the Agency official rant and rave about the lost helicopter and men. Racine could care less. What he was concerned about was the reports he would have to make to both Nero and Collins. Ying and yang, he thought. Opposite ends of the same crap.

And the bitches. They'd escaped the landing trap *and* the chopper. Goddamn Gant. He'd taught Neeley well, Racine had to admit. Still, she was only one person—and a woman at that—and she was dragging along the blonde bimbo housewife.

Racine reached into his pocket with his free hand, the tinny words of the CIA bureaucrat echoing out of the cell phone an irritating buzz, and pulled out a bottle of pills. He flicked the top off and tilted the bottle into his mouth, tumbling a half-dozen pills in. He chewed on them, anxious for relief from the pain throbbing in his temple.

Racine was still in Kansas City, having figured to let the Agency scoop up the two women and bring them to him. Plan A and Plan B had crapped out.

Luck. That was it, Racine finally decided. The bitches had just been damn lucky. Even the CIA guy had admitted their pilot flew into the wires. Very lucky for the bitches, but one could only ride that wave for so long.

"Enough," Racine snapped into the phone, jabbing the off button. He leaned his head against the window of his hotel room blindly staring at the parking lot. He found it difficult to think and was uncertain of his next step.

He walked over to the bed on which he had tossed his briefcase. He dialed the combination and opened it, pulling out the laptop and bringing up the encoded file on Gant that Nero's secretary had given him.

The bitches were heading west. That was all the Agency could give him. No wonder they hadn't been able to kill Castro, Racine thought. How many years had that Cuban son-of-a-bitch been in power and they couldn't put a damn bullet in his brain? Fucking exploding cigars.

Racine scanned the documents, all emblazoned with Top Secret, Q-Clearance. After all these years *and* his death, Anthony Gant was still Top Secret Q. The Cellar. Nero had it all. Everything about Gant. Everywhere he'd been. Everything he'd ever done. Racine shook his head. The poor son-of-a-bitch must have thought he was free of the Cellar the last ten years or so, but Nero hadn't let him go.

A cruel smile twisted Racine's lips as he noted an entry about Gant and the scant property he owned. A cabin in Vermont. A house in Boulder. Racine opened his little black book and searched for the person he wanted.

NEELEY COULDN'T REMEMBER ever being as exhausted as she navigated I-70 into Denver. She had driven all night and only the eye-catching view of the front range of the Rockies kept her from slumping over the wheel. Hannah was asleep with her tote serving as a lumpy pillow. She had slept through the long straight drive across the flat eastern half of Colorado.

As Neeley got on the Denver-Boulder Turnpike, her thoughts drifted to Gant and the first time he brought her here. They had been together a few years and it seemed he would never be satisfied with her training. He had brought her to Boulder to check out how well she could climb. After practicing a few days, Gant had accepted that they were at least equal partners on the rock and they'd moved on to more difficult routes.

They had spent a wonderful spring and summer in Boulder and Gant had purchased the house. It was a small rock cottage near the downtown area and they leased the basement apartment to a professor at CU who maintained the main floors of the house in exchange for rent.

Every day they made their way into the mountains. At first she clung awkwardly to the chalk-covered surfaces, her muscles trying to remember the skills they'd once had, but eventually she relearned the rhythm of the rock and the joy of a perfect fingerhold. When Gant was comfortable with her movements on the rocks, they moved to Boulder Canyon and began to aid climb using ropes and other gear for protection.

Finally, they went a few miles south to Eldorado Canyon. The canyon was a world-renowned rock climbing Mecca and their last months in Colorado were spent exploring its various climbing routes.

She had never been here without Gant. Driving into the town she maneuvered the streets as if she'd never left, feeling his absence. At last she turned due west toward the foothills and the little house that had been one of only two places in the world to offer Neeley safety and comfort.

She parked in front of the house and sat still for a moment, staring at the small stone and wood cottage. Then she woke Hannah up and got out of the truck. Her road partner was quiet, as if sensing the emotion and respecting Neeley's memories.

After unlocking the door, Neeley pushed the front door of the house open with her boot. Her arms were laden with gear and she was beginning to think she would end up carrying this stuff all over the country. Hannah approved of the house but seemed more excited at the thought of a shower. Neeley wondered if the basement tenant was in. She decided to give him a try while Hannah went into the bathroom.

Neeley went around the back of the house and knocked on the sliding glass door that was the basement access. She looked around the quiet backyard and admired how well kept it was. She noticed that the spring perennials were beginning to bloom.

The professor didn't seem surprised by her sudden appearance. He offered condolences about Gant's death and explained that Gant had written him a few months ago telling him he was very sick and saying the Neeley would probably be coming soon. Gant had also included a letter for her.

Neeley felt herself growing dizzy. She grabbed the envelope, issued a quick thanks, and hurried back around the house. She could hear the water running from Hannah's shower stop as she sat down and stared at the envelope. It took her several moments to muster the energy to open it.

"You all right?" Hannah had a towel wrapped around her.

Neeley reluctantly looked up from the letter in her hand. "What?"

"Hey," Hannah said, looking closer, "you look terrible. What's wrong?"

"Gant left a letter downstairs." Neeley was in a daze, fingering the edges of the paper. She showed it to Hannah.

Hannah began gathering her clothes. "I don't know about

this Gant guy," she said. "Pardon me for saying, but any allusion to him seems to bring you down."

Neeley looked at the single sheet of paper from Gant's letter. Her eyes burned for a moment at the sight of the familiar writing. She read it to herself and tears slowly escaped her blinking eyes.

"Well?" Hannah asked.

Neeley shook her head and stuffed the paper in her breast pocket. "It just says that I made him very happy and that he loved me. Says to remember the rules."

Hannah was already dressed and tying her shoelaces. "What rules?"

Neeley shot her a weary look. "Oh, just a bunch of rules to live by."

Hannah got up and moved toward the bathroom. "So, nothing about a tape? I don't get it. If this guy loved you so much, why didn't he just give you this tape that the Cellar seems willing to kill you for?"

Neeley watched her disappear into the bathroom. "Actually, Hannah, I think he told me where it was before he died."

Hannah's head popped out from behind the door. "When were you going to let me in on this?"

Neeley was silent as she went to one of the bedroom closets.

"Well?" Hannah demanded. "Are we going to start working together? Combining our brain power?"

"Rule number seven. One man who thinks can beat ten men who don't."

"Rule number seven is Shaw," Hannah said. "And it doesn't apply here, because I can think."

Neeley paused with the door open. "What?"

"Gant's rule seven is a paraphrase of George Bernard Shaw. I read it." Hannah noticed Neeley's dismayed look. "Hey, cheer up. So far it seems to be the only thing we both know. That means something, right?"

Neeley started pulling gear out of its neatly packed rece...

Hannah came over to help. "What are you do...

"We're going to find the tape."

Hannah stepped toward the pile of ropes and slings. "What's this for?"

"It looks like we're going on a little climb."

Hannah shook her head. "Wait a minute. What do you mean we? I can barely climb out of bed. Speaking of which, shouldn't you be tired? You mean like climb a mountain?"

Neeley kept pulling gear from shelves and stacking it neatly around Hannah's feet. "A rock, Hannah. We're going to climb a rock."

Hannah stared at the ropes and belts and helmets piled around her feet. "This is a stupid question, I know, but why couldn't he hide the tape here in this closet with all this stuff?"

Neeley's look was what Hannah expected. Neeley grabbed one of Hannah's hands. "You're going to have to cut off these nails." Her thumb rubbed the surface of Hannah's long perfectly shaped red nail.

Hannah looked at her hands as if seeing them for the first time. "They're acrylic. Do you have any idea what these cost?"

"Hannah, get them off. Do you have any idea what it feels like to rip your nail out at the root?"

Hannah picked up one of the harnesses from the floor, looking at it. "I don't care about the fingernails, Neeley. It was just an observation. You've got to calm down. This has not been easy and I've done my best so far."

Neeley sat down with an exhausted look on her face. "I'm sorry. I know I've been hard on you. I feel like I'm all alone and I'm not up to this. Can you understand that? Gant was always there and now he's not."

Hannah dropped the harness. "I'm hungry and tired." She rubbed a hand across her face. "My husband got shot the other night. I know he ran out on me and left me in a bad place, but we spent a lot of years together and some of those were decent years. At least no one was trying to kill me all the time. That's looking pretty good right now.

"In the past couple of days I've been stabbed, shot at, and crashed a plane. Geez, what else?" Hannah looked at

Neeley. "I try to be observant and pick strange things to talk about sometimes to protect myself, okay? Because I don't want to feel what I'm supposed to feel about the real shit in my life. At least that's what my shrink said once."

Neeley nodded. "I understand. Let's get this stuff together and we'll eat, okay? Then get some sleep. I know this has been hard but we have to keep pushing. We have to find that tape Hannah, or we're dead. We climb first thing in the morning. You'll do fine. I promise. We'll take turns standing watch tonight."

Hannah focused on one part. "Eat?"

"Yes."

"Great," Hannah pulled herself and the look was back in her eyes. "I can fall off a cliff for breakfast tomorrow. That's how they'll find me. Splattered on a rock with nubby fingernails."

RACINE WANTED TO congratulate himself. His instinct had been to fly to Boulder, wade in, and blow the bitches off the face of the planet. But the rational part of him knew that would not have been acceptable to Nero and much as he hated the old bastard, he knew he couldn't afford to make him an outright enemy—not yet at least.

The whispers were out that Nero's reign was coming to an end. You'd think the old fart's lungs would have given in like his throat had. Some said Bailey would take his place, but Racine couldn't see Bailey sitting in that room day after day reading reports and thinking. Bailey was an action man. From what Racine had heard, Bailey was the son of some Brit that had gone into France with Nero during the last Great War. Bailey was ex-SAS, Special Air Service, who'd cut his teeth doing the nasty stuff in Ireland and somehow crossed the pond to work for Nero. Racine did grant that the SAS were some hard-ass dudes, so he gave Bailey some space.

Racine took the elevator from the second floor to the first and went to the bar. He ordered some food and looked around. A sparse crowd of losers was his summation. A bleached blonde two stools down gave him a quick once over.

A stewardess, Racine figured. Or an office manager who had to fuck her boss to keep her job. Sliding into middle age and not happy at all about it. Just perfect for what he needed tonight. He turned to her and smiled.

NEELEY STOOD on the small deck in the back of the house and looked up at the stars. She remembered being in this exact same spot with Gant. She heard Hannah come out.

"Memories?" Hannah asked.

Neeley nodded.

"Good ones?"

"I don't know now." Neeley tensed, waiting for Hannah to probe with more questions but there was only silence. They stood silent, staring at the stars.

"DO YOU HAVE SOMETHING to drink?"

Racine shut the door, bolted it, and slid the chain on. If he concentrated he could make her look like the blonde, Masterson's wife. She turned toward him, a quizzical look on her face as she heard the chain rattle.

"What are you—"

Racine hit her with the knife edge of his right hand directly across her throat. Not full power, just enough to smash her larynx and keep her from saying another goddamned word.

She staggered back.

Racine followed the first hit with an open palm strike to her solar plexus while his other hand pulled a slim, double-edged commando knife from behind his back.

His third strike was the knife.

Within minutes Racine was splattered in blood.

He was not satisfied.

CHAPTER

18

HANNAH STARED UP at the top of the rock wall and shook her head. "You've got be kidding. That's straight up. I couldn't get up that if it had stairs."

They were along the north wall of Eldorado Canyon. The wall was practically vertical in most places, with cracks and crevices interspersed among the smooth rock. The crest of the face was over two hundred feet above their heads. It was a beautiful day. The sun was shining and the temperature was an unseasonable fifty-five degrees. In Boulder, at over a mile in altitude, the sun made all the difference as far as temperature went.

"What did you say it was called again?" Hannah asked.

"The route we're going to follow is called Thin Air," Neeley said.

"Great name." Hannah looked about. "Isn't there an easier way?"

"No." Neeley finished arranging her climbing rack and tried for the tenth time to reassure Hannah. "You can do this. It's mostly your leg muscles that do the climbing, not your arms. Remember, you have to push away from the rock. Your tendency is going to be to cling close to the wall, but that changes your gravity vector and will make you slide off. You have to push away, putting your vector into the rock."

Hannah stared at her as if she were speaking Swahili.

Neeley slapped the rope and her rack. "Besides, we have the rope and I'll be putting protection in the whole way up."

"And from what you said, I'll be taking the protection out," Hannah argued.

Neeley shook her head. "The climb is longer than the rope. You'll be freeing the rope so we can make it to the top." She tapped the assortment of gear on her rack. "My protection is what will hold the rope if one of us falls."

Hannah reached over to Neeley's rack and lifted one of the small metal nuts that were on a loop of thin metal cable. "*This* is supposed to hold me if I fall?"

"It's rated for ten thousand pounds vertical stress," Neeley said.

"What if we both fall?"

Neeley looked at Hannah. "You think we weigh that much?"

"Very funny, smart-ass."

"Only one of us moves at a time. The other is on belay."

"Why can't I just watch you?" Hannah asked. "I'll take pictures. Or we can just let that guy go up and we can both watch him."

Hannah was pointing at a young man who had just started a route forty feet to the right. He was hard and supple. All his muscles were taut as he went from one hold to the next. His climbing shorts were brightly colored and his hair was long and thick and hanging loose. His only equipment was a chalk bag tied around his waist.

"How come he doesn't have all this gear?" Hannah asked.

"He's doing what's called free climbing." Neeley admired his technique for a moment. He looked like one of the dozens of young climbers who made Boulder their home and lived only to climb. Besides him, it appeared they had this part of the canyon to themselves, prime climbing season being a few months away. He'd arrived shortly after they had, parking a beat-up pickup not far from their truck.

Neeley knew that Hannah was right about the difficulty of this route. She doubted that the man was going to be able to free climb to the top. Only a fool would do that. He was "bouldering," going up thirty or forty feet, then coming back down. To go higher on this route, appropriately labeled Thin Air and rated 5.10 in the guidebook, required at least two climbers and the safety gear. Neeley had the safety gear, but glancing at Hannah, her helmet precariously perched on her blonde hair, Neeley knew she didn't have the two climbers. She granted that Hannah had done very well in the plane yesterday but this was a very different venue.

Neeley cupped her hands to her mouth. "Hey, want to make some money?" she shouted.

The climber turned and looked down, two fingers of one hand curled around a tiny bump on the rock face. "How much?"

"Three hundred."

Neeley was amazed how quickly he retraced his path down.

The young man stuck out his hand. "I'm Mitch."

Neeley took it, feeling the powerful grip. "I'm Sue." She pointed at Hannah. "That's Sara."

Mitch smiled. "Sue and Sara. How interesting."

Neeley pulled a sling off her rack and handed it to him. He looped it over his shoulder. She then split her rack, giving him some of the pieces he would need.

Mitch looked up. "Thin Air?"

Neeley nodded. "All the way. I need you to bring up the rear and give Sara a hand. She's kind of new at this." Neeley slapped Hannah on the shoulder. "Just do as I told you."

Neeley turned toward the rock and reached up, her fingers curling around a small ledge. She slid one of her feet up, feeling through the thin toes of the climbing shoes and she was on her way.

After fifteen feet, Neeley hit a small crack in the rock face. She put a nut in, and then hooked a snap link to the ny-lon loop attached to the nut. She pushed the rope through the gate in the snap link, then put a second snap link through the rope-nylon juncture, making sure the gate on that one was facing the other way. Then she continued up.

On the ground, Hannah's neck was hurting from looking up and watching Neeley climb. As soon as the second piece of protection was in, Neeley halted and looked down. "I've got belay."

Mitch swept an arm toward the rock. "After you."

Hannah didn't see how she could possibly get two feet off the ground. She put one of her hands on the rope and was ready to give it a tug when Mitch gently put his hand over hers. "Don't do that. You might pull your friend off the wall. The rope is only for protection, not to climb on."

"That's the stupidest thing I've ever heard," Hannah mut-tered. "The rope is here, why not use it?"

"There with your left hand," Mitch pointed.

Hannah reached up over her head. Mitch kneeled and grabbed her right foot. "Put this here," he said, guiding it. He placed her other foot and suddenly Hannah realized she was off the ground and on the wall. Mitch was right beside her, pointing out new holds. Neeley pulled up the rope, making sure there was very little slack until Hannah was there, right next to her.

"Very good," Neeley said. "Now you wait here."

Mitch did something to Hannah's harness, hooking her into the protection itself, and taking her off the rope. He then belayed as Neeley climbed up.

And that's how they went up. Neeley leading, a spider clinging to the rock, putting in protection every ten or fifteen feet. Then belaying Hannah up to her. Mitch was also hooked in to the rope but he didn't seem to need it. Hannah appreciated him being close to her, hovering right next to her skin, his hands moving her feet and hands to the proper places.

Halfway up, there was a long stretch of bare rock. No

cracks, no crevasses, and almost vertical. Neeley used everything she had ever learned in climbing to get up the twenty feet to a small ledge. By the time she got there, sweat was pouring down her back and her fingers and forearms were sore from the holds she'd used. She put in two pieces of protection: a bolt into a vertical crack just above the ledge right at her feet and a loop of nylon over a rock spur just above her head. She hooked in to both. Then she slid the rope over the figure eight in the front of her harness.

"On belay."

Hannah couldn't believe Neeley expected her to traverse the stretch above. As far as she could tell, it was a sheer rock wall.

"Left hand, there," Mitch said, pointing.

Hannah looked in the direction his finger indicated. "There's nothing there."

"There's a small knob," Mitch said.

Hannah looked again and shook her head. "I don't see it."

Mitch edged around her, his body pressing against her. "Here." He took her left hand in his and extended it. Hannah felt something hard pressing against her rear. Probably one of his snap links, she thought.

Her fingers felt the slightest protuberance from the rock. "You've got to be kidding me," she said. "I'm supposed to use that?"

"Try it," Mitch said. "Move your left foot up about eight inches. Push slightly away from the rock and let the rubber toe grip."

Hannah did as she was told and was amazed to find that she could actually move up the eight inches. Slowly, she continued up until she was in the middle of the twenty-foot stretch. But at that point, the next hold was just out of her reach. Neeley with her extra height had been able to make it, but for Hannah, her fingers came up an inch and a half short, no matter how she stretched.

"Come on, Sara," Neeley called out. "You can make it."

Hannah glanced down. Mitch was pulling out the protection from the place they had just left. Then her eyes traveled past him. The ground was suddenly a long way down. She had been so caught up in moving inches she hadn't realized that she was ninety feet off the canyon floor.

"Sara!" Neeley called out, her voice concerned.

Hannah quickly looked back up. She wanted off this bare stretch. She looked at the small indentation in the rock that she knew was the next hold. Then she moved, pulling her right hand off, left hand extended, pushing up hard with her left leg, her right one dangling in space. And then she was holding nothing but air.

Hannah fell eight feet, then the slack in the rope was gone. She bounced off the rock wall and went down another six feet as the rope did as it was designed and stretched, keeping her from experiencing an instantaneous braking which was as dangerous as falling. Hannah slowly bounced against the rock wall like a pendulum, almost twenty feet below Neeley. Mitch was to her right and slightly below.

"Hang on," Mitch said.

"I've got nothing to hang on to," Hannah shot back, her hands desperately searching for a hold.

Up above, Neeley could feel the pull through her harness, going out to the two pieces of protection. She glanced up. "Oh shit," she muttered. The nylon loop had popped up during the fall and was now hanging by just an inch, still caught at the very top of the spur. And that was taking all the weight of Hannah and herself. The nylon strap leading to the lower protection was slack since it was angled down. If the top loop went, Neeley wasn't sure the bottom nut could take the impact. She dug her heels in tighter to the small ledge.

"Come on, Sara!" she called out.

Hannah shook her head to clear a lock of hair and the helmet slid down over her face. "Great!" her muffled voice came out through the small holes in the helmet. She felt a pair of hands grab her thighs, slowly pulling her to the right. Then the hands slid down her legs until they reached her feet. Mitch placed her feet on some small support and Hannah was no longer hanging.

Neeley breathed a deep sigh of relief. She leaned back against the rock and carefully snapped the slack in the upper nylon loop. It went back down over the spur.

"I'll give you some support with the rope," Neeley said. As Hannah traversed the rest of the bad pitch, Neeley left no slack in the rope. In fact she aided Hannah as much as she could, straining her arms to help pull her partner up. Soon Hannah was at her side and Mitch soon followed.

"I'd like to go down now," Hannah said.

"We're almost there," Neeley reassured her.

"The more we go up," Hannah pointed out, "the farther away the ground gets."

"That's the concept," Neeley said and then she began the next pitch.

Before Hannah had completely recovered from her fall, Neeley was in place, beckoning her up. Hannah climbed.

Soon even Hannah could begin to see that they were going to make it. The top was only twenty feet away. Neeley climbed up and then disappeared over the top, the rope trailing her. Hannah followed, Mitch at her side. Then Mitch smiled at her. "Race you to the top." He unhooked from the tail end of the rope.

"You win," Hannah immediately said.

Mitch shot up and was over the top in twenty seconds. It took Hannah that same amount of time to find her next hold.

Finally, as Hannah pulled herself up the last overhang, she could hardly contain her enthusiasm. She slid over onto a rocky ledge, ten feet wide. There was another rock wall in front and the ledge disappeared to the left. To the right the ledge widened and a bunch of large boulders were tumbled there, caught from falling farther. Neeley and Mitch were nowhere to be seen. Just the rope, locked in to several anchor points in the rock at the very edge and then disappearing behind the boulders to the right.

Hannah turned and looked back down the way they had come. "This is incredible. Wow, look at the view," she called out. "Hey, where is everybody?" she asked as she turned her attention back to her own altitude.

Hannah dropped her backpack and walked toward the boulders, following the rope. Neeley came from behind the nearest boulder, holding a small waxy packet. "Congrats on the climb, Sara. Good news, bad news."

"What do you mean?" Hannah asked. "Where's Mitch?"

Neeley nodded. "Oh, the bad news. Mitch is right behind me."

Hannah saw the gun the same moment she saw Mitch appear and the nasty look that covered his face.

"Oh for crying out loud," Hannah muttered. "Where'd you get the gun, Mitch? There's barely enough room in your shorts for your testicles."

Mitch shook his chalk bag. He pointed at the rock wall and walked toward the edge. The maneuver got the sun out of his eyes and gave him a nice target of both women against the wall.

"Give me the package and I promise I won't kill you. A shot in the legs should do for now."

Neeley glared at him. "Who are you working for?"

Hannah snorted. "What a stupid question. He's working for the guy who paid him six hundred dollars, of course."

"Racine requires that I acquire the tape and papers. Beyond that, I am free to let you go."

The gun focused on Neeley's left knee. She held up the package. "All right. It's yours." She tossed the package onto the rocky ground near the edge to Mitch's right.

"Nice try," Mitch said. "Pick it up. Give it to her," he said, gesturing at Hannah, "and she gives it to me."

Neeley stepped forward. She bent down to pick the package up, and then suddenly threw herself forward and off the ledge into space.

Hannah screamed and Mitch turned to follow Neeley with the gun. The rope that was tied around Neeley's waist quickly ran out of slack and snapped tight into Hannah's harness, in the process whipsawing Mitch in the thighs. He staggered and held against Neeley's weight on the rope for a second and then he was gone, tumbling out into space.

Hannah was dragged to her knees by the taut rope, sliding toward the edge.

"Hold on!" Neeley cried out from twenty feet down, where she was swinging back and forth on the end of the rope.

"Hold on," Hannah muttered to herself as she looked around.

"Grab the protection!" Neeley yelled.

Hannah looked at the anchor points that Neeley had put in. She reached out with her right hand and grabbed hold of a sling attached to cam jammed into a small crevice.

"Now what?" she gasped.

"I'm climbing up," Neeley said.

Hannah felt the weight lessen on the rope. Soon Neeley's hands appeared and then she was up. Hannah stood. They both looked over the edge. Mitch had fallen all the way to the bottom, his broken body lying on top of a boulder. She looked around; there were no other climbers in sight and no one on the ground in the immediate area.

Hannah shook her head. "That poor boy. What a waste."

"Oh yeah," Neeley said. "He's one of Nero's people. Don't waste any tears on him."

Hannah shook her head. "He said Racine. Not Nero."

"Same thing."

"No, it isn't," Hannah disagreed.

"It doesn't matter," Neeley said.

Hannah thought it did, but didn't say anything. "Why the hell did you jump over the side?" she demanded, changing the subject.

"It was the only way to stop Mitch," Neeley said. "Rule fourteen. Desperate times call for desperate measures."

" 'It's a characteristic of wisdom not to do desperate things,' " Hannah quoted in turn.

Neeley looked up from the package. "What?"

"Shakespeare. Beats Gant hands down in my book."

"Oh, shut up," Neeley said. She ripped open the waterproof wrapping and pulled out a small square of paper.

"So where's the tape?" Hannah asked.

"Damn," Neeley exclaimed. "It's only half a cache report."

"Cache report?" Hannah dully repeated.

"It's a format that gives directions to where something is hidden. In this case, it must be the tape."

"So where is the tape?"

"This only gives the IRP," Neeley said.

"IRP?" Hannah wearily asked.

"Immediate reference point," Neeley said. "It's the final fixed point from which you go to recover the cache. In this case it's a bridge abutment. The only problem is we don't have the FRP, the far reference point, and the area which tells us where the hell in the world the FRP is, which in turn leads us to the IRP."

"I don't have a clue what you're talking about." Hannah sat on a rock and leaned forward, putting her face on her knees. "Why wouldn't he leave the whole report here? For that matter, why didn't he leave the tape here? Hell, he could have left it all at the house in the closet with the climbing gear."

Neeley used a handkerchief to rub the sweat out of her eyes. "Come on, Hannah, think about it. Gant had to make it hard to find the tape. The only reason I knew about this place is because I lived with him for over ten years and climbed this route with him. But he couldn't put all his eggs in one basket. We need to find the other half of the cache report."

Hannah shook her head. "I don't buy that. Gant could have cached it—as you call it—somewhere and told only you where it was. He has—had—another reason to make you go through all this."

Once more Hannah's words struck a chord of truth in Neeley, especially as she hadn't told Hannah about the second note in the packet.

Hannah stared at Neeley. "How old are you?"

"Is that important?"

"It's just a question."

"Thirty-two."

"You don't look it."

Neeley shifted uncomfortably.

"Maybe there's something to be said for living a life on the edge," Hannah said. Sensing the other woman's uneasiness, Hannah looked over at the wide expanse of plains to the east and the towers of Denver on the horizon. "So where else did he tell you to go?"

Neeley held up the second piece of paper from the packet.

"Not another climb."

"No, this is on flat ground."

"All right."

"It's in France."

"Oh." Hannah considered that piece of information. "France? Really?"

"Yes." Neeley motioned for Hannah to follow. "We have a lot to do. Let's go. Hey, come on, don't you feel good about yourself knowing you got up here? Do you realize how difficult that climb was? It's a miracle really that you made it with no experience at all."

Hannah retrieved her backpack. "How come at the bottom you told me it was so easy and how anybody could do it? Does this mean I can't trust you?"

Neeley paused. "No, Hannah, it means you can trust yourself."

Neeley turned and made for the rappel point. She figured with luck they'd make it back to town before dark and Mitch's body wouldn't be found before the next day.

Neeley looked at the piece of paper and shivered at the thought of returning to Strasbourg and all the memories there. The "Goose Girl," was all Gant had written on the paper. Neeley knew exactly what that meant. She had told Gant many times about the statue in Josephine Park in Strasbourg. She had always called it "Goose Girl," even though the statue was annointed with a greater, but long-forgotten name. Even about her niche in the rock wall where she hid her treasures as a child. Could it be that Gant had had the piece Nero thought she had? And he had put it there along with the video?

Looking behind her, she gave Hannah what she thought was an encouraging smile as she hooked up the rope. Hannah was looking down at Mitch's body.

"Let's go," Neeley said.

C H A P T E R
19

THE DESK IN NERO'S OFFICE was now covered with Braille folders. Racine had said the women wanted a trade. Nero had been right so far. She had Gant's videotape or knew where it was. It was exactly what Nero had predicted Gant would do. The tape and papers had been sitting for over ten years; a few more hours would be inconsequential. Indeed, what was difficult was reining in Mr. Racine. He had apparently put the women on his ever-growing personal vendetta list. Nero wondered again how such an emotional man could have functioned so long in his profession.

While all appeared to be developing the way he had planned, there was an aspect about this that bothered Nero. He had thought he'd known the full story so many years ago. But he considered one of his greatest strengths to be the ability to admit that he was wrong. Maybe something had escaped his notice. He was disturbed by the Racine-Collins connection. The Senator would not have pulled Racine out of a hat to do the job in Baltimore. That indicated a prior relationship; perhaps one outside the province of the chain of command of the Cellar at even an earlier date. He had thrown the Sudan connection at the Senator to probe for more. What else had the two done together? Had the Senator been riding his own agenda for the past couple of decades, and if so, what was the agenda, and was it good for the country or just Collins?

Had they been together as early as the Sudan or even before? Nero had never considered the possibility before recent events because things had turned out the way they should in the long run from that event. Until 9-11 that was.

Nero saw a definite connection between what happened in Mogadishu and 9-11. Even bin Laden had admitted as much, saying on record how he had felt seeing the Americans turn tail and run after a handful were killed in Somalia. Nero now felt there was more to Collins being in the Sudan and Racine disappearing for several months around that time. He had to wonder if an extension could be drawn to Mogadishu.

This angle was why he had brought Racine in on this operation, rather than another operative. He'd always found that thrusting someone into a crisis tended to expose their true nature. If Mogadishu had not been as he thought, then many subsequent events that had wavered from the path Nero had aimed for could be explained.

All Nero had been able to find so far was that Racine had been seen in Berlin later that October in 1993. Gant had also been in Berlin working under cover for a covert Special Forces unit. In fact, that was when Gant had "resigned" and brokered his deal with Nero.

There was something interesting in Senator Collins's classified file. The French Directorate of Territorial Security, the DST, had a flag on a bank account the Senator held in Geneva. Regular withdrawals were made from the account at a French bank in Paris and it was assumed that Collins had a mistress he was paying so no further inquiries had been made. Collins was a United States senator after all.

Nero checked further into Collins's file but if the senator had a mistress in France, he saw very little of her unless she came to the States. Nero considered it, then pressed the intercom, instructing Mrs. Smith to get a hold of his contact in the DST. He wanted to know who the money was going to.

Nero lit another cigarette. It was early morning in Paris and he knew it would take Mrs. Smith a little bit of time to track the man down. Nero's doctor had left the office earlier, still preaching about imminent death due to smoking, high blood pressure, bad diet, and some words too long for Nero to consider. Nero found the idea of death not disturbing in the least. He had the contented repose of the lifelong atheist who had lived without the threat of hell and would die basking in the surety of his convictions.

All his life, Nero had believed that religion was merely a vehicle to protect people from their true nature. That without the shackles of the spirit, one could thoroughly indulge himself or herself in the task of living, which was a nasty business when done correctly, except very few could do it correctly, thus the need for religion.

In fact, Nero had very much appreciated the purpose of religion. He liked Jung, who said that if God did not exist, then man would have had to invent him. Religion was very important. The breakup of the Soviet Union, Nero laid to the fact that the communists had ignored the very effective purpose of religion. Much more effective than communism for keeping the masses in their place.

Man was an animal, Nero believed. Left to their own devices, the majority of men and women would destroy themselves rather quickly. Religion helped. So did the Cellar. It kept the country on the straight path of sanity against the powerful people driven by emotion who would just as easily destroy it for their own selfish, shortsighted reasons.

There had often been times in his life where Nero had pondered the difference between him and his fellows. At an early age he'd simply accepted that differences existed. Then he'd accepted he wouldn't change. Even that he didn't want to change. What could have been a distressing turbulent existence became instead a rather calm, calculated life with the occasional turbulent event.

What had happened to him in France at the hands of the

Gestapo had only deepened this belief system. He'd felt no resentment upon his return to the States and meeting the man who had occupied this office and agreed with the decision that had cost Nero his eyes and his teammates their lives. It had been a smart decision with a large payoff in favor of the United States and its allies that clearly outweighed the handful of men knowingly parachuted into the meat grinder. Those who had thrown tens of thousands onto the beaches of Normandy knowing many of them would die had been hailed as heroes and been feted with ticker-tape parades after the war. Numerous statues had been cast in their honor. What was the difference? His predecessor had accomplished so much more with less loss of life. As had Nero over the decades since. Only for the Cellar there were no statues or parades or medals; the Cellar had no need for recognition.

Knowing he might be so close to ending this entire messy business put Nero in an oddly reflective state of mind. He found it odd because it was new to him. He had simply never dwelt on the past to heal wounds or relive joys. And this was not because he had problems with the past; it was because he felt nothing. Nero had lived his entire life without feeling any emotion except for occasional anger, which seems the one human emotion able to birth itself in a void. Nero felt no real joy to be sure, but he had also never really experienced emotional pain or regret. A person like that was capable of amazing things, or nothing at all.

Nero, by accepting his lack of humanity, had made himself indispensable to that same humanity. Every country needed a few men who could accomplish what was necessary and unlike the sociopaths whom he passingly resembled and frequently employed, Nero could stop when that was necessary. That's why he could anticipate having the tape and papers but not feel the anxiety of not having them. After all, they were minor compared to what was really at stake here.

The phone rang and his contact in the DST, an old-timer who had been part of the Resistance team that rescued Nero so many years ago was on the line. Without preamble or giving a reason, Nero made his request.

CHAPTER

20

"CAN'T I AT LEAST TAKE A SHOWER?" Hannah asked. "I need a break."

"We can rest when we're dead," Neeley muttered as she threw a duffel bag full of equipment into the bed of the pickup truck.

"Oh, that's nice," Hannah said. "The words of Gant again?"

"No, Warren Zevon," Neeley paused in loading the gear. "They're after us. They know we're here and Mitch was just the point man. You can bet there will be more. Racine is probably on the way as we speak."

"No."

Neeley stopped and looked at Hannah, surprised at the certainty of the word. "Why not?"

"Because he sent Mitch after us."

"And?"

"Racine didn't expect Mitch to fail, but if he did, then there's a backup plan. If *that* fails, then Racine will come."

"Why do you say that?"

"It's been his pattern so far and he'll continue it."

Neeley thought through what Hannah had just said and realized the other woman was right. Racine would have a backup in place. It was what Gant would have done, although she knew Gant would have made himself the primary on any mission. "Okay. I buy that. But we still have to get out of here before his backup plan kicks in." She went into the house.

Hannah looked up and down the street Neeley's small house was on. She was tired from the climb and the adrenaline rush had worn off during the drive back from Eldorado Canyon. Neeley had jumped out of the truck as soon as they'd arrived and started loading the gear.

"Are we going to drive to France?" Hannah asked as Neeley bustled past her with another load.

"No, we're flying."

"Not another one of your friends, I hope," Hannah said.

"We'll fly a commercial airliner," Neeley said.

"What about passports? I didn't pack mine in the rush."

"I'll take care of that," Neeley said. "Listen, you mind giving me a hand here?"

Hannah eyed the growing pile of equipment in the truck. "We're going to take all that with us?"

"No, we're not taking it with us," Neeley said, "but I don't want to leave it here for Racine's goons."

"Then what are we going to do with it?"

"We're going to cache the money." Neeley was attaching a pair of skis to the rack on the top of the camper shell. "Just help load the truck, Hannah. Please."

"Are we going skiing?" Hannah asked, a concerned look on her face.

"Just load!"

Hannah bit the inside of her lip and helped. Twenty minutes later, Neeley was driving through Boulder. She pulled into a crowded shopping center and parked. "Wait here," she ordered Hannah. "I have to get a few things in McGuckins." Neeley jogged into the hardware store and shortly reemerged with a shopping cart full of supplies, most of which she quickly piled into the back of the pickup.

As Neeley slid into the driver's seat, she thrust a box of plastic garbage bags and a roll of duct tape at Hannah. "Start bagging the money," she ordered, pointing at the briefcase right behind Hannah's seat. "Break it down into stacks of fifty grand and then triple-bag each stack. Tape each bag shut and make sure they're tight. Try to leave as little air in each as possible. Make the bags narrow enough to fit inside the PVC pipe. Leave about thirty grand to take with us."

Hannah opened her mouth to say something, then thought better of it and got to work. Neeley drove to Broadway and turned right. After three miles Broadway linked up with Colorado 36 and the end of town. She turned onto 36 and drove north, paralleling the foothills of the Rocky Mountains. She checked her rearview mirror constantly and once pulled over to let a row of cars pass her. After ten miles she was sure no one was following them.

Route 36 turned left into the foothills at the small town of Lyons. The road narrowed and started twisting and turning, following St. Vrain Creek into the mountains. They began gaining altitude.

Soon they could see the town of Estes Park ahead, and behind it the white peaks of the continental divide. Looking down into the town, Neeley could see that the old Stanley Hotel, where she and Gant had spent some nights a long time ago, had undergone a renovation. It was the hotel Stephen King had based the one in the *The Shining* on, something Gant had found amusing considering there was a McDonald's less than a quarter mile down the road from the entrance to the hotel.

As they passed through Estes Park, Hannah bound the last of the money. She was immersed in black bundles. "Hope we don't have an accident," Hannah said. "This would be hard to explain."

Neeley hardly heard her. She was playing with the control for her side mirror, angling it up. "We've got company."

Hannah spun about, but the road behind them was clear. "Where?"

"Above us," Neeley said. "There's a chopper above us."

Hannah tried looked to look but couldn't see anything. "You sure it's following us?"

"I'm sure. It's been shadowing us since we passed Lyons."

"Great," Hannah said. "Who are these guys?"

"The Cellar," Neeley said.

"You've told me that," Hannah said. "But who is exactly is this Cellar? Some supersecret part of the CIA?"

Neeley shook her head. "I don't think the Cellar is part of the CIA. I think the CIA may be part of the Cellar. Or they're totally separate. I don't know."

"What now?" Hannah asked.

"I'm getting tired of following their lead," Neeley said. "Time to take the initiative. I'm going to make them play on our terms. First thing is to get that chopper down on the ground."

"How?"

In reply Neeley pointed at a sign that indicated that the entrance for the Rocky Mountain National Park was less than five miles ahead.

"So?"

"Trust me," was Neeley's answer.

The entrance to the Park was barricaded and the small booths were empty. A sign hung on the metal bar said the park would be opening Memorial Day weekend, which was still several weeks ahead. Neeley drove the truck off-road to the right of the gate. She regained the road on the far side and they headed into the park.

Hannah twisted her head as they entered a large meadow with mountains on all sides. "What are those?" she exclaimed as several large brown animals crossed the road in front of them.

"Mountain sheep," Neeley said. She was looking in her mirror. The chopper was hanging in the air several miles back. Neeley pointed across the meadow toward the snow-covered peaks while they waited for the sheep to cross. "See that thin line up there?"

Hannah craned her neck and stared. "Yes."

"That's Trail Ridge Road. That's where we're going."

"How high is that?"

"At that point? About twelve thousand feet."

"And then?"

"And then we take care of business."

They rounded the far end of the meadow and the road began going back and forth in long, forested switchbacks. Hannah sat silently and watched the scenery change with the climb. The first traces of snow started as they passed Many Peaks Curve. Despite the fact that the road had been plowed since the last snowfall, Neeley had to shift into four-wheel drive to deal with patches of snow blown across the asphalt. Hannah took a look out her window at the meadow, which was now over two thousand feet below them.

"See the chopper?" Neeley asked.

Hannah nodded. "It's over the meadow." As she continued to watch, the aircraft touched down briefly on the road they had traversed ten minutes earlier, bounced back up into the air, then settled down on the road, this time to stay.

"It's landed," Hannah said. "What's wrong with it?"

"Helicopters have low ceilings," Neeley said. "If they've got more than two or three guys in that thing it won't have the power to go much higher. They'll have to find some other means of transportation and that will give us enough time."

Neeley made another switchback and the meadow disappeared from view. Soon they passed a sign indicating they were going through twelve thousand feet in altitude. To the right, Hannah could see all the way back to the town of Estes Park beyond the park's entrance and four thousand feet down. The helicopter in the meadow three thousand feet below looked like an ant. To the left, the side of a mountain stretched up another thousand feet, the slope covered in several feet of snow.

Neeley pulled the pickup truck over. "We go up from here," she announced. "That's Sundance Mountain. We'll cache the money near the summit. It's only another thousand feet."

Hannah eyed the snow-covered slope and shook her head. "Uh-uh. No way."

Neeley handed her a set of small metal snowshoes, ski boots, and a heavy parka. "Put these on. The boots are an old pair of mine. They should fit you. The snowshoes attach to them."

"Listen—" Hannah began, but Neeley cut her off.

"Do it. Now!"

With a grimace, Hannah put on the heavy plastic boots and began strapping the snowshoes to them. Neeley took the black bundles of money and shoved them into foot and a half sections of eight-inch PVC piping that she'd purchased. She screwed caps onto each end and then sealed the ends with duct tape.

Neeley stuffed a folding entrenching tool and the PVC pipes into a backpack. She took out one of Gant's weapons cases and attached it to her backpack. She slung an MP-5 submachine gun over her shoulder and put extra magazines in the pocket of her parka. "Here," she said, extending the Berretta 9mm pistol to Hannah. "Stick this in one of your pockets."

Before Hannah had a chance to protest, Neeley handed her a set of skis. "Balance them on your shoulder. Let's go." Neeley kicked the toe of her snowshoe into the plowed snow on the side of the road and began climbing. Hannah stood there, skis in hand for a few moments, and then grudgingly followed.

After two hundred feet, Neeley paused and looked back. Hannah was fifty feet behind. Neeley scanned Trail Ridge Road. She spotted a Park Service Suburban coming their way, a thousand feet below and four miles away. She opened the weapons case and took out the sniper rifle that she had used in the Bronx. She quickly bolted the two parts together. She had taken off the suppressor earlier. She removed a ten-round magazine with a thin piece of red tape wrapped around the bottom, indicating these were hot loads, not the blue taped subsonic rounds. She slammed it home.

Neeley put her eye to the scope and twisted the focus. The men inside were dressed in black fatigues and had weapons. They must have stolen the parked vehicle from one of the closed Ranger Stations. Someone was staring back at her with binoculars from the rear seat of the truck.

"Let's go!" she called out to Hannah.

Hannah didn't have the breath to reply. It was like climbing a never-ending sand dune with boards strapped to her feet. She could feel sweat pouring down her back and her lungs were straining in the thin air to grab oxygen.

Neeley picked up the pace. The slope they were climbing was concave. There were trees on both sides, but their position at the center was clear. Neeley didn't figure it would help telling Hannah the reason there were no trees here was because it was an avalanche area. The top of the mountain was really a four-hundred-yard-wide ridge, completing the top of the concave slope. When Neeley got within fifty meters of the top, she halted. She threw her pack down in the snow. Hannah was a hundred meters behind.

Neeley took the two ski poles and stuck them in the ground forming a waist-high X. Sitting on her backpack, Neeley placed the forward stock of the rifle on the junction of the poles and put the scope to her right eye. She zoomed past Hannah's tortured face. The Suburban was less than a quarter mile from the pickup.

Neeley pulled back the bolt on the Accuracy International, chambering a round. She zeroed the crosshairs on a point on the front windshield and pulled the trigger. The round hit the shatterproof glass and an explosion of cracks emanated from the impact point. About two inches to the left of her aiming point Neeley calculated as the truck slid to a halt and four men piled out, crouching on the far side of the Suburban, pistols and submachine guns drawn. Neeley made the necessary adjustment to the scope so that it would be zeroed.

Hannah had thrown herself to the snow when Neeley fired. Now she stood, dusting herself off and continued up as Neeley yelled to her it was safe. "Their guns can't reach this far," she assured Hannah.

For good measure, Neeley fired a round into the left front tire, blowing it out. Then she waited, keeping the truck in her scope until Hannah reached her side.

"What now?" Hannah gasped, collapsing into the snow.

"Dig a few holes, here and there," Neeley said.

"What?" Hannah demanded.

"Just dig a few holes, not too deep, just enough to disturb the snow and make it look like something's been buried," Neeley unfolded and handed the shovel to Hannah, then went back to her watch.

Hannah leaned on the handle and stared at her companion. "I'm dying."

Neeley sighed. "You'll be happy while they waste their time looking here."

"You never planned on caching anything up here, did you?" Hannah said. "You just wanted to be able to shoot at those guys who were following us."

Neeley shook her head. "I came up here to get the helicopter out of the picture and give us the high ground, but I do plan on caching the money in the park. Just not here."

"Couldn't we have just buried it in the backyard next to the perennials?" Hannah asked as she thrust the spade into the snow.

"It would be found there."

"Well, what about in the woods around town? Could have saved ourselves the drive."

Neeley was watching one of the men edging his way to the right rear of the truck, getting ready to make a dash to outflank her. "The National Park is the best place. We're guaranteed that it won't be disturbed. Any place else and they can put a shopping mall on top of your cache site before you get back to it."

Neeley drew in her breath and held it. The man started his run and she fired. The 7.62mm round tore through his right thigh and knocked him over the edge of the road, tumbling down into the pine trees on the slope below. The other three men fired futilely with their pistols and submachine guns but the rounds fell well short.

"I thought you said the helicopter couldn't fly this high," Hannah said, pointing.

Neeley pulled her eye away from the scope. The chopper

was about a kilometer away to the northeast, and gaining altitude.

"Not with all those men on board," Neeley said, "but with just the pilot and one other man, it looks like it can." She shifted the muzzle of her weapon toward the new threat. As she did so, the three men all burst from cover and dashed into the trees to Neeley's right front, eight hundred feet below. Neeley snapped a quick shot but the round ricocheted off the tarmac and the three were safe under cover.

"Shit," Neeley muttered. She looked back. Hannah had turned over snow in about a dozen places. "Enough."

The helicopter was closing, less than half a mile away. Neeley aimed and fired three rapid shots at the engine. She was rewarded by a stream of smoke pouring out of the cowling.

The helicopter banked left and disappeared out of sight downslope. Neeley turned her attention back to the trees on the right side of the slope.

"All right," Neeley said to Hannah as she broke the sniper rifle back down. "Time to go skiing. We'll head through those trees to the left." She put the gun into the case. "They're on foot and we'll be long gone before they get back down."

Hannah stared at her. "I don't know how to ski."

Neeley froze. "*Why* didn't you tell me that before we climbed up here? Why do you think you hauled those skis up here?"

"You didn't give me much chance to say anything," Hannah said. "It was, do this, Hannah, do that. I tried to tell—"

"You've never skied?"

"Never."

"Great." Neeley looked down at the pickup truck, and then across at the trees where she knew the three gunmen were making their way, trying to get in range.

"Listen," Hannah said. "The whole idea of skiing is to get down the hill fast, right?"

Neeley absently nodded, her head filled with tactical considerations. She pulled an MP-5 submachine gun out of the pack and slipped the sling over her neck.

"Then I think this will work," Hannah said.

Neeley finally paid attention and turned. Hannah was kneeling on her parka, the smooth Gore-Tex side face-down in the snow. "See you at the bottom," Hannah said as she pushed off and lay belly down on the material.

"Hannah, don't!" Neeley cried, but it was too late as Hannah accelerated down slope.

"Shit!" Neeley exclaimed as Hannah pulled away. In another hundred yards she would be in range of the men in the trees. Neeley threw on her backpack, strapped the sniper rifle case to it, and grabbed the ski poles. With a shove of the poles, Neeley was off. She headed directly for the trees to her right front.

Neeley dropped her poles as she reached the trees, trusting to the edges of her skis and her skill to keep her from doing a face plant into one of the trunks. She pulled back the charging handle on the MP-5.

Hannah was literally flying down the steep slope. She tried digging the tips of her boots into the snow to slow down, but it did little good. She notices little puffs of snows popping up in front of her and momentarily wondered what they were. Then she heard the echoes of the guns going off. Hannah rolled to her left, tumbling off the parka, but her speed was such that she continued downhill, a gaggle of arms and legs and flying snow.

Neeley flashed between two trees almost right on top of the first gunman. He heard her skis on the snow and was turning, but much too slowly as she fired a quick three round burst into his chest, slamming him against a tree, staining it with blood as he slid to the ground.

Neeley bent low at the knees, digging her left ski edges in and turned, hooking around a thick grove, then reversed course in a spray of snow. The other two men were suddenly twenty feet in front of her, turning from firing at Hannah. Neeley pulled the trigger on the MP-5 and nothing happened. She couldn't stop, heading directly for the two men. There was a small ridge between her and them and she pointed her tips straight for it, leaning forward to gain speed but also to make as small as target as possible.

Both men fired as she hit the ridge. She pushed off, into the air and flew right between them. They continued firing but the jump caught them by surprise. Before they could correct they were shooting at each other. The man on the left took several rounds in the chest from his partner. The one on the right took a round in the shoulder and pirouetted into the snow as Neeley crash-landed less than fifteen feet away.

Neeley's feet popped out of the bindings and she rolled, letting go of the useless submachine gun and pulling her Glock out of her coat pocket. The wounded man was on his knees, bringing up the muzzle of his gun when Neeley fired, double-tapping as Gant had taught her. Both rounds hit the man in the center of his forehead and he flopped back into the snow, his blood and brain spreading out below him in a red stain.

Neeley slowly stood. She checked the MP-5. Snow from the turn she had made was jammed in the breech. She looked behind her toward the open slope as she recovered her skis.

Hannah was slowing down but the plowed road was rapidly approaching. Hannah hit the ridge of snow that the plow had left. The impact knocked the wind out of her and she almost stopped but tumbled over the edge onto the side of the road. Hannah lay there gasping for air.

"You bitch!" a man's voice caught her attention from the other side of the road near the Suburban. The first man Neeley had wounded was pulling himself around the back of the truck, his wounded leg leaving a trail of blood. All Hannah had eyes for was the large gun in his right hand. He centered the muzzle on her forehead and was pulling the trigger when a small black hole appeared on his chest. It was quickly followed by several more. The sound of a gun being fired rolled downslope.

Hannah slumped back against the snow and looked to her rear. Neeley was skiing down, her pistol held with both hands leading the way. She halted just before the road with a swift turn to her left, spewing snow over the edge onto Hannah.

"*Next* time, don't do anything until we agree on a course of action," Neeley hissed.

"You never told me the course of action until it was too late," Hannah said, dusting snow off her sweater.

Neeley was trembling as she popped out of her bindings and joined Hannah on the road. "Damn, Hannah, that was close."

"Let's get out of here. Now." Hannah walked toward the pickup ignoring the body and Neeley followed.

Once they were in and driving back the way they had come, Hannah reached across the cab and poked a finger in Neeley's shoulder. "Next time you decide to set up an ambush, tell me, okay?"

"All right." Neeley sighed, and then looked over at Hannah. "Listen, I'm just not used to explaining—" she paused as Hannah yelled: "Watch out!"

The helicopter was astride the road in front of them, less than sixty feet away on a bend in the road. The pilot was just as startled by their appearance, looking out his door at the truck. Another man was standing in the cargo bay, a submachine gun in his hands.

Neeley automatically brought her foot off the gas toward the brake, and just as quickly slammed her foot down on the gas pedal. The V-8 engine roared and the truck accelerated.

The man with the submachine gun put the stock in his shoulder and was aiming. He was getting ready to pull the trigger when he realized the truck wasn't slowing down. He dropped the sub and turned to jump, just as the front grill of the truck smashed into the side of the chopper.

Neeley slammed on her brakes as they hit. The impact neatly bounced the lightweight chopper off the road and into the abyss on the far side of the turn. The gunman went flying out farther, into open space.

Neeley and Hannah stepped out of the stopped truck and followed the course of the helicopter down. It was over a thousand feet to the valley floor below. Neeley blinked as she heard the whine of engines and the blades on the falling aircraft slowly started to turn.

"No way," she muttered. And there was no way the damaged engine could get up to speed in time. The chopper hit bottom in a blossom of flame.

"Let's go," Neeley said, getting back in the truck.

They peeled rubber around the turn.

"What about the money?" Hannah asked.

Neeley didn't say anything for fifteen minutes, until she pulled into a roadside parking area at Beaver Ponds, a nature walk area well away from the scene of their recent battle. She grabbed the PVC pipes with the money and got out of the truck.

"Stay here," she ordered Hannah. "I'll be right back."

Neeley had learned the art of caching from Gant who'd been taught it at the Special Forces Qualification course at Fort Bragg over two decades ago. He'd shown her that it was a much more complicated skill than simply digging a hole in the ground and chucking something in. The first concern was to make sure that whatever was cached would be recovered in usable condition.

The next priority was to find a good spot to put the item. Neeley looked about. Approximately fifty meters away she spotted a pine tree that towered over the other trees. Neeley shot an azimuth to the pine from the corner of the parking area. Forty-seven degrees magnetic. She drew the parking lot on a piece of paper and an arrow, labeling the direction. She then stepped out the distance to the pine, using the pace count Gant had worked out with her—every seventy-two strikes of her right foot equaled one hundred meters. It was thirty-one right steps to the pine. Neeley labeled the arrow with forty-five meters.

From the base of the tree she looked about. The pine needle floor was perfect. Neeley put the pipe down. She stepped out four paces from the tree due south. She laid a garbage bag down on the ground and carefully began the hole. First she slid a piece of cardboard under the needles and scooped them up intact, putting it off to the side. Then she removed the topsoil and placed it on the plastic bag. Each different layer of earth was placed on the plastic in piles, to be put back in the same order it came out. Neeley dug a three foot round hole, down almost three feet. She put the tubes in. She replaced the dirt, making sure to put the top layer back on last and then slid the needles back on top. A bit of careful rearranging and it looked undisturbed.

Neeley put the dirt displaced by the PVC piping into the garbage bag and brought it back to the truck, tossing it in the back. She transcribed the map she had drawn into a Special Forces cache report format as Gant had taught her.

Neeley copied the report onto the lower part of the paper and then quickly tore it in half. "Here," she handed the scrawled copy to Hannah who had watched her in silence.

"What do I do with this?" Hannah asked in surprise.

"Isn't it obvious? If something happens to me, dig the money up."

Hannah shook her head. "Neeley, I'm touched, really, but you don't know me. We only met a few days ago."

Neeley held out the report. "I know you better than anyone on the planet. Besides, you knew your husband for years and what did that get you? I want you to have the report, Hannah, and that's all that matters."

Hannah took the report. "What now?" she asked.

"We go to the airport."

CHAPTER

21

HANNAH AND NEELEY stepped out of the airport parking lot shuttle with a surprisingly light load. They couldn't very well haul everything with them so they had spent most of the past hour cleaning and oiling and carefully repacking the guns in the back of the truck.

They had then left the truck in long-term parking at DIA where it would not be noticed for months at least, given the volume of vehicles that went through that lot. They didn't have enough clothes between them for one person to be out of style in France, much less two. Neeley had offered the limited contents of a back closet that she described as having a few things. It turned out to be skiing apparel, a wet suit, and some stuff Emma Peel would have loved. So now they were searching for their gate in the jumble of Denver International Airport wearing a lot of tight black clothing. Hannah noticed that when your butt was poured into black ski pants, men hardly noticed ragged nails. Neeley was wearing a one-piece catsuit with a wide black belt that she said she had only worn once before: to crawl through a long narrow pipe. Hannah believed her.

They had an hour before the flight so they stopped at the European Café on Concourse B and had a combination of the last five meals they had missed. For the first time in years, Hannah ate her fill without counting fat grams. She and Neeley looked fit and healthy, their tummies as flat as boards and their complexions glowing from exercise and the sheer stress of imminent death. Neeley spent most of the lunch in disbelief that Hannah wasn't sore from the climb and the incident in the Rocky Mountain National Park.

Neeley made all the flight arrangements at the counter. She knew she was on the right track, but she wondered if they would live long enough to find Gant's cache.

Then she excused herself from Hannah to make a phone call. She took a stack of quarters and sat down at a pay phone. She pulled out the 212 number that Gant had given her.

She dialed it and the operator told her how much she needed to pay. Neeley slid the coins in, then the phone rang. It was picked up on the third ring.

"Yo!" a voice boomed into Neeley's ear.

"Is this Joe?"

"You did the dialing, sweetie. You make a mistake? And you got the advantage because I don't got a fucking clue who you are."

Despite the harsh words, the tone was light, the accent clearly New York City.

"I'm a friend of Anthony Gant."

"My little Tony! How's he doing?"

Neeley closed her eyes tight. "He's dead."

"Fuck."

A long silence reigned. Then the voice came back, all lightness gone. "How?"

"Cancer."

"Mother of Mercy. That's a bad way to go. You the woman he's been with these past ten years or so?"

"Yes."

"You there when he died?"

"Yes. I buried him."

"Good. That's good. He wasn't alone. His mother know?"

"I don't think so. I haven't told anyone but you just now."

"Then his brother doesn't know either. Okay. Damn. I guess I'll have to tell her. And Jack. That ain't gonna be good." There was a short pause. "But you're calling for another reason, right?"

"I need a little help. Gant said I should call you if I needed help."

"Did you visit the Bronx recently?"

"Yes."

"You done good there. Helped me out what you done. What you need, sweetie?"

"Passports."

"When and where?"

"I'll be landing in Atlanta in about four hours. Then heading to France."

"A passport got a short shelf life these days," Uncle Joe said. "You can get out of the country and have maybe forty-eight hours, but then it will be hot."

"That's good enough."

"You coming back?"

"I hope so."

"Good. Good. I'd like to meet you sometime. Tony was a good boy. A good man. I'm glad you were there for him. Okay. Here's the deal. There's a guy who owes Gant from their time in the service. He does the best. Real deal. Checks out. But I can't guarantee that the names used won't roll into the system. Like I said, maybe forty-eight hours, then someone's going to see your name. Maybe quicker if your name is hot and on a list. I don't know if that's good or bad for you, but I'm just telling you like it is."

Neeley knew it was bad, but she also knew they had no choice. She hoped they could get to France and back within forty-eight hours. Neeley quickly copied down the instructions Uncle Joe gave her. He ended by telling her to call him when she got back in country and thanking her for being there at the end for Gant.

Neeley didn't talk to Hannah as they waited to board. On the plane, Neeley scanned the other passengers, wondering which one was the shadow. It could be anyone, Neeley decided, even one of the crew. Given the stricter security, she would have to wait until France to arm herself and that made her nervous.

Hannah was talking to a woman seated across the aisle. She was leaning into the open space to the irritation of the other passengers who were still finding their seats and putting away luggage.

Neeley watched in fascination as Hannah continued to chat with her newfound friend. If Neeley leaned a little closer she could catch pieces but it seemed to be meaningless talk. They finally stopped for takeoff and once the plane was airborne, they seemed to forget about each other.

Hannah pulled some cream from the tote to rub into her ragged cuticles. Neeley watched her in silent wonder. She looked so normal despite all that had happened in the last few days. "How do you do that?"

Hannah turned in surprise. "What do you mean? This?" She motioned with her cream-colored fingertips.

"No, well, partly. I mean how do you do all these normal things? Like talk to that woman and do your nails with all this stuff going on?"

Hannah continued massaging her nails. She was thoughtfully using her thumbnail to push back the dead skin around the half moon of her nails. "I do day-to-day living well. I've had to."

Ignoring Neeley's confused expression, she continued. "My parents died in a car crash when I was six. There was no family for me to go to since they were both orphans. I guess they were drawn to that aloneness in each other, but sometimes I see it as very selfish: to have had a child who had no real connection to anyone. When they died no one was responsible for me except some bureaucrats, the ones who step in and take care of children like me.

"I was lucky in a way. My first foster parents were decent enough. No hanging me upside down in closets or anything, but they were joyless people. They did day-to-day living as if life is a series of tasks that you just finish, not for any particular reason other than you can't live anymore if you don't do it right.

"It was a very quiet way to grow up, if you can call it growing up. Sometimes I think I just got physically bigger and that was the extent of my maturing. Because I had done the right thing for so many years I was able to go to college. I met John in my second year and that was the end of Hannah as a coed.

"By then I was too dependent to see my own life as an opportunity, an adventure. I took the security and direction he offered and helped him make his life the center of our lives. Men like John need women like me; anchors to boring reality, partners in the mundane."

Neeley shook her head. "Hannah, if you believe that your personality was basically fixed and John married you for that reason, then how can you allow for what happened between you and him?"

"What do you mean?"

Neeley tugged on the tight jumpsuit to find a more comfortable fit. "It's pretty obvious, isn't it, that if John had married you for your placid acquiescence, he would have told you about his past. Why should he hide all that if you're the obedient little wife living vicariously through your successful husband?"

Hannah shrugged. "I was the obedient wife. I just existed."

"What changed?" Neeley asked. "That's not what you've been the last couple of days."

"Besides you coming into my living room with a gun? And John getting killed?" Hannah didn't pause for an answer. "The change really happened before that. When I truly accepted what John had done to me when he split, taking everything, that was all too much. I got mad. Angry. Pissed.

I could have lived with all the wasted years being his wife but the son of a bitch should have been grateful for that. Disappearing the way he did and leaving me with nothing; acting like it had all been nothing, now that was going too far. Something snapped in me."

"You want to know what I think?" Neeley said. "I think you just existed until someone like John came along and programmed you. Maybe we're a lot alike. Maybe most women are like this—the way society, despite its proclamations to the contrary, wants us to be. Notice that they still make Barbie dolls and in the Super Bowl it's the guys on the field and the women on the sidelines swinging the pom-poms. What's the female equivalent of the Super Bowl? You don't see a stadium full of women watching the Miss America Pageant.

"It's like you have a computer just sitting there. It's a good piece of equipment, works fine, no glitches in the hardware, but there's no program loaded in. So along comes some guy needing a computer to support him in living his life. Depending on who they are they're going to have their own software.

"The accountant has his tax stuff, the lawyer's got all the case history stuff, and an architect would have some cool drawing software. The point is that now the computer only has the ability to do what they need it to. It could have done anything but instead it ends up very specialized. That's the way it is for so many women."

Hannah nodded. "Is that what happened to you?"

Neeley cocked her head sarcastically. "No, actually my childhood dream was to be a professional assassin with no identity."

"Sorry. Sometimes I forget you kill people, you're so nice to me."

Neeley turned to look out the window. Nothing but clouds and blue skies. "I never forget."

"But remember," Hannah said, "computers can be reprogrammed. I think what John did to me blew a fuse and I'll never function that way again, making someone else more important than me." She reached out and put a hand on Neeley's arm. "But now you'd better get some rest. We've got a lot to do in a little time and I have a feeling France is going to be a pain in the ass if the last couple of days are any indication."

CHAPTER
22

NERO WAS ALONE in his office. He sat in the dark smoking and pondering his soul. Or rather the soul of the country, which he considered one and the same.

The last several phone calls were most interesting. The freelancer's body had been found in Eldorado Canyon. On top of that, he'd just received news of the debacle in the Rocky Mountain National Park from the Agency. Seven dead, two destroyed choppers, and the women were still on the run. Not at all what might be expected from the two women by anyone other than Nero.

Nero was the keeper of all the secrets and when he died, they would be in the possession of his successor. His predecessor had told him there were only two prerequisites for this job: to be able to keep a secret and to be loyal to a higher concept. Nero had none of the burning drive found in most people to share all they knew for profit or position. He got no pleasure from shocking people and he detested the simpering idiots who traded information for acceptance. He would be a hard man to replace, something he had spent many years pondering.

His job was simple—keep the country safe—from enemies foreign and domestic, and police the covert world. It was the latter job that Nero had found most difficult to accomplish over the years, especially since Vietnam. The misguided decisions that had to be corrected; the out-of-control politicians who had to be corralled or covered for; the sociopaths who had to be terminated before they destroyed too much; the terrorists, home grown and those from abroad, who could not be dealt with through normal channels and whose threat was so great they demanded the attention of an organization as efficient and ruthless as the Cellar. Nero had seen it all and more over the decades in the shadow. If he had not been ill for the six months preceding the 9-11 disaster, things might have turned out much differently. That illness had caused him to look at something he had put on hold until then—his own mortality and what the lack of his presence would mean for his country.

He also had been forced to accept that he, like the others in the covert world, had misread the signs and failed the country.

It wasn't that he had not previously considered his death and what it would mean. He had put things in place decades previously in preparation for that possibility. But he had finally accepted it was time to move those preparations forward. Anthony Gant's death had helped greatly in that matter.

Nero's reverie was broken by the demanding ring of the phone. Nero hit the on button and listened as his Paris contact told him who Senator Collins's money was going to. It was not, as Nero had suspected, a mistress. His contact had done an efficient job and Nero memorized the name, address, and phone number he was given.

Breaking the connection, Nero then dialed the number in France. A man answered and Nero identified himself as Senator Collins's representative. A long silence followed, the live connection indicating the man was hooked. Nero informed him that the payments would be ceasing.

The man exploded with a flurry of vague threats.

Nero's dull metallic voice filled the office. "I called you out of courtesy for past services rendered."

Nero listened a while longer, but the man grew no more specific with his threats. "You are free to do what you want." He smiled at the thought. The man was a fool. People were so naive, especially when it came to themselves.

The voice stridently went on for a few more minutes.

Nero finally interrupted with a question. "Do you know a man named Racine? Have you ever met him?"

The denial was the slightest bit too strong.

"You are certain?" Nero asked. He always believed in giving someone a second chance to jump out of the grave they dug themselves.

The man immediately went into another tirade of threats and denial.

Nero would have sighed if his throat could have handled it. "Of course the Senator has much to fear and of course I know that if you go down, we shall all go down. Dear Sir, that has been the refrain I have heard from many my entire professional career."

Nero finally hung up the phone, disgusted with the conversation. He tilted his head toward the door opening. He could smell the gum and follow the man's movements from the chewing.

Nero was curious to see how this next act turned out. These two women were doing quite well. He felt it was time they received some breathing room. From the latest information he'd received, they were on their way to France, which could prove to be most interesting given his last conversation.

"Mr. Bailey, I have some things I would like you to do."

C H A P T E R

23

RAY SUGGS WAS NOT a happy man. Earlier he had received a call from some connected guy in New York saying he needed papers for some chick who was a friend of Anthony Gant's. The guy had told him she'd pay twice his usual fee for a couple of sets of papers. It sounded like an okay deal and Ray had let his anticipatory greed rise.

His van was gliding without much mental energy on his part toward the Atlanta Airport. He was eating a veggie bagel sandwich purchased before he got on the highway. There were some alfalfa sprouts hanging on his beard as he lit his after-lunch cigarette. He was a vegetarian smoker, something that drove people crazy. Ray couldn't see the problem; not much different than being a Christian soldier, he thought.

He remembered Anthony Gant well, or as well as you can remember the guy who saves your ass from frying.

Ray could hardly think about that disaster so many years ago in Africa without his blood pressure spiking. As it was, he had been toasted enough that his beloved Army had declined his services any further, thank you very much.

He had never met Anthony Gant before October 3, 1993, but he had met his brother Jack, who was a captain in the Rangers in Mogadishu. How Anthony Gant had arrived there, no one, not even the Delta commandos, seemed to know.

Suggs was flying one of the support Blackhawks for the raid and he was brought in to pick up some of the wounded and one of the prisoners. To Suggs it looked like everything was falling apart with the amount of incoming fire that was being poured into the friendly forces.

As he prepared to take off from a dusty street in between two buildings, an RPG round hit his helicopter. The next thing he knew, he was engulfed in flames as the chopper hit the ground. His copilot was gone, out the window, saving his own butt. Ray knew right then and there he was a dead man. A couple of the guys in the rear and the rag-head prisoner they had just loaded were dead.

That was when he met Anthony Gant. This crazy-looking guy, fire extinguisher in hand, had appeared in the passageway leading to the rear of the chopper, carving out a small opening in the flames with the device.

"Come on!" Gant had yelled after checking the bodies and confirming they were gone.

Ray's burned hands couldn't unbuckle his harness and Gant had slid between the pilot seats, unsnapped him, and dragged him out. Ray clearly remembered being over Gant's shoulder as he ran from the chopper, seeing the aircraft burst into flame even as he felt the pants of his flight suit burning. Gant threw him down in the dirt and extinguished the flames but the damage had been done.

Gant had saved him then, and several months later he had shown up at the VA hospital where Ray was recuperating.

"I hear you're pretty good with photography and calligraphy," Gant had said. And that had been the beginning of Ray's new life although he never found out how Gant had learned about his hobby.

It wasn't so bad working on the edge of the edge. Ray couldn't do covert special ops but by God he was one of the

people who made them possible. His passports and papers
were recognized as the best. He worked for the government
sometimes and he worked for others beyond the law. He ful-
filled a need on both sides and because of that he was basically left alone.

After the quick phone call he was looking forward to the
whole business, especially news of Gant, when the bottom
dropped. He'd put the information into the computer to pre-
pare the passports and get the proper numbers and names
into the system in time for the women's flight. Less than an
hour later, that incredible, rotting fuck Bailey, Nero's
hatchet man, had called with a request from his boss. Ray
could feel the tendrils of hate and fear intertwine in his gut
and drop to his scarred useless legs. He'd nervously wheeled
his chair back and forth, keeping the phone cocked under his
chin. He'd listened and nodded and the only word he had
spoken was an affirmative. It was the only possible answer
when Nero asked something.

So Ray wasn't happy. He was gonna crap on someone
who was a friend of Gant's and gonna pay him well and he
was doing it for Nero. Bailey had also told him Gant was
dead, which hadn't made the whole thing any happier. And
then there was the connected guy in New York who wasn't
gonna be too happy about this either.

He hoped the woman was a bitch. In his experience it was
always easier to betray shitty people. But she was a friend of
Gant's and Ray couldn't see Gant being too tolerant of a
bitch hanging around. 'Course, she could be a good-looking
bitch. He supposed Gant was like any other man in that his
tolerance for difficult behavior was directly inverse to the
size of the tits involved.

The airport exit caught his eye and, as he switched on his
blinker, he tried to put aside the bad feeling.

HANNAH COULDN'T BELIEVE they were already landing in
Atlanta. She had slept the remainder of the flight, but instead

of feeling rested, she felt sluggish and swollen, wondering if her face was imprinted with the pattern of the tweedy seat cover.

She tried to keep up with Neeley but the latter was being pressed by the tight schedule of their next departure. Neeley hurried out to the parking concourse, searching for her objective. Hannah struggled with her big tote and her too tight pants all the while trying to rouse herself from her lethargic state. "Slow down a little, Neeley."

"Just a sec, I think we're almost there."

Suddenly Neeley halted next to a battered van and dropped her bag.

Hannah inspected the rumpled metal. "Look, it's even parked in a handicapped spot."

The soft whir of a motor caused her to step back as Ray's wheelchair cruised around to their side of the vehicle.

"Oh." Hannah decided to remain mum. The man was eyeing them both in a manner usually reserved for cattle purchases.

"Thought you weren't going to make it," he snorted.

Neeley apologized for their lateness and reiterated their needs.

Without saying another word, he motioned toward the van. Neeley seemed unconcerned but Hannah was hesitant. Something felt wrong to her but she wondered if it was just the squalidness of the entire situation. Following Neeley's lead, she climbed into the darkened interior. After a moment to adjust her vision, Hannah drew a sharp breath. The inside of the van was quite a contradiction to the outside. The interior was clean and modern, with a bank of computers and printers lining one side. Hannah felt her anxiety lessen as she granted Mr. Suggs his degree of professionalism. In a moment he had joined them and began the task at hand.

Hannah brushed her hair vigorously for the photo, giving her some time to feel things out. Hannah decided that Suggs was relaxing a bit although he still had difficulty ignoring their breasts. He seemed genuinely troubled by Neeley's story of Gant's death, withdrawing for a moment and then not really looking at them again.

Hannah noticed his hands were trembling as he gave them the finished products. Neeley gave him the money and that was it, except Hannah stepped forward. "Are you going to fax our passport numbers to the Cellar?"

Ray seemed surprised, and hurt, but he nodded. "Bailey already called."

"Who's Bailey?" Neeley asked.

"Nero's right hand," Ray said. "They must have had an alert on the computer for your names. Showed up right away when I did a run through to get the paperwork started."

"I was told you owed Gant," Neeley said.

Ray wearily nodded. "He saved my ass. But he's dead now." He didn't lift his head to meet her eyes.

"Is that all it comes down to?" Neeley asked. "Nero runs everything?"

To that, Ray had no answer.

"Do you know who called you to set this up?" Neeley pressed.

She didn't think it was possible, but he sounded even more morose. "Yeah, Gant's uncle. I'm screwed coming and going on this. And then there's his brother."

"What about his brother?" Neeley asked.

Suggs lifted his head. "You think Tony Gant was a hard man then you never met Jack Gant. He was there too. Mogadishu. I hear they never spoke again after it."

Despite the time constraints of their next flight, Neeley couldn't walk away. "Why not?"

"Jack was a captain in the Rangers. He led most of the men who got caught on the ground there. Lost seven guys. He took their deaths hard."

"But why wouldn't he talk to his brother?" Hannah asked.

"The raid was fucked and Tony was part of it in some way." Suggs shrugged. "I don't know. It was a bad time and a bad place."

Hannah didn't buy it. One thing she had learned in her social circle was what appeared to be the situation between people was rarely the reality, as her own recent experience had clearly pointed out. She tugged at Neeley's arm. "We've got to go."

As they walked away, Suggs called out: "I'm sorry."

Hannah was letting it all sink in by the time they got to their gate with the boarding passes. "Does everyone work for the highest bidder?"

"Ray doesn't have much choice." Neeley held the passports up. "These are real, Hannah. The numbers are recorded in the State Department and Ray can access the computer and put our identities in there so we won't get stopped at customs if anyone decides to check. It's virtually impossible to travel on false papers these days. The only way they can be real is if Nero and the Cellar helps Ray. He has to pay them back otherwise he could never stay in business. Giving up our names is part of his payback. It's not that big of a deal; at least from his point of view."

"It's a big deal from my point of view," Hannah said.

Neeley looked around, trying to spot their tail. "No, then we'd be dead. We're just point men, picking our way through the trip wires." She smiled grimly. "Plus, I think he's going to have to deal with Uncle Joe and that might not be pleasant."

" 'Uncle Joe'?"

"Forget about it."

Hannah's depression was beginning to settle in for a longer stay. "Look, I'm tired. This is pointless. The only reason Nero is letting us go to France is to get the tape. They're going to kill us as soon as we find the tape and if we don't find it, they're going to kill us anyway. All we're doing is having a bad time before we die."

Neeley slowed down and turned to her companion. "We still have a chance. As long as we're breathing, we have a chance. Besides, they want us to give up. They think because we're women we can't take it. They're wrong."

Hannah straightened up and tried to feel a confidence that wasn't real. "Well, just remember they're a little righter about me."

Neeley shook her head. "No, I think you're the one everyone has been most wrong about."

RACINE STARED AT THE NUMBER on his secure cell phone through three rings before he answered it. "Yes?"

Besides the number, there was no mistaking the raspy, metallic voice. "They're heading to Europe, Mr. Racine. France. Does that mean anything to you?"

Racine's grip on the phone grew tighter. "Neeley spent a lot of time in France as a kid, according to the file you gave me on Gant."

"Yes. I suppose. But why go now?"

"Recapturing memories?"

"Do not jest with me, Mr. Racine.

"I have no idea."

"I want you to stay clear of them," Nero said. "I want to see what they're trying to find."

"Sure."

The phone went dead and Racine tossed it on the passenger seat and then gave it the finger. He headed for the airport.

C H A P T E R

24

NINE HOURS AFTER Ray Suggs faxed his copies of their passports to Nero, Hannah and Neeley were packing their gear in the trunk of a rented car in Frankfurt. It was a couple of hours before dawn and though Neeley could sense some jet lag, the flight had been boring enough to be restful. Hannah had spent hours in conversation with a young man wearing a T-shirt announcing *I have a liberal arts degree. Will that be for here or to go?*

Neeley had decided that Hannah could carry on a conversation with a tree stump. That there might be some jealousy in her observation was not lost on Neeley. She wondered how Hannah did it. With Gant and those who he associated with, conversation had been limited to the essentials. She also was beginning to realize there was a method to everything that Hannah did. She talked to gather in information from people just as she apparently had learned so much from all those books in her house.

It was much cooler in Frankfurt but Neeley knew that the

sunrise would take care of a lot of the chill. The big heat tab in the sky, Gant had called the sun until the day he died.

The sky had been overcast and sickly gray that day. Gant had gestured weakly and Neeley had bent low to hear what were almost his last words, surprise and a little fear that he would never see the sun again. He felt the clouds were cheating him. Watching Gant's slow death she wondered how much of his career choice had simply lain in the fact that he had hoped for a fast, though brutal, death over the slow calculating dying that most people could look forward to. She'd wept for him as every day he experienced the fear anew.

Hannah and Neeley decided to stop for some breakfast before they got on the autobahn for Strasbourg. Hannah was surprised at the Americanization of Europe as they pulled into the IHOP parking lot.

As they had their breakfast, Neeley thought of the last time she had been in Strasbourg. The floodgate of memories kept her quiet for a while until finally Hannah poured them both more coffee and said: "Okay, so tell me about this Jean-Philippe guy."

Neeley played with her coffee cup. "Jean-Philippe. I wonder how I survived knowing him. Some people are so poisonous to the human soul they should have a big warning label on their forehead. But they don't, of course. They are usually wrapped in beautiful packages because beauty and sweetness tend to make us forget about danger. Haven't you ever noticed that's the way with snakes too? The most deadly are so brightly colored?"

Neeley didn't wait for an answer. It was as if she were talking to herself, verbalizing thoughts that had always lurked in her brain. "I was entranced by those bright colors. He was poison and he killed the best part of me. Sometimes I think it's because people like that are so dead themselves they destroy those who are alive out of jealousy. Other times I think they do it because they're mean and it's a sport. All I know for sure is my part, and I know my loving him destroyed something in me. I miss it every day."

Neeley was caught in her narrative and paid no heed to

anyone in the bustling restaurant. "You know how you can tell if you are with a poisonous person? You begin to commit acts which are completely, totally foreign to you. Of course you can't see this, but your friends can and your family too, the people who know you're good and special, they recognize when something in you is dying.

"But here's the weird part. You start to think those friends are the enemy. Instead of seeing them as saviors, you see them as bitter, jealous cynics trying to deprive you of happiness and you get rid of them instead of the real poison.

"It wasn't hard for Jean-Philippe to turn me from a schoolgirl into a conspirator. I would be lying if I said that I wasn't responsible for my part. Today, what I hate so much is that he used all my flaws to destroy my strengths and then what am I left with? You tell me?"

Hannah signaled the waitress for the check and reached her hands across the table for Neeley's cold fists. "Neeley, can't you see that he didn't kill your soul or your spirit? He hurt it, he angered you, he filled you with a rage you've never felt before and therefore didn't know how to handle. He didn't hurt you as much as he made you aware of hurt. Your flaw, and mine, is that we can't deal with that pain so we ignore it. You let Gant cover up that hurt with his attention as surely as I did with a house and reading books."

Neeley smiled mournfully. "Isn't that the worst part? Being so responsible for your own fall? Isn't that a tragedy?"

"It is very tragic of course, but the whole point of tragedy is to rise again from the very qualities that destroy you. It is to seek redemption."

Neeley stared at Hannah, trying to reconcile the person in front of her with the woman she had spied on in St. Louis just a few days ago. "You are so amazing. How can you be so positive about things you don't understand?"

Hannah let go of the other woman's hands. "See you are doing just what you did before. Pushing away the person who knows only the good and strong in you."

"But I said I pushed away the people who tried to pull me

away from Jean-Philippe. There is no poisonous person in my life now."

Hannah gathered her things and stood. Looking down at Neeley she said: "But of course there is—Gant's ghost."

Neeley felt a stab of pure pain explode in her chest and squeezed her eyes shut as if that small gesture would soothe the turmoil within her. "Let's go," she said curtly.

The traffic on the autobahn was so thick and treacherous that the breakfast conversation soon receded to a place where both women could ignore it for a while.

CHAPTER
25

NEELEY STOOD with Hannah at the edge of Josephine Park. Neeley's grandmother had brought her to this park every day as a child during her summers in France and later she had come with Jean-Philippe.

The drive into Strasbourg, on top of the recent conversation she'd had with Hannah, had stretched Neeley's emotions to the limits. The city was on the west side of the Rhine, just over the border from Germany. Getting to the park had required driving across the Rhine, into the southeast part of the city, through the center, to the northeast suburbs, activating all the attendant memories of the time Neeley had lived there.

The park was bordered on the north by the Marne-Rhine Canal and spread over numerous acres with paths winding through thickly forested terrain. It, at least, had not changed much from her childhood memories.

She led Hannah to the southeast section of the park and the statue of the Goose Girl. As a child she had been drawn to the fountain.

There were few people about since it was early and the weather was not conducive to hangers-about. Just a few nanny types quickly walking through with their charges braving the chill because of duty and a gray-haired man on a bench opposite the fountain.

Neeley walked around the bronze figure. The little girl was pulling her basket away from the attentive goose. As a child, Neeley's mood had dictated whether she saw fear or playfulness on the frozen face. Now she stared at it and felt the chills erupting as bumps on her arms and legs.

Hannah was ignoring the fountain and staring at Neeley. It was the first time she saw fear in Neeley and Hannah was immediately worried. Her eyes darted back and forth, scanning the area for the threat that her senses recognized even if she didn't.

"Let's get out of here, Neeley. This place gives me the creeps."

Neeley ignored her and was walking backward away from the fountain, her gaze still focused on the statue. Her head was a jumble of all the things Gant had taught her over the years. She was starting to shake all over and when she turned to Hannah she saw the woman's face was a mask of concern.

Hannah pulled Neeley toward one of the benches arranged in a circle around the little frozen girl and forced her to sit down.

"What's wrong with me?" Neeley could only gasp the question.

Hannah put her arm around the shaking shoulders. "It's the fear you've always run from. You're supposed to be afraid, Neeley, so am I. This is a good thing. You're just showing on the outside what's always been on the inside."

"My, God, I couldn't function if I was always like this; how can this be a good thing?" Neeley's teeth were chattering now, making it even more difficult to talk.

Hannah just kept holding her. "Now you see why everyone isn't a professional killer. I guess you did pretty good to get this old without feeling the fear that rules the rest of us."

"But I was this afraid before, the day in the airport, when I met Gant."

"And Gant was there for you," Hannah said,

Neeley looked up. "And now you're here for me."

"Let's get whatever we came for and get out of here." Hannah was trying to be chipper but the effort was wasted on Neeley.

Neeley leaned forward until she was staring at the ground between her feet. She took several deep breaths, then looked up. "Okay."

Hannah waved her hand about. "So what did you tell him about this place? What did he think was important enough for you to remember always?"

"You know, typical childhood memories. My grandmother bringing me here, buying me a milk chocolate bar. I would run around and play mostly. Sometimes I'd walk on the rock wall over there in those bushes but I had to stop because it was loose. Some people yelled at me one day and I was mortified.

"Once my grandmother even got upset because I was despoiling the park, as she said." Neeley stopped and looked at the bronze girl. One hand was pulling the basket from the playful goose and the other was thrust forward as if for balance and the fingers were pointing across the park. She followed the tips of the fingers to the low rock wall and stood.

Hannah had to jog to keep up.

"That's where it has to be. I told Gant about my grandmother getting so angry when she found out that I was stashing paper from my chocolate in the loose stones. One day I put a flower in the foil and wrapped it tightly and stuck it there thinking that someday I'd be back. A little time capsule of my childhood. I just hope we don't have to tear the wall down."

But they didn't have to do that at all. Amazingly, the stones and their arrangement were very familiar to Neeley even after so many years. The tightly bound packet was where Gant had left it, close to Neeley's first childhood cache buried under a couple of loose stones. With trembling fingers she opened the foil and looked at the dried flower. Tears dripped down Neeley's face. Reluctantly she opened the small package that had been on top and extracted two pieces of paper. She read Gant's spidery handwriting.

"Well, what is it?" Hannah asked. "Where's the tape?"

"It's the rest of the cache report. But there's also a note here. I don't understand."

Hannah glanced around nervously. "Okay, good, forget the note. Do you know where the tape is?"

"Yes. This says the bridge from the other half of the report is in West Virginia. Near where his ex-wife Jesse and his son live." But Neeley was more interested in the address written in Gant's hand on the note. There was nothing but the street and a number. "We have to go to some address here in Strasbourg." Her voice had gone cold and flat.

"What?"

"Shit, Hannah, I don't know. It says Rue d'Adelshoffen in Schiltigheim, which is a part of Strasbourg."

Hannah looked up at the overcast sky. "Let's just go to West Virginia, get the tape, make a deal with Nero, and forget this note." Hannah reached for the paper just as a shadow fell across the stone wall.

Neeley was facing Hannah, her hand resting on the stone wall. "It's the guy from the bench, isn't it?"

Hannah watched his arrival from behind Neeley's right shoulder. He appeared quite brazen in his approach but then his gun was walking point. "Uh-huh."

Neeley remained perfectly still. "Does he have a gun?"

"Of course."

"Does it have a silencer?"

"Yes."

"Put the paper in your pocket."

Hannah started fumbling along the sides of the tight ski pants. They both heard the sound of the gun's slide being pulled back. Hannah realized the man was staring at her empty-handed fumbling. Before she could throw herself to the ground, Neeley had turned to throw the loose stone that was in her hand as hard as she could in the direction of the noise.

They both heard the light pop of the gun and the bullet pinged the wall, slicing shards of stone, one of which clipped Hannah across the cheek.

Hannah fell to the ground clutching her face. Neeley jumped the wall as the man once more pulled back the slide on the silenced weapon. She snap-kicked, catching his wrist and the gun went flying. He immediately assumed a professional fighting posture and easily blocked Neeley's next two kicks.

They circled, each looking for an opening, when he quickly reached down and pulled a knife from a sheath on his right calf. Neeley had left her own personal arsenal back in Denver, knowing she wouldn't get it through airport security, and now she regretted not having taken the time to rearm herself here in Europe.

He was stepping forward, throwing his left hand in a jab toward Neeley's face. She took the punch, knowing it was the knife hand that was all-important now. The blow brought a sharp pain, but she caught his right hand in a perfect X block, her forearms crossed. She twisted, trying to disarm him, but he'd been trained well and he slithered his arm out of her grasp, the blade slicing cloth on her arm but not skin.

He slashed, and then continued the move, spinning, swinging a backfist with his left, which Neeley ducked. She hit him hard with her open palm in the chest and heard the air rush out of his lungs. As she went in to finish him off, he jabbed up with the knife, the point piercing her jacket, and causing her to abruptly change course and leap back or be spitted on the blade.

The man straightened and took a deep breath before speaking in French. *"No more games."*

He pulled a second knife out from behind his back and whirled the two about, the steel glinting. Neeley realized she was finished now. This man knew what he was doing and with two blades it would literally be a process of him whittling her down, a cut here, a piercing there, until he got with a fatal blow or she was so disabled she couldn't defend herself.

Neeley's eyes narrowed. *"I'm going to kick your teeth down your throat,"* she growled in French.

The man smiled, but the smile froze as she leapt forward, feinting, kicking. He backed up to get an angle on her attack and that's when Hannah smashed the stone down on the top of this head from her position on the wall.

The man dropped.

Hannah vaulted off the wall and stared at their attacker. Neeley recovered the pistol and chambered a round, before joining Hannah. She searched his pockets.

"Is he dead?" Hannah asked.

"He will be in a second," Neeley said, pressing the end of the muzzle against his temple. She paused to see if Hannah would protest, but the other woman said nothing.

Neeley pulled the trigger and the head rocked from the silent internal explosion.

Hannah nodded acceptance. "Was he from the Cellar?"

Neeley looked at the body. "I don't know. I don't think so. It's strange, he didn't ask about the tape or the papers. This guy just wanted us dead. But if it's not the Cellar, how did he know we'd be here?" Neeley grabbed Hannah's arm. "Let's get out of here."

The two women made it out of the park without speaking to each other. Neeley cleaned the wounded flesh of Hannah's cheek once they were safely at the car.

"The question is what do we do about Rue d'Adelshoffen in Schiltigheim?" Neeley asked.

Hannah kept gingerly poking her face and checking it in the rearview mirror. "Let's have an early lunch and maybe find a plastic surgeon."

Neeley grabbed the other woman's hand. "Leave it alone. You'll infect it for God's sakes. You want to go have lunch while armed men are lurking about?"

Hannah rolled her eyes. "Every meal I've had with you has been life threatening. I say we find a very public place. The

Cellar wouldn't shoot through the lunch crowd. I think we need a little time to catch our breath and think for a moment."

"If it wanted to bad enough, the Cellar would blow up the lunch crowd," Neeley said.

Hannah shook her head. "There's more going on here than we know. Don't you sense it?"

"What do you mean?"

"This magical mystery tour we're on. You say it's because Gant needed to protect you and hide things. I don't buy that completely. And my husband. Disappearing like that all of a sudden. Why did Nero send him running?"

Neeley frowned. "Good question. Why would Nero do that?"

"I don't know yet," Hannah said, "but before this is over, I think we need to find out." She nodded. "Let's do lunch."

Neeley agreed to a quick lunch but had to add: "I wonder what's at that address?"

Hannah pulled Gant's message from her waistband, the only place she could stick it during her frantic search for a pocket. "By the way, I know what you did."

"What do you mean?"

"Don't be coy, Neeley. It's not a good look for you. I know that you set me up to dig through my clothes so that man would think I had a gun. What if he'd shot me?"

"With the silencer and the locked breech I knew he had to work the slide to chamber a second round. I knew I'd have time. I threw the rock to screw up his aim on the first shot."

Hannah pushed her fading blonde hair away from her face, careful not to disturb the stinging slice there. "Well, I think that's a little presumptuous. What if you'd been wrong or he hadn't been distracted?"

"You'd be dead." Neeley started the car and leaned back to check traffic. Neeley pulled the small car smoothly into the heavy traffic. "I want to go to that address before we leave. If we're lucky, we have a few hours before they find us and we can't stay in public places forever. Eventually the public goes home. We need to be in the air before nightfall."

"Neeley," Hannah said, "if we only have a few hours, don't you think we should leave France now? Getting that tape is our only chance, not running off on some goose-chase, no pun intended."

Neeley remained silent and Hannah knew it was hopeless. Hannah also had a very good idea what was at that address and she was surprised Neeley didn't. But she kept her peace, not wanting to ruin the upcoming meal. The lunch traffic was so chaotic that Hannah soon forgot her complex thoughts and concentrated on learning and using the obscene gestures directed toward them by the irritated French drivers.

THE PUNGENT ODOR OF FLOWERS made Racine want to gag. His nose had always been sensitive and what others found sweet he found cloying and vaguely frightening.

He hated parks and this one was the worst. Fucking traffic getting here was a nightmare and it seemed that once again he had lost the bitches. He was definitely grateful that he wouldn't have to contact Nero with more bad news. This time he knew where the women were going thanks to his directional mike and their big mouths.

Racine was chewing on a piece of French bread, a long, thin baguette. A small piece of the crusty loaf fell to the ground. Racine snarled as a squirrel darted across the grassy expanse and poked at the bread. These park squirrels were pretty daring and it only scampered off when Racine's foot swooshed the air alongside its quivering tail.

He looked around and caught a few looks of disdain. A good time for a tower and a sniper rifle. He was muttering as he tossed the remaining bread into the lake. Let the rodent work for it.

As he sauntered off, he tried to steady his anger with two thoughts: Nero didn't know he was in Strasbourg and the two bitches were having their last day. Screw the tape. Nero needed another tape like Congress needed another asshole. Fucker probably had the entire twentieth century on tape or that dotted paper he was always running his fingers over. Besides, this was personal now. Racine had only to think of Kansas City and his guts would twist until he thought he could kill with just the pure energy of his hate.

Racine's car was on the other side of the park but he was in no hurry. His directional mike had picked up the women's conversation clearly. Going to lunch, he thought. Maybe they'd do a little shopping again. Women. Never would a woman be a true professional.

He worked his way through the park, backtracking the women, and discovered the body of the man they'd killed. Racine stared at the corpse. He'd never seen him before, but that didn't rule out the Cellar employing him.

He checked the body and noticed the close-range death shot. Had to be Neeley. The matted brains from the knock on the head he gave to the blonde. A bloody mess she was. Bash in some guy's brains and want to eat. That was sick for a civilian. Yes, Racine decided, as he continued to his car, that woman was very sick for a civilian. He couldn't wait to kill her.

C H A P T E R

26

LUNCH WAS PRETTY much symbolic as neither woman could muster up much of an appetite. Neeley toyed with the fruit tart on her plate and tried to get past all that had happened in the park.

"Who do you think the man was?" she asked Hannah.

"I don't know," Hannah admitted, her thoughts elsewhere.

"If he was from the Cellar why didn't they stop us in Atlanta? Or have someone waiting when we got off the plane?"

"Good questions," Hannah said. "I need more data before I can give you an answer."

" 'More data'?"

"More information," Hannah said. "We're behind on the old information curve here."

" 'Information curve'?"

Hannah stared at Neeley. "Do you have a problem with me? I'm doing the best I can."

Neeley backtracked. "I'm sorry. Let's not get into anything right now or right here."

"No, Neeley, I've listened to your story and while parts of

it horrify and even anger me, it is not what I see in front of me now. And I don't know for sure what you see in me but I don't think you know enough. Everything in your past put you in a place where you chose to save my life. So it couldn't have been all bad."

Neeley put her napkin on the table. "We need to go."

"No." The retort was harsh enough that Neeley dropped obediently back onto her chair.

Hannah's voice was cold. "I have a story to tell, too. One I've never told before because my first foster parents warned me that no good could come from anyone knowing my past. They were simple, ignorant people who didn't know any better, but I was an obedient child who became an obedient adult.

"In the past few days I've realized my entire life has been dominated by only one desire: I wanted no shit in my life. That was important to me because as a young child, shit was all there was. Well, given the fact that we just killed some man over a piece of paper, I would say I now have plenty of shit in my life, so the old rules don't apply anymore."

Hannah's words were coming out steady and the tone brooked no interruption. "My parents didn't die in a simple car crash even though I've told the lie so often that it seems more real to me than the truth.

"I was six the night my parents died. My mother woke me up to go to the sheriff's office to pick up my father. He was drunk as usual and he had been arrested in a bar fight. My only real memory of her is the smell of her cream and the varying hue of her bruises. I guess she was pretty hopeless. She had no one but my father.

"That night I sat in the backseat in my cotton nighty and asked him what had happened. He reached back and slapped me so hard my head hit the side window. Then he passed out and my mother started the drive home.

"We drove for a long time, much longer than it should have taken. She talked, but my head hurt and I didn't understand a lot of what she said. I finally fell asleep and I don't know what happened to my mother's mind then. When I awoke, it was to a huge thundering noise and a glaring light.

"I sat up and shouted for my Momma and she turned and grabbed my hand and held me. The noise was so loud I couldn't hear her at first and then she shouted 'Forgive me' and her hand was torn out of mine."

Neeley was perfectly still listening to Hannah's quiet voice. The noise of the restaurant had faded to a distant murmur.

"That was all I remembered," Hannah continued. "In the hospital everyone whispered 'dreadful accident' and 'what a miracle for such a small child to survive.' But I knew my mother was waiting for the train and the only accident was that the car had sheared in half rather than crumpling into a pile of jagged metal. I was barely injured. My parents were destroyed."

Neeley stared at Hannah, not quite wanting to believe her but knowing it was true. "Oh my God, Hannah. Why didn't you tell me this before?"

"Because now you'll understand the end of the story. Nothing from that night, the train, the hospital, nothing was as bad as months later when I tried to explain to my first foster mother what had happened. The look on her face when I told her of my mother's holding me in that car was terrible. That was the worst.

"I swore that no one would ever look on me with such appalled pity again. But we both know that was an empty promise."

"Why would I know that?"

Hannah signaled the waiter for the check. "Because you've been motivated by pity since you first discovered what a sham my marriage and my life were and how screwed I was that John had left me in the hole he did."

Neeley held up a hand in protest. "I never meant that. I think you've been incredibly strong and I wouldn't have made it without your help. I don't pity you."

Hannah put a fistful of francs on the table with the careless American gesture that signals, 'your money means nothing to me.' "I didn't say you pitied me. I said you were motivated by pity. The pity is for you. Really it's for the you in that airport holding a bomb and knowing Jean-Philippe didn't give a shit about you."

Hannah wasn't done. "I learned some things over the years from those women you listened to at the golf course—my bitch brigade. I bet you ten to one your Jean-Philippe could hand you that bomb and kiss you good-bye because he had someone else ready and waiting to take your place. That's the way men are."

Neeley's hands were clenching into fists and she dropped them into her lap as if they were untrustworthy and could at any moment cause her acute embarrassment. "Why did you tell me your story now?"

Hannah pushed her friend into the beautiful spring afternoon. "Because I know betrayal too. But I know something you don't. Sometimes betrayal is the only love left. Remember that."

CHAPTER

27

STRASBOURG WAS AN AMAZING CITY, fascinating enough to cause some of the bad emotions of recent events to fade as the two women drove through it. Neeley was reminded again and again of its magnificence as she and Hannah searched for the Rue d'Adelshoffen. It was in a part of the city, Schiltigheim, she was not familiar with, being far north of the suburb where she and Jean-Philippe had lived before they moved to Berlin. After they left the restaurant, she had driven down a street just a few blocks from the Parc Orangerie. She passed the large apartment where she had spent so many wonderful summers bathed in her grandparents' adoration. Neeley had been devastated by their deaths, but at least they had not lived long enough to watch her destroy her life with Jean-Philippe.

Hannah consulted the map and groaned hopelessly at the maze of canals and bridges that made up the city. Finally she gave up and assumed the air of tourist. She took in the old center of the city with admiration. The towering cathedral and the four-hundred-year-old houses met with her approval.

as did the endless blooming flowers hanging from every window and adorning every pot.

She thought of the austere Kansas countryside that had been her birthright, the endless miles of nothing and wondered about Neeley even more.

"How could you grow up here and become caught up with Jean-Philippe?"

"Remember, I only spent summers here until I graduated high school. The rest of the time, I was caught in the happy bosom of my family in the Bronx."

Hannah craned her neck to catch a glimpse of the Kammerzell House built in 1467, one of the oldest houses in Europe. The narrow streets were clogged with traffic and pedestrians so their progress was slowed considerably.

"Tell me about your mother."

Neeley momentarily gave up maneuvering the small car through even smaller breaks in the traffic. She leaned back and thought about an answer. "My mother lived her entire life waiting for my father to have a good mood. Eventually she got tired of waiting and she tried to make him have one. She pretty much became an extension of him, a parasite to his emotion. Mostly I just remember a lot of tension and manipulation. It was like something was always about to happen, but never did. My mother just wanted him to be happy no matter what."

Hannah whistled. "Polar opposite of my mom, eh? I find it fascinating how different people are. Look at us: nothing in common, yet look how great we get along."

Neeley saw an opening for one of the small canal bridges and went for it. "We have to get along great. The same people are trying to kill us."

"Well, yeah, that may be what brought us together but you have to admit our personalities mesh well. You could have dumped me along the way, tossed me to the wind so to speak, but you've stayed with me and protected me."

"Oh, my God, not this again. Hannah, your personality would mesh with anyone's. You're the universal donor of relationships, but hey, I'm not complaining."

"Neeley, do you have any idea where you're going, or better yet, why we're going there?" Hannah was watching her partner closely.

"I'm just following the note. It was from Gant, so I know it's important. Gant obviously wanted me to go there. I just don't know why. Maybe it's the mysterious third piece that Racine thought I had."

"The third piece," Hannah mused. "You said Gant wrote it was the 'why' in his note?"

"Yes."

"What do you think that means given we have the what—the pipeline deal; and the who—Senator Collins and bin Laden?"

"I don't know," Neeley admitted.

"I think the why takes this whole thing to another level," Hannah said.

"What level is that?" It was indicative of the new nature of their relationship that Neeley's question was straightforward.

"That the who and the what is only the tip of the iceberg," Hannah said. "The why is the bulk that's hidden from sight right now."

"Well let's not be the *Titanic*," Neeley muttered as she pulled the car to the curb in front of an ultramodern office building. The building appeared out of place amid the ancient city, but Neeley had to admire its clean, elegant lines as being aesthetically pleasing.

A small sign on the door front advertised the building as the offices of Dr. Bernard Wiss and if Neeley's French was a match for the complicated medical lexicon, then Dr. Wiss was a straightener of teeth: the proverbial orthodontist. The two women entered the lobby and approached the receptionist area, which was empty of customers.

"Are there any other practitioners in this building in addition to Dr. Wiss?" Neeley's French was not as succinct as she would have liked.

The young woman looked up from her computer screen and shook her head in the negative.

"May we see Dr. Wiss then?"

The girl, whose plump breast proclaimed Gaby on a plastic smile of a nametag shook her head. *"It is our day to do paperwork. The doctor does not see patients today."*

"I need to see the doctor." Neeley and Hannah's perfectly straight teeth seemed to belie any medical emergency.

"I am sorry but—"

Neeley finally gave up on the respectful strategy and reached across the perky red-and-white counter to grab a handful of Gaby's shirt.

Hannah noticed that Neeley's French sounded much better when it contained the element of threat. *"Get the doctor, now!"*

Gaby was evidently not paid enough to serve as bouncer because she quickly used the phone to do as she was told.

Hannah was worried about their presence in the office. It certainly didn't look like the kind of place Gant would send Neeley. Maybe it was a mistake, maybe the address was wrong, or there had been some move or change that Gant didn't anticipate. All Hannah knew was that Neeley was acting stranger than normal. Her aggressive behavior with the receptionist was to be noted as well as the loaded pistol in her jacket pocket. Ultimately, Hannah hoped she was wrong about why they were here.

The door to the inner office opened abruptly and a very handsome man appeared. He looked at the receptionist with some irritation and it was obvious that his French was about the sudden interruption. Gaby merely shrugged her shoulders and pointed at the two troublemakers.

Later, Hannah would remember that the irritated orthodontist appeared to swoon. Just like in one of those British costume dramas. Except it looked ridiculous happening to a man over six feet in a white smock.

Hannah wasn't surprised by the change in Neeley. She quite literally energized, as if she had grabbed a live wire and popped it in her ear. The roots of her hair crackled with an energy that seemed to bolt right through to her toes. Her hand was fumbling for the gun she'd taken from the man in the park and that was what dragged Hannah's attention from Dr. Wiss.

"What are you doing?" Hannah's voice was louder than a whisper.

Dr. Wiss swiftly turned and slammed the door behind him. Neeley was already after him.

Hannah was right behind her. "Jean-Philippe, oui?"

Neeley had the doorknob in her hand, ready to blow it off the door if there were resistance. There wasn't and she and Hannah were chasing the white-coated figure down a hallway.

Neeley was cursing under her breath. Hannah was more fascinated with Neeley's demeanor than the sudden appearance of Jean-Philippe, which she had suspected would be the case.

So much for cold and calculating. At the moment Neeley looked like the model for female rage. Neeley reached the door at the end of the hallway as it shut in her face. She didn't even pause. She slammed her foot into it and the jam splintered. And then the three were in a small room cluttered with clay impressions of heads and crooked teeth and piles of wicked-looking metal appliances.

Jean-Philippe's voice was magical and lilting. Hannah had no idea what he was saying, but the tone and hand gestures seemed to be saying, 'please don't kill me.'

Neeley's answer was rapid-fire and caustic, so much so that Hannah waited for the red stain to form somewhere on the white-coated chest.

Hannah was sorely regretting taking Spanish in high school when Neeley abruptly switched to English. It seemed that her level of anger had forced her frontal lobe to revert to its native tongue. Jean-Philippe followed suit with that marvelous French accent that sounded so sexy. Hannah looked at this man who had so affected her friend's life and could well imagine how things had happened. Hannah stared at his blatant good looks and thought she might have carried a bomb for him too when she was nineteen.

"Cherie, I thought you were dead!"

Hannah winced and decided it was a poor opening line.

"Well, no shit, you worthless pile of puke. You hand me a damn bomb, kiss me on the top of the head, and push me on a plane. I thought you were writhing in some private circle of hell reserved for total sons of bitches and here you are straightening teeth on Rue d'Adelshoffen."

Jean-Philippe was either a brilliant actor or his shock was genuine. "A bomb? What are you saying? I gave you no bomb. I loved you."

"Cut the crap. The box, big red bow. Remember?"

"But that was not a bomb!"

"Right. I forgot, once the C-4 and wires were pulled apart it was not a bomb. Just a box of clay and electronics."

Jean-Philippe wiped a hand across his dampening forehead and found a chair so that Neeley's gun was no longer aimed squarely at his heart but rather was pointing at the smooth stretch of skin between his lovely blue eyes.

"You must believe me, Cherie. I did not know it was a bomb. They told me it was papers. Secret papers that had to get to London."

Neeley's voice was losing its hysteria and she spoke in measured, deep tones that Hannah found even more frightening. "Who is they, Jean-Philippe, and why would a box of papers have weighed a couple of pounds?"

"I thought they weighted the box so it would appear to be something other than a box of papers."

"Tell me you weren't this stupid when I was sleeping with you."

"You think that is what it was, that I was stupid? Okay, maybe you are correct. I prefer you think I am stupid than a murderer."

Neeley leaned against an instrument cabinet for some support and kept the gun steady. "Just tell me what happened. Start at the beginning."

Hannah found a small stool in the corner of the room and pulled it over to Neeley's side. She perched herself on its shiny top. Neeley glanced at her and Hannah kept her face noncommittal, allowing her friend latitude to work this out in her own way.

Jean-Philippe watched the silent communication between the women and he seemed to relax. Gaby's concerned voice through the door was answered with a relatively calm voice, full of reassurance that must have satisfied the bewildered receptionist. At least the cops wouldn't be busting down the door, Hannah thought with some relief.

"To begin with, Neeley, you must remember those were turbulent times and I was an idealistic young man."

"Skip the bullshit, Jean-Philippe. We were young and dumb and if I remember correctly, we all spent a lot more time fucking than spouting ideologies. And all you gave a damn about was making money. There was no idealism there."

He seemed diminished by her harsh words and shook his head. "We spent much time making love and I was trying to make my mark on the world, yes, I admit that."

Neeley laughed bitterly. "Skip to the part where you decided to blow me up."

"It was not like that, I told you. The man representing the American said they needed a courier to take some papers to London. He offered a lot of money. Money that we could have used to be together."

"The American?" Neeley cocked the weapon. The cold, hard sound was more effective than any words. "Tell me what happened."

"Okay, Okay, he offered money or death. I needed the money to get away." Jean-Philippe swallowed. "I was sleeping with that blonde girl, Helga. Remember? The one whose boyfriend was a psycho? He was starting to get suspicious and I was afraid. I thought the money would get me away and then I would go to New York and find you."

Neeley had looked at Hannah when he mentioned Helga. Hannah, fortunately for her, given Neeley's current emotional state, continued to keep an impassive face.

Neeley took a deep breath and forced herself to ease the pressure on the trigger.

Jean-Philippe's head was bowed and Hannah found the story partially believable. In her limited experience, his cowering two-timer alibi seemed to hold water, but people sometimes admitted to one thing to cover up something deeper and she had no doubt that was what Jean-Philippe was doing.

"You must believe me. I had no idea that it was a bomb. If I am guilty of something, it is of holding back about the money and that I was with sleeping with Helga. Please believe that!"

Neeley ignored his pleas. "Tell me about this American."

"I only met him once. The man who worked for him pulled me off the street and drove me to a house, to the basement. He threatened to kill me if I didn't do as he said. He just wanted someone I trusted to take the box to London. That was all."

"How much money did you get?"

"Enough, all right, Neeley? I got enough to get away from Berlin and go to school and start over here. And the payments continued over the years."

Neeley gave a tired, sad nod. "Enough to start a new life, right, Jean-Philippe? A new life you choose, one that you wanted to live." Her voice sharpened. "You don't get to start over in this business. Not unless there is a reason for someone to let you."

"I tell you the truth," Jean-Philippe said.

"No, I don't think you do," Neeley said. She switched the subject abruptly. "Do you have a family?"

His look was a curious mixture of pride and fear at her interest. "Yes. My wife and I have two sons."

Neeley's voice was tight and full of obvious hurt. "And your wife? What is her name?"

Jean-Philippe hung his head. "Helga."

Neeley drew a deep breath that had an audible hitch at the end. "You son of a bitch. I could kill you now just to feel good, but I won't. I think your American will do that. Someone seems to be trimming away all the loose ends and you appear to be a big one."

His head jerked up. "What do you mean?"

"You figure it out."

Hannah's voice caught both Neeley and Jean-Philippe off guard. "Did someone tell you we were coming?"

The shifting of the man's eyes answered the question for both women. "You bastard," Neeley whispered. "You sent the man after us. The man in the park."

"I had to protect myself," Jean-Philippe pleaded.

"Who told you we were coming?" Neeley demanded.

"Someone from the American's office called me," Jean-Philippe said.

"Who is this American?" Neeley asked. "Nero?"

Jean-Philippe frowned. "No. The man behind it all is Senator Collins. I do not know the name of the man he sent to me. Who gave me the bomb. But he was a dangerous and crazy man. You could see it in his eyes."

"Racine," Hannah said.

"That might have been his name," Jean-Philippe admitted.

Neeley stood. She crossed the distance between her and her former lover and put the gun to his forehead. "If you tell me the truth, I will let you die quickly. If you lie to me again, I will make you hurt for a long, long time. Then I will find Helga and your children and kill them. The truth and they get to live."

Jean-Philippe was sweating profusely now. "You have changed, Neeley."

"I've become what you made me," she replied. "Did you know about the bomb?"

He paused, and then answered. "Yes."

Neeley's eyes closed briefly. "Why did you want to kill me?"

"It was not me. It was the American."

"Why did he want me to kill me," Neeley amended.

"It wasn't for you."

"Who was it for?"

"Another American on the same flight. Some soldier going home. This man—Racine you say his name is—who paid me said this soldier had information that the senator wanted destroyed. The only way to do it was to destroy him and everything he had with him."

"Gant," Neeley whispered.

"Pardon?" Jean-Philippe said.

"What information?" Neeley demanded. She blinked a few times trying to absorb all she had just learned. Even through her shock, she realized that Hannah seemed to be at least one, if not two, steps ahead.

"A videotape," he answered.

"What is on it?" Hannah asked.

"I do not know."

"You're lying," Hannah said.

In response to her partner's accusation, Neeley moved the barrel of the gun a few inches closer toward her former lover.

"It's a videotape of a meeting. About some oil pipelines."

"Are you on it?" Neeley asked.

"Yes."

Neeley focused on Jean-Philippe. "Why did Racine and Collins let you live and pay you?"

"Because I gave you the bomb."

"That's not enough," Neeley said. "As we all know, it didn't work. I'm here aren't I?"

Jean-Philippe licked his lips. "Because of the papers."

"What papers?" Neeley demanded.

"Papers with Collins's name on them. And other names. Names of people who are very important now. Papers that show they dealt secretly and illegally with the Taliban and others. And more. Pictures of Collins meeting with people. People who have been very prominent in the news—bad news—lately. People he would never want anyone to know he ever spoke and dealt with. All of this was very dangerous information. It's become even more dangerous in the last several years. It was what my partners and I collected as I— we worked on the pipeline deal behind the scenes."

"There were no papers or pictures in the package," Neeley said. "Just the bomb."

"Of course not. I kept the papers for my own insurance. I did not trust Racine or the Senator."

"You set me up," Neeley hissed. "Not once, but twice. With the bomb and then by telling them I had the papers."

"Ah!" Jean-Philippe protested, "you must understand. It

all worked out for the best. Once the Americans thought you gave the papers to Gant, the situation changed."

Hannah cut in. "And you sold out the others, didn't you? Your fellow black market financiers? Those involved in the Afghanistan deal."

Jean-Philippe weakly nodded.

"What happened to them?" Neeley asked.

"They—" Jean-Philippe seemed to search for the right words, then finally shrugged—"disappeared. I do not know exactly."

"You scum," Neeley hissed.

"Where are the papers now?" Hannah asked.

"I keep the originals in a safe place."

"And copies?" Hannah asked. "Do you have any here?"

"I have copies here," Jean-Philippe confirmed.

"Get them," Neeley said.

Jean-Philippe turned on his stool. He picked up a small hammer and smashed it down on a plaster skull that was on a shelf. He pulled out a plastic-wrapped package.

"How convenient," Neeley noted as she took the packet. "That's why you ran back here, isn't it?"

"You can have the papers," Jean-Philippe said. "In exchange—"

Neeley's laugh was harsh. "In exchange? You've got nothing, *nothing* that you can use with regard to me. All that was gone when you handed me that bomb. When you told Racine I had the papers."

"What are you going to do now?" Jean-Philippe asked.

Neeley stuck the gun in her pocket and turned away, heading out the door. Hannah followed. They walked away without looking back and the two women were silent as they made their way through the suddenly still office and by the glaring receptionist.

On the sidewalk Neeley stopped for a moment and looked at Hannah. "That hurt."

Hannah patted the trembling shoulder of her companion. "I know."

"What now?" Hannah asked.

"We have John's part," Neeley said numbly. "We have copies of Jean-Philippe's papers, which they thought I had all along. Now we get Gant's tape and end this."

Hannah didn't say anything, realizing her friend was still in shock. Hannah knew now that it wouldn't end with Gant's tape. She was getting glimmers of the why and it chilled her but also brought a tinge of excitement.

CHAPTER

28

RACINE WATCHED THE WOMEN emerge from the office building. He was safely tucked behind a thickly flowered lilac bush in a park across the street. The scent was overwhelming. It tugged at his memory and made him slightly sick at the same time. Through his trained eye, the specially designed scope on his pistol framed Neeley's bitch face perfectly. He drew a breath, held it, and his finger tightened on the trigger.

He smelled the man's gum before he felt the dull pressure of a muzzle pushing against the slow pulsing of his carotid artery.

"I don't think Mr. Nero would like this. Do you?"

Racine felt the barrel press even harder into his flesh as his own gun was lifted from his hands. He recognized the English accent as well as the smell. Nero's pet. The old man must be getting tired of the whole situation to have sent Bailey.

Racine looked up at his colleague and tried a weak smile. "I haven't seen you in years. I'll take it apart if you like," he added, pointing at the specially designed pistol and the lead-lined case at his feet that he had transported in the hold of the Concorde in a diplomatic pouch.

Bailey pocketed his own gun and dropped the pistol at Racine's feet. "Fine."

Racine tried to ignore the smell of the lilacs around them. It was giving him a headache. That and the fact that he despised an interrupted kill guaranteed a bad day.

Racine watched the two women drive away. "Where are they going?"

Bailey reached into his coat pocket and pulled out a pack of Juicy Fruit and extended it to Racine. "I suppose back to the airport. Seems like the logical thing."

Racine shook off the gum and watched as Bailey stripped the paper and rolled the stick of gum into a tight little log before he popped it into his mouth.

As Racine put away the last of the pistol, Bailey spoke again, spraying tiny bits of sugary saliva into the lilac blooms. "Let's go do this last bit here and get to the airport ourselves."

Racine equated sitting next to Bailey for five hours on par with letting a cobra spit in his eye. "Okay."

The men walked through the small park and stood at the curb, waiting to cross the street. Bailey continued to chew loudly and occasionally pop the wad of gum. "So, how have you been?"

Racine thought that if Bailey popped the gum one more time it would be acceptable to push him under the large Mercedes truck bearing down on them. "I've been Okay. You?"

Bailey nodded. "Good, bloody good." He spotted a break in the traffic and plowed forward, Racine following closely behind.

Bailey paused before they entered the building. "What are you doing here?"

"Finishing the job Mr. Nero gave me," Racine said.

Bailey shook his head. "Nero didn't tell you to come here. In fact, I believe he specifically told you the opposite. How did you know the women would end up right here in Strasbourg?"

"I'm good at my job," Racine said. He stared back into the other man's pupils. They remained like that for almost a minute, ignoring the people who walked around them. Racine was the first to break the standoff. Finally, Bailey turned for the door. "Let's get this over with, shall we?"

This time Gaby didn't even seem surprised as the two men with no appointment approached her counter and asked for the good doctor.

"He's in there." She pointed to the office door. As they headed down the corridor she gathered up her purse and left.

Bailey and Racine had only to follow the sound of the doctor's voice as he hurriedly tried to plot his flight to safety. The door to the examining room was ajar and they could hear his frustrated attempts to get a flight anywhere, the destination didn't matter, the only requirement that it must leave now.

Racine pushed the door with his foot and the two men made themselves known to Jean-Philippe.

"So fast! How did you get here so fast?"

Behind Bailey's back, Racine put a finger to his lip and shook his head as Jean-Philippe recognized him.

Bailey popped his gum. "English please. We saved your ass in the war, the least you could do is speak English."

Jean-Philippe was sweating again. A few beads were breaking clear of his hairline and starting the slide down his classic features. His eyes shifted from Racine to Bailey. "How could you find me so fast?"

Bailey pulled over the swivel stool that had earlier been Hannah's. He put his gun on the cluttered table so he could swivel it up a few notches. Once seated he retrieved the gun, popped his gum, and smiled. "Why, we're the Cellar, laddie. We can find anyone if we want to. You think no one knew you were here?"

Racine was feeling lightheaded. The addition of acidic, nervous sweat to the collage of aromas wafting from Bailey was causing him acute discomfort. He wished he had thought of the stool first. He detected a lackadaisical attitude in his partner that indicated urgency was not a critical factor.

His head was truly beginning to throb and he needed to take a leak. He could have pissed at the lilac bush if he'd known Bailey was going to dawdle.

Bailey was swiveling back and forth, his English accent filling the small room. "You see that, right? You punched your ticket years ago, mate. The meter just ran out, that's all."

Jean-Philippe backed into the corner, his arms held out in a pleading gesture that both Bailey and Racine had seen many times before and ignored. Just as they ignored it now.

"My dear Doctor, this can't be a surprise," Bailey said. "Surely you have anticipated someone arriving someday? No? Well, I do have a few questions that if you would take the time to answer would give us all the opportunity to restore some dignity to the afternoon."

Jean-Philippe looked ashen. "You're crazy."

Bailey spat his gum a couple of feet toward the plastic lined wastebasket. He had misjudged the distance and the wad stuck to the top rim of the plastic and began to sag outward, pulling the liner. All three men watched this display of gravity until the liner won and the gum dropped to the tiled floor.

Bailey focused his attention back on his captive. "I prefer antisocial personality. I do a service, Dr. Wiss, much like your career here. But I am more valuable because there's a lot of you and not many of me. You see that has always been your dilemma—you are expendable.

"Take Mr. Racine here. We need Mr. Racine. Every country needs people like Mr. Racine and here's the interesting part—there's no one else exactly like him. See the simplicity of that?

"You were kept around because there was no need to get rid of you. It appears you entered into a mutually satisfying relationship with Senator Collins and now that it's over you won't answer some questions?"

Racine stiffened at the mention of the Senator's name.

Bailey pretended to ignore Racine as he continued to speak to the Frenchman. "You've had many free years to enjoy. How about a little appreciation?"

The doctor was dumbfounded. "I have the papers and the pictures. If you do anything to me, they will become public."

Bailey shook his head. "Son, you're going to tell me where these papers and the pictures are."

Racine perked up at the mention of the papers and pictures. The few times he'd worked with Bailey it had been like this. Yack, yack, yack. Racine didn't understand why someone who called himself antisocial always got so frigging social with everyone he whacked. However, he didn't like where this was headed at all.

"I would be insane to give you that," Jean-Philippe argued.

Bailey nodded in agreement. "I see. You have a point. How about this? You tell me everything I need to know in a truthful manner I can absolutely believe, give me what I ask for, and I will leave you your life, but nothing else. How's that?"

Racine watched as the Frenchman filled with hope. He seemed to grow larger and his face lost the haggard look of dull acceptance. Racine knew that Bailey had won. Racine also noted the various implements of the Frenchman's trade on the tables. This could turn interesting if the Frenchman didn't stay hooked on Bailey's bullshit. Racine picked up a metal probe and turned it in the light. Jean-Philippe noticed and his skin went a shade paler.

Bailey smiled. "Now, Doctor, first tell me everything you know about Neeley and the woman with her, Hannah, and what happened in here. Then we'll go get the stuff."

Jean-Philippe jerked his head in recognition of the first woman's name. And he slowly began to talk. Racine wondered if even the doctor was aware of the slowness of the words. Racine finally decided a part of Jean-Philippe knew that the bullet would come when the words ran out and he gave up the papers. As he twirled a shiny implement in his hands he listened carefully to the Frenchman, waiting for him to say something stupid.

But he didn't. He told them what little he knew of the two women. It took less than five minutes. The only part that was of interest was the fact that he had given a copy of the papers to the women.

"No pictures?" Bailey checked.

"No, just the papers."

Bailey stood. "Now the originals?"

"You must promise that my family will be left alone," Jean-Philippe said.

Bailey calmly rolled another piece of Juicy Fruit.

Jean-Philippe stuck a finger out, pointing at Racine. "You said that—"

The Frenchman never finished the sentence as Racine slammed the point of the probe into his chest. Jean-Philippe stared in disbelief at the metal implement sticking out of his white robe.

Bailey had swung around on the stool, pistol at the ready. Racine was ready for this, his own backup gun on Nero's pet. Jean-Philippe staggered back against the wall and slid down to a sitting position, with a confused expression marring his good looks. He was struggling for breath, the probe twitching. Both men ignored the body between them as they focused on the gun in each other's hands.

Racine backed up, finger caressing the trigger. He smiled into Bailey's muzzle. "Not today."

Bailey didn't blink. They both knew this was a lose-lose situation. "Not today," Bailey agreed.

Then Racine was out the door, running.

In the room, Bailey turned back to the doctor. A pinkish froth had appeared around the man's lips. Bailey leaned close.

"Your family will be left in peace. But I have to have the documents."

He put his ear next to the Frenchman's lips and listened as the man spoke his last words.

CHAPTER

29

THERE WAS A SIX-HOUR WAIT in Frankfurt for their red-eye flight to Pittsburgh and Hannah had voted for shopping. Neeley had been shocked. She'd wanted to unwrap the package Jean-Philippe had given them and read the copies, but Hannah had disagreed. "Wait until we get the tape and have it all," had been her advice. "Or at least when you're on the plane and have nothing else to do. Here's one of my rules— there's a time for everything and right now is not the time to be dealing with any more shit."

She had finally persuaded Neeley that spending a few hours grooming was a necessity. "It's not normal to wear the same clothes every day or have dirty hair. That's what civilization is all about, Neeley. Being clean."

They bought some new clothes of Hannah's choosing and were able to discard the tight, black ninja look. As Neeley modeled a navy blazer over the white T-shirt and soft linen slacks, Hannah nodded in approval. "You can wear it forever. The style is perfect."

Neeley put her hand on her hip. "So you think it makes

sense to begin my wardrobe collection the day before my probable death?"

Hannah gave her a look that said, *don't start.* "It is never too late for a woman to begin collecting a classic wardrobe."

Neeley had to admit the clothes were comfortable and efficient. She decided that if she survived she would buy more of the designer clothes. Their next stop was at a salon where Hannah arranged for them to have the complete spa treatment. Neeley decided, after a few tense moments of trying to relax while someone else handled her body, that maybe this was just the right way to spend your last hours. Hannah was right, she had a lot to teach her about living that was just as important as everything Gant had taught her about surviving.

Her mind wandered to Gant as she sat basking in the attention of a pedicurist, manicurist, and hair colorist. She tried to imagine Gant seeing her with foil wadded in her hair and cotton balls between her toes. He would have dismissed this as unimportant just as Hannah hadn't at first realized the significance of the Eldorado Canyon climb. Neeley decided that they were both important to her now.

Neeley shifted her mind to more immediate concerns. Gant's tape had been so critical that someone had been willing to blow up an entire airliner of civilians, which was rather an extreme step to put it mildly. And since they had failed in that attempt, why had they not tried again? And how did that connect with Jean-Philippe acting as messenger boy for Collins so many years previously? She suspected that Collins's involvement explained the extreme reaction of the Cellar to this entire affair but beyond that, little was clear.

Neeley pondered all this while she formulated their next step. It was clear to her where they had to go. Gant had sent her to Jean-Philippe to finish old business just as he had sent her up the cliff wall. She even remembered the rule: there's no such thing as unfinished business. It had been important to him that she learn that before she went to West Virginia.

That had been his destination the day they met in Templehoff Airport. He had been going to his wife with knowledge and something that others wanted. Now it was time for Neeley to go to the woman whom Gant had once loved. Only then would she go for the nearby tape.

West Virginia was her final connection to Gant. He had given her Jean-Philippe. Neeley knew that it would have mattered little to Gant whether she killed her betrayer or not. What mattered is that she let go of the past and move into her own world. A world where she was no longer molded by men. Whether the molding was for her benefit or detriment mattered little compared to the losing of herself. This she was learning from Hannah or rather they were learning it together.

And with the tape, John's contracts, and the papers, Neeley knew that she could strike a deal with the Cellar and Nero. But only if she got the tape in her hands before they got to her.

When the women left the salon hours later Neeley was surprised at the attention they received. She was used to frank looks from men but had never experienced the silent compliment from both sexes that were directed to her entire person and not just certain parts of it. Neeley realized people were responding to her attitude about herself. It was almost more powerful than holding a weapon. It was simply being.

Neeley was totally relaxed as she looked out the window as the plane taxied down the runway. Hannah's eyes were drooping when she ruined Neeley's mood. She too had obviously used the last few hours to do some thinking. "Nero's not behind what happened in the past."

"What?" Neeley spit the word out.

"Some of it, but not all of it. We know now that Senator Collins and Racine were behind the bomb that Jean-Philippe gave you."

"But Racine works for Nero."

"I think he was working only for Collins when he did that," Hannah said.

"What do you mean?"

Hannah closed her eyes. "There's something else going on. You have the papers. You might want to read them."

Neeley stared at Hannah for a few seconds then was startled to realize the other woman was already asleep so she settled into her own thoughts of the next day. Her plan would have to be a good one because Neeley knew all the players were finally coming together and the end of the game was in sight.

She pulled the papers Jean-Philippe had given them out of her pack and began reading.

CHAPTER
30

NERO DIDN'T LIFT his head for Bailey. He was simply too tired. He was glad he didn't have to worry about budgets and expenditures. In any other agency they would have had to justify the seat on the Concorde that had gotten Bailey back to the States while Gant's woman and Hannah were having their legs waxed.

Nero's voice was so low that Bailey had to lean across the desk to hear his words. "Do we know where the women are going?"

Bailey cleared his throat. "I would assume Neeley is going to see Jesse. They're flying to Pittsburgh and they have a rental car waiting. Morgantown is close by."

Nero smiled, a most rare occasion. "Ah, yes, Jesse."

"And the boy."

"A man now."

"Yes. Physically at least," Bailey amended.

"Yes. That was—is—a terrible shame," Nero said. He was reflective for a few moments. "You need to talk to Jesse," Nero finally said.

"I will. I might have to slow Hannah and Neeley down a little."

"Do whatever is necessary."

"And Jack Gant?" Bailey said.

"What about him?"

"I've gotten a call," Bailey said. "Jack's heard rumors his brother is dead. He's asking questions."

Nero nodded weakly. "Neeley must have called the uncle in New York for the connection with Suggs. I didn't think of that. Jack's on his island, right?"

"Yes."

"But he hasn't been contacted yet and I would prefer it stay that way until this problem is resolved." Nero paused. "Where is Mr. Racine?"

Bailey shifted his feet uncomfortably. "We don't know."

"You don't know?" Nero repeated.

Bailey shrugged. "Racine is good at certain things. I will take care of Mr. Racine later. He won't stay hidden long."

Nero's head shook very slightly. "Racine won't go away. Perhaps you should have finished him in Europe when he was there against my wishes."

"I had other priorities and I wasn't aware of the entire situation until I interrogated the doctor," Bailey said simply. The two men had worked together for so many years that they wasted no time on recrimination, but rather focused on reality.

"Racine will show up," Nero said.

"I know. How would you like me to handle it?"

"Racine has run out of chances. The women bested him enough. He might get lucky, so I would appreciate it if you could even the odds a little. Jack Gant might help in that matter. There was never any love lost between the Gant brothers and Racine, even though the love between the two of them was greatly strained by Mogadishu and even more so by Jesse. However," Nero added as he considered it, "hold off on Jack unless absolutely necessary."

"So Racine is a Sanction?"

"Yes."

Bailey nodded. Then he tossed a folder on the table. "There's what Jean-Philippe had to say and his precious papers and photographs."

Nero didn't pick it up. "The gist?"

Bailey sank down into one of the hard seats, an indication of the seriousness of the situation. "Racine has been working for Collins for a long time. Since 1991 at least."

Nero had already guessed that much. "He was the one who arranged the bomb with Jean-Philippe?"

"Yes." Bailey looked at his old companion. "But there's more to it than that."

Nero waited.

"Racine was ordered by Collins to ensure that the snatch mission failed. Not just failed, but was an embarrassment. A disaster to cover things up."

Nero rubbed his forehead. "Racine shot down one of the choppers?"

Bailey nodded. "To kill al-Turabi, Gant, and Masterson. And destroy the tape and papers. Except Gant and Masterson, along with the tape and papers, weren't on the chopper."

"So Racine initiated the disaster in Mogadishu," Nero said simply. "And Collins didn't trust I would do my part to cover his ass," Nero added, almost to himself.

"He had his own agenda," Bailey said.

"Neeley and Hannah are getting closer to the truth even as I get closer," Nero murmured. "And they have copies of Jean-Philippe's papers."

Bailey nodded. "I think Jean-Philippe double-crossed Racine and Collins though. I think he told them that Neeley gave Gant the papers and pictures and was going to go public on Collins."

"Interesting," Nero said.

Bailey waited as Nero sat in a cloud of smoke after lighting a cigarette. Finally the old man spoke again. "When you have the videotape, give me a call. Do you understand?"

Bailey nodded. "You can count on me, Mr. Nero."

Nero sagged back onto his chair. "I always have, Mr. Bailey. I always have."

Bailey paused. "What about Senator Collins? And the papers?"

"That will depend on what exactly Neeley has," Nero said. "This has gotten out of hand. There are others besides Collins involved and they are not pleased. I think the events of the past week and this new information clearly show that my judgment—not Collins's—should be trusted."

Nero leaned his head back. "Parallels. That is what is important about studying history. To see the parallels between current events and past events and thus be able to project forward and anticipate the future. Do you know why the Japanese bombed Pearl Harbor?"

Bailey had been through many history lessons in this office. "No, sir, I don't exactly."

"Most people don't remember," Nero said. "It's the same reason most of the wars in this century have been fought. One word. Quite simple. Oil." Nero paused as he caught his breath, the air wheezing through his tracheotomy. "Oil is power. And wars have always been fought over power. On July 25, 1940, the United States government decided to limit its export of oil to Japan—curious isn't it, that we were actually once in a position to export oil?

"This put the Japanese in an untenable position. Their economy was just beginning to recover from the Great Depression. But without U.S. oil, and no source of their own, they would have to look overseas. They cast their eyes upon the Dutch East Indies and Malaysia. Thus setting themselves on a collision course with the European powers who controlled those lands, and because those powers were embroiled in fighting Hitler, the United States, which was trying to pick up the slack in the Pacific.

"Yamamoto knew it was a mistake to attack Pearl Harbor. He'd lived in America and he knew the true character of the American people. While those around him who only knew the United States secondhand saw the Americans as weak and cowardly, he felt differently.

"Bin Laden made the same mistake as those around Yamamoto. Bin Laden watched what happened in Mogadishu, how quickly we pulled out after a handful of our soldiers were killed, and he thought us weak and vulnerable. So he attacked us. But he might also have known we shot our own helicopter down and figured we were so screwed up we were vulnerable in our greed.

"But behind it all was the power of oil." Nero fell silent, lost in thought.

Bailey had seen his boss do this before, think out loud to a certain point and then go inside his head, sorting through all that had been learned. He stood to leave and cleared his throat. He knew he should just leave, but he too had spent many years preparing for this. "The women?"

"Yes?" Nero was distracted.

"Are they—" he left the rest of the question unsaid.

Nero nodded ever so slightly. "They just might be, Mr. Bailey. They just might. But let's not get ahead of ourselves."

CHAPTER
31

PITTSBURGH WAS WINDY and chilly and raining. Morgantown, West Virginia, was an hour and a half from the airport. Neeley had spotted their trailers before they got to the rental car counter. Pretty incompetent Neeley decided. As the women loaded the compact sedan the men kept well out of sight. Neeley decided to forget about them for the moment. She had not yet told Hannah what she had read in the papers.

Hannah pulled the small bag of cookies she had saved from the flight from her tote. She offered one to Neeley, who refused. "So where exactly are we going?"

"To Morgantown, West Virginia. It's near the Pennsylvania state line. It's Gant's hometown."

"And the videotape is cached there?"

Neeley tried not to look exasperated. She had not slept the entire flight like Hannah had. "Yes, near there. It's also where Gant's wife and son live."

"Have you ever been there before? Do you think we could stop and get some coffee?"

Hannah was eating one cookie after another.

"Yes and no. Gant and I visited Morgantown every year. On the sly of course. We came at different times and surveilled the place. Gant wanted to make sure Jesse and his son, Bobbie, were safe."

"Why can't we get some coffee?"

Neeley shook her head in wonder. "Has anybody ever told you that you are an odd duck?"

Hannah stopped chewing, her eyes widening with surprise. "No, why?"

Neeley smiled. "You know, I believe you."

They drove for a few miles in silence before Neeley spoke again. "I've read the papers Jean-Philippe gave us."

"And?" Hannah asked.

"The bomb Jean-Philippe gave me was made by Racine on orders from Collins in order to kill Gant and destroy the video and the papers which were supposed to be in the package also."

"We knew that," Hannah said. "We probably should have killed Racine in Kansas City." She said it flatly, as if discussing the weather. Neeley realized Hannah had a very quick learning curve.

"Racine also used an RPG to shoot down one of the helicopters in Mogadishu thinking he was getting Gant's chopper, along with Masterson, the video, and the papers. He made a mistake."

"That's a good chunk of the iceberg," Hannah murmured. "How many men got killed because of that?"

"Eighteen all together," Neeley said.

"So what else was in those papers?" Hannah pressed. "There was more than just a note about Racine."

Neeley nodded. "There were copies of money transfers. Stuff I used to do for Jean-Philippe. Collins was helping Cintgo negotiate for rights for two oil pipelines from Turkmenistan across Afghanistan. One would terminate in Pakistan and one on the Arabian Sea. The problem wasn't so much the pipelines, but rather security for them. It would make no sense to invest billions of dollars in building them if they got blown up every other day as the Taliban had done to the Russian pipeline."

"So?" Hannah said. "That's all out there in the open. I even remember talking about some of that with my husband. The pipelines were never built."

"True," Neeley said. "But to get a guarantee of security from the Taliban—"

Hannah sat up straight. "They paid them off."

Neeley nodded. "Three hundred million dollars. Fifty million of which was the good senator's own money, illegally redirected from campaign funds and payoffs."

"Geez," Hannah whispered. "No wonder he wants this squashed. He paid that money to the people who blew up the Trade Center and Pentagon. He helped finance the 9-11 attacks."

"Right. And we've been caught in the middle over a decade later."

Hannah tapped a finger on her lip. "Nero didn't know about the money transfer or Racine shooting the helicopter down."

"How do you figure that?"

"Because Collins and Racine wouldn't be around if he did," Hannah said simply. Her finger continued to tap as she thought. "But—" she drew the word out.

"But what?" Neeley pressed, glancing at the rearview mirror and catching a glimpse of the car that had been trailing them since the airport.

"There's still more to this," Hannah said.

"What more?"

Hannah shrugged. "I don't know yet."

"That's helpful," Neeley said, but without an edge of sarcasm.

"I will never again trust that what I see in front of me is the truth," Hannah said. "I've learned my lesson."

"Amen, sister," Neeley said. She spotted the car once more. Neeley kept one hand on the wheel and put the other in her jacket pocket. She handed Hannah the small cassette recorder.

"What's this for?"

"The guys trailing us."

Hannah's head whipped around. "Where?"

"For God's sakes, they're not in the backseat. Let's just say they know where we are. I need to get rid of them. We need to get to Jesse alone. I have to talk to her."

Hannah was playing with the buttons on the recorder. "Okay, what's the plan?"

She started to nod as Neeley told her. "You're learning," she said when Neeley was done. "We have to use our strengths and their weaknesses."

C H A P T E R

32

JESSE GANT WAS VACUUMING so she didn't hear the doorbell. Bobbie had had some friends over the night before and they had left the kitchen littered with junk food remnants. Jesse enjoyed cleaning it up. It was a normal thing and normal things still gave Jesse great pleasure. She could remember a time in her life when there had been very little that would be considered normal.

She was a tall, slender woman with short red hair. Her face was etched with lines, most oriented in a way that indicated she smiled and laughed much more than she frowned. Freckles were liberally sprinkled on her skin and her green eyes were following the progress of the vacuum sucking up the remnants of chips and cookies.

Most women would have screamed the moment they felt the hand touch their shoulder, but Jesse merely reached down and shut off the vacuum as she turned to face the man standing behind her. "So he's dead?"

Bailey nodded. "Yes."

"When did he die?"

The dour face never changed expression. "We think a few weeks ago. We're not sure."

Now it was Jesse's turn to nod. "I knew Tony was sick. I was secretly hoping he would try to see Bobbie but he never did. How did I have a kid with such a screwed-up guy? It's really the most important decision a woman makes."

Bailey sat down in one of the kitchen chairs. Jesse pushed the vacuum cleaner away to give her access to her own chair. The man stared at her, trying to decide if she had changed much in the years he hadn't seen her.

"Anthony kept you both alive all these years."

"But if I had married a nice doctor or something I wouldn't have had to worry about that. You know not everyone has to worry about getting assassinated."

"I don't believe we can choose who we fall in love with." The words coming from Bailey were almost comical, but Jesse knew they were to be taken very seriously. Men like Bailey didn't stop by for chats and didn't say things idly to make conversation.

Jesse rose and got a couple of cups for coffee. She still knew how he took his.

"The woman, Neeley, is coming here. I arranged a diversion so we could talk, but she will be here soon."

Jesse's hands tightened on the coffee mug. "Why is she coming here?"

"For the package you have apparently been keeping for Gant all these years. She believes she needs it to survive."

"I don't have it," Jesse said.

To that, Bailey made no comment.

Jesse looked at the hard face. "And does she need it to survive?"

Bailey sipped the steaming coffee. "We all need insurance. Tell me, Jesse. Why did you leave the Cellar? You were one of the best. I know I was quite fond of you."

Jesse leaned back in the ladder-back chair, causing the cane bottom to squeak in protest. "Mr. Nero asked me to leave. He assured me I would have lifelong safety if I would retire. I was only twenty."

"My, that is surprising." To Jesse he sounded not at all surprised. "Why did Mr. Nero want you out?"

Jesse stared out the window, watching the slow movements of the clouds and let her thoughts return to that long ago day in Nero's office. "He said he had made a mistake in selecting me. That I fit the profile he needed but that I had something extra that made me unfit for duty."

Bailey was very interested. "And what was that?"

Jesse spoke with no embarrassment. "I apparently generated the emotion of love in people who were supposedly not capable of it."

Bailey nodded. "Yes, fascinating. I always suspected something of that sort. Bad for business. It was bad for Anthony—and his brother Jack."

"But remember, I brought Tony in," Jesse said. "It wasn't my fault that the robots in the Cellar began hearing violins. I didn't do anything on purpose. Besides, Mr. Nero got reams of psychological studies from the whole business. I'm sure he never recruited anyone like me again. I do regret that Tony and Jack never spoke again."

"Some of that was due to Mogadishu," Bailey said.

Jesse shook her head. "No. Jack understood that. He works for the Cellar now, doesn't he? So he understands necessity. More than marrying Tony, my greatest regret in my life was splitting the two of them. But I have Bobbie so screw 'em."

Bailey put down his empty cup. No more coffee was offered. "Please believe that my interest was purely that, and I am offering no judgments. It's just been a curiosity. Mr. Nero speaks of you warmly."

Jesse spoke slowly. "Yes, I know. I've always been grateful to him. And to Neeley, even though I never met her. It was good to know Tony wasn't alone. Especially at the end. He would have been afraid of the darkness."

"Why did you leave Anthony? Because of Jack?"

Jesse carried the two mugs to the sink. Speaking softly she said: "Not because of Jack. Because Tony—and even Jack who was very like him—and I didn't want the same things. If I'd have gone with Jack, I would have been repeating the same mistake. I did learn that lesson from Mr. Nero."

Bailey watched her, deciding that she had changed very little. "I understand."

"What will happen to me and Bobbie?"

"I can assure you that you will continue to be safe. Just give Neeley the package."

"I told you I don't have it. It was Tony's insurance, not mine. He knew Mr. Nero well enough to know that for me to have it would only be dangerous. If I had it, wouldn't Mr. Nero have sent you here the minute Tony was dead to claim it?"

Bailey pursed his lips and then slowly nodded again. Whether he believed her, she couldn't tell.

"Where's Racine?" Jesse suddenly asked.

"Don't worry about him. I'll take care of him."

Jesse turned to look at her guest. "I always worry about Racine. I never understood why Mr. Nero tolerated him."

"He is a man with useful talents and few scruples. The very thing you fear is an asset to many. But even the most useful assets have their own particular shelf life and I can assure you, Racine's has expired."

"If he gets within two states of Bobbie, I'll kill him."

Bailey nodded. "That's completely understood."

Jesse led him to the door.

He paused. "There's some new information that we have just learned that puts the past in a different light."

Jesse considered her guest. "A new perspective on the past is only important if it changes something in the present."

Bailey smiled, something Jesse could never remember him doing. "I knew I could count on you." He stepped onto the porch. "Don't mention my visit to Neeley and her companion."

"What companion?"

Bailey smiled for the second time. "A most interesting woman, very versatile."

Jesse led him to the door. "Versatility is a good thing."

CHAPTER
33

HANNAH AND NEELEY had hidden the car behind a large pile of brush. They had left the main road twenty minutes previously and were on the northern shore of Cheat Lake. The Lake had been formed by a dam on the Monogahela River. The towns that had been in the valley had been flooded, the people moved elsewhere. It was a gloomy place and the town still lay beneath the lake's gentle swells.

The dirt road they had taken ended at this lush greenery-covered shelter. One of the hundreds of old brick furnaces that dotted the state stood to their right. Farther to the left was a small cropping of boulders forming a natural fence. It was from this area that the noises were coming.

Bailey's trailers arrived within ten minutes and only the tires crunching on the graveled rocks announced their arrival. The motor had been silenced farther back and the car allowed to roll the last part of the way. The men left the car cautiously, their guns drawn.

They seemed to hear the faint noises simultaneously because as if synchronized, they moved together toward it.

They heard soft laughter and throaty whispers. As the men drew closer it was obvious they couldn't hear the words but they understood the tone. Their weapons lowered a bit as their anxiety dropped replaced by a baser instinct.

Crawling closer to the rocky stone wall, the men gave in to natural curiosity. Over the wall they could hear moans and whispers.

The younger of the two men put his hands up on the edge of the natural formation to pull himself up. The other man followed suit. Looking over, they both saw the same thing— nothing but the small cassette recorder.

Hannah and Neeley waited for them to turn around. Neeley had a gun pointed at them. Hannah walked up and took their weapons. She even patted them down, noting that their ruse had worked well. She tossed the guns to Neeley.

"Okay. What now?"

Neeley braced herself. "Now I shoot them."

Hannah looked at Neeley. "It's not necessary. They're only here to slow us down."

"How do you know that?" Neeley demanded in frustration, but Hannah didn't answer. After a few seconds, Neeley stomped a foot in frustration. "All right, all right. Jeez, you make me crazy. You wanted to kill Racine not long ago."

"Racine is different."

Neeley motioned for the men to approach and handed Hannah one of the other guns. "We'll put them in the old furnace, but I swear Hannah, if they make any moves, we shoot."

"Agreed."

The walk to the brick furnace was short and uneventful. By squatting, the men managed to squeeze in the front. Neeley stood guard as Hannah backed their car up against the opening, effectively imprisoning them. She left the keys in the ignition. On the way out she spotted a kit bag of gear in the backseat. She pointed it out to Neeley and they took it out of the car and placed it in theirs.

Hannah and Neeley drove toward Morgantown, free of surveillance for the first time in quite a while.

They went the rest of the way in silence, each lost in their own thoughts. Neeley knew exactly where to go and she pulled up in front of the small house on the edge of town a little before noon.

Hannah and Neeley got out of the car, just as a tall woman stepped out the front door of the house. She held a sawed-off shotgun in her right hand, the comfortable way she handled it indicating she would have no trouble firing it and hitting whatever she pointed it at.

"Neeley?" the woman called.

Neeley nodded. "This is Hannah," she added.

"I'm Jesse." She lowered the shotgun and led the way into the house, sliding the shotgun into an umbrella stand as she went by. The three women went into the kitchen where they awkwardly arrayed themselves around the center counter. Hannah looked from Jesse to Neeley and decided that Gant must have been an exceptional man to have had both these women in his life.

"I know Tony is dead," Jesse said by way of opening the conversation. "I assume you have been continuing my payments from him," she added, looking at Neeley.

Neeley nodded. "Where's Bobbie?"

"He's at school." Jesse looked at the clock. "He'll be home in an hour. I'd like you to be gone by then. What are you here for?"

"We need help," Neeley said. "I don't know how much you know about what Gant did for a living but . . ." Neeley started to stammer.

Jesse gave a sad smile. "You want Nero off your back?"

"You know about the Cellar?" Neeley was surprised. Gant had never hinted that his ex-wife knew.

"I worked for it for a little while," Jesse said. "Then I had Bobbie and the two didn't go together. I had something more important than the Cellar and Nero knew it. He wanted to keep Tony though, so we struck a bargain. Tony stayed, I was allowed to leave."

"Do you know about the tape?" Hannah asked.

Jesse nodded.

"But you don't know where it is?" Hannah continued.

"No." Jesse looked at her, sizing her up. "You do, don't you?"

"We have the cache report," Neeley said, a bit surprised once more at Hannah's sharp perception and understanding of a situation she herself found confusing. She took the piece of paper out and put it on the counter.

Jesse glanced at it. "Your FRP is the bridge on route forty-two. Now you need to leave right away. Bringing that report here puts my son and my life in danger."

"Do you know what's on the tape?" Neeley asked.

"Yes."

The other two women waited, but Jesse didn't say anything else for a little while, then she faced Neeley across the counter. "Did you love Tony?" she asked.

"Yes."

"Do you know what the Cellar is?" Jesse asked both of them.

"I know some of what it does," Neeley said.

"But you don't know its overriding objective, do you?"

"I don't care," Neeley said.

That brought a faint smile to Jesse's lips. "I felt the same way, especially when I saw what happened in Mogadishu."

Hannah shook her head. "The Cellar was involved to the extent that Gant—Tony—and my husband, tried to recover the videotape. But it was Racine, who fired the RPG that downed that helicopter. It was he who killed those men and initiated the problems that led to all the other deaths there. And Nero didn't order that. It was Senator Collins."

Jesse assimilated that information. "Tony never knew?"

Neeley shook her head.

"Stupid question," Jesse said. "If Tony had known, Racine would be long dead. Gant had all those rules." Her hand flew to her mouth. "Oh my God. Jack."

"Jack?" Neeley asked.

"Tony's twin brother. Jack was in the Ranger Battalion there in Mogadishu. He never forgave Tony for what happened. For his dead men."

"Is that why Gant—" Neeley caught herself—"Tony never spoke to his brother."

A sad smile played over Jesse's face. "No. That was because of me."

"Oh." Neeley's sharp intake of breath was audible.

Jesse looked at Hannah. "How are you involved in this?"

"John Masterson was my husband," Hannah said.

"The men in our lives," Jesse said wonderingly, shaking her head.

"You had Gant," Neeley said, pointing at Jesse, "I had Jean-Philippe, and Hannah ended up with John. And here we all are so many years later."

"Do you think it was all chance?" Jesse asked.

Neeley frowned. "What do you mean?"

"There is no such thing as chance when you have Nero involved," Jesse said.

Hannah was nodding. "I think Mr. Nero wanted us all to end up here, the three of us sitting together."

"Why?" Neeley asked.

"I have an idea," Hannah said. "But now is not the time. Let's get out of here and get the tape."

Jesse nodded. "Yes, please go. Your presence here can only mean trouble."

Neeley slowly stood. "Gant—Tony—was a good man."

"I know," Jesse said. "He—" she paused as the phone rang. Jesse picked it up.

The other two women could immediately tell something was wrong by the way Jesse's face went white as she listened. Then she simply said three words and hung up: "We'll be there."

"Who was that?" Neeley asked.

"That was Racine," Jesse said as she reached under the countertop and her hands came back up, an automatic pistol in her right one. She pulled the slide back, chambering a round. "He has Bobbie. He wants all three of us to meet him. He said he'll give me Bobbie if I give him both of you and you give him the papers from Jean-Philippe and the video."

She pointed the gun at the other two women. "You're coming with me."

Hannah held her hands up. "Hey, whoa, take it easy. We'll come freely."

CHAPTER

34

NEELEY DROVE, Hannah was in the passenger seat, and Jesse sat in the back, her gun pointed at Neeley's head.

"We'll help you," Neeley said.

"Racine's not stupid," Jesse said. "He's waiting for us and he has Bobbie. I'm not going to do anything to jeopardize my son. You brought Racine here and you brought that damn cache report here. I'm going to give you to him and take my son back."

"He won't give you Bobbie back," Hannah said in a level voice.

Jesse glared at her. "Why do you say that?"

" 'Cause Racine's nuts. You've met him, right?"

Jesse reluctantly nodded.

"So have we," Hannah continued. "Listen, I know you're upset, but you've got to think this through. It's us against him. Don't let him split us up against each other."

Neeley continued to drive in the direction Jesse had indicated. Both women in the front seat relaxed slightly as Jesse lowered the weapon. "All right. But no matter what, we get Bobbie out of there. Clear?"

"Clear," Neeley and Hannah said in unison.

"How old is Bobbie?" Hannah asked.

"Twenty-two."

Realizing that Hannah didn't understand something, Neeley hastened to explain. "Bobbie is—" she searched for the right words and Jesse stepped neatly in.

"Bobbie has Down's syndrome. He's up to about a sixth-grade level now. After a lot of damn hard work."

Hannah was nodding as if she understood completely.

"He goes to a special school in town," Jesse continued and both other women could hear the pride in her voice. "He's doing good. Real good."

"We'll take care of Racine," Neeley said and Hannah nodded at the blunt words.

"What is this place we're going to?" Hannah asked.

"An abandoned quarry," Jesse said. "We're to meet him on the top, at the back." She pointed. "Turn there."

Neeley took the dirt road indicated and the car rumbled over the bumps.

"Hold on a second right here," Hannah said. "We need to be ready. Stop the car."

FIVE MINUTES LATER, they could see a large open pit to their left, about a quarter-mile wide. It was so deep, that twenty feet away, on the road, they couldn't make out the bottom.

The trees gave way and they came to an open space, about forty feet wide, by twenty across on the edge of the pit. There was an old metal crane bolted to the edge and a derelict bulldozer rusting away, twenty feet to the right of the crane.

Jesse took a sharp intake of breath. A young man was tied to the blade of the bulldozer, facing the crane. Racine stood under the crane, a gun in his hand and a smile on his lips as the car came to a halt. There was a rope going from behind

Racine up into the framework of the crane, the purpose of which none of the women could immediately determine.

"That's Bobbie?" Neeley asked.

Jesse tightly nodded as she stepped out of the backseat, pistol pointed at Racine.

"Steady, now, steady," Racine yelled. "Let's not be getting hasty."

The three women spread out facing him. Jesse looked over. "Are you all right Bobbie?"

There was no answer. Bobbie appeared to be unconscious, held up by the rope around his chest.

"What did you do to him?" Jesse hissed, her knuckles white around the pistol grip.

"I just knocked him out for a little while. I didn't want us to be distracted from the task at hand. A simple shot. No pain or nothing."

Jesse raised the pistol until her sight was set on Racine's forehead.

"Hold on! Don't do it or he dies!" Racine cried out. He pointed above him, at the rope. "Follow," he said, his hand pointing along it until it disappeared behind a generator.

"You," he said, pointing at Hannah. "Move over there so you can see what the rope is tied to."

Hannah did as she was told. When she got about ten feet in front of and to the right of the other women, she could see that the rope was attached to the trigger of a rifle that was clamped down on a tripod.

"Tell them," Racine said.

"It's attached to a gun," Hannah said.

Racine turned slightly and they could see that the other end was attached to his belt. "There's six inches of slack between me and the trigger. I can assure you that the rifle is zeroed in on your son's chest, Jesse. I took several practice shots to settle in the tripod before I tied him to the blade. If I happen to move more than six inches, the rifle goes off, and your son is dead."

"You bastard," Jesse hissed. "Nero promised me that we would be safe."

"Nero!" Racine spit. "Fuck Nero. He was getting ready to terminate me. I may be a bit eccentric but I've lasted a long time in this business. Longer than our mutual friend Mr. Anthony Gant.

"Give me the papers!" he yelled.

Neeley reached into her coat and drew out the papers, bound by a rubber band. She threw them onto the ground.

"Good." Racine said.

"Now the tape," Racine said.

"We don't have it," Neeley said.

"Not the right answer," Racine said.

"I have a cache report for the tape," Neeley said. "It's located not far from here."

"Put it next to the papers."

Neeley pulled that out of her pocket and put it on the ground.

"Let my son go," Jesse said. "You've got what you want."

"Shoot Neeley," Racine said, "and I'll think about it." He raised his free hand and ran it up and down the rope. "I'll give you five seconds."

Jesse turned to Neeley, the gun shaking in her hand. "Why did you have to come here and draw us into this? Why?" The muzzle wavered, then centered on Neeley's chest. She pulled the trigger and the round hit Neeley in the chest, knocking her to the ground. Her body twitched for a second, then was still. The muzzle wasn't wavering any more.

"Now the other bitch," Racine said.

She aimed at Hannah and fired. As Hannah fell, Jesse dropped the hand with the gun in it to her side.

Racine blinked. "A mother's love. Pretty powerful stuff." He reached behind and unfastened the rope, but kept it in his hands. "At last, someone who understands the way things work. Now drop the gun."

Jesse did so. As soon as Racine had the rope clear, her hand went inside her coat, pulling out the sawed-off shotgun. She charged forward, a feral scream emanating from her lips as she pulled the first trigger. The first blast hit Racine right between the eyes, taking the top of his skull off.

She pulled the second trigger and the second swarm of pellets hit the body in the chest, slamming the already dead body back so that it fell off the edge of the quarry.

Neeley slowly stood up; ripping open her shirt and rubbing her chest under the vest she wore. One of two vests that had been in the kit bag they'd taken from their trailers' car. "Good shot," she told Jesse.

There was a moan and they both turned and looked as Hannah rolled on her side. "Jeez," Hannah said with great difficulty. "Someone give me a hand here."

Jesse ran over to her son as Neeley knelt next to Hannah.

"I think my rib is broken," Hannah said, trying not to take a deep breath. Jesse had untied Bobbie and was cradling him in her arms.

They all watched as two cars raced into the open area and stopped close to the edge. Bailey leaped out of the front one, pistol at the ready along with three other armed men.

"You're too late," Jesse said.

Bailey walked forward as the other men waited at the cars. "I'm sorry, Jesse," he said. "We lost Racine," He looked at the body in the quarry. "We'll take care of that. Is Bobbie all right?"

"No thanks to you," Jesse said. She looked up at the two women and Bailey. "I want to be left alone. Do you understand that? Leave my son and me alone! I don't care about the past." She pointed at her son. "He's the future. Let him have his own."

Bailey holstered his pistol. "We understand, Jesse. I'm sorry this happened. Like I said, we lost Racine and—"

"Just leave us alone." With that she walked away, holding her son.

Bailey turned to Neeley. "The tape, if you don't mind."

Neeley shook her head. "I don't have it here, but I know where it is. Gant left everything he had to me. I say that includes the tape. It's as safe with me as it was with him. Tell Nero that Hannah and I will use it to protect ourselves."

Bailey looked old and tired. "Mr. Nero will be displeased. He's not a man who likes loose ends."

Neeley stood close to Hannah, her voice a ragged whisper. "You know, I really don't give a shit. Our lives depend on that tape and you know it."

"I—" Bailey began, but Hannah cut him off.

"Nero made a mistake a long time ago. He knows that."

Bailey stared at her, then reached into his pocket and pulled out a secure cell phone. He punched in a number, waited a moment, then spoke into it. "Mr. Nero, I have Neeley and Hannah Masterson here." He nodded, looked surprised for a second, and then turned toward the second car and its dark windows. He indicated for Hannah and Neeley to come with him. "He wants to talk to you."

Hannah didn't seem surprised. Bailey opened the back door and the two women slid in. It was dark inside and they could barely make out a form seated across from them.

The metallic voice was a surprise as it rasped into the sudden silence. "Do you know why I'm here?"

Hannah nodded. "Yes."

There were several moments of silence. Neeley was looking between the old man and Hannah, waiting to be clued in.

"Please tell me, Mrs. Masterson."

"You want me to work for you."

"Not quite."

Hannah could see the surprised look on Neeley's face at hearing this. Hannah's eyes were beginning to adjust and she could make out a little bit of Nero's face. The scars were shocking, but she kept her reaction from her own face. She realized he was waiting for her to speak.

"You want me to be you," Hannah finally said.

"Very, very good. I knew I was right about you. And Neeley also. Mr. Bailey is getting on in years as I am. We need new blood. And more importantly, a different perspective."

"A woman's perspective?" Hannah asked.

"The world has changed greatly in the last sixty years," Nero said. "I've made mistakes. Allowed people like Collins to thrive. Bad things have happened on my watch. My fault."

"How long have you tracked me?" Hannah asked.

"Since the accident when you were six."

"Why?"

"You were betrayed at a fundamental level. But you didn't turn against that which betrayed you. That was key."

"Like you were in some way?"

"Like I was, indeed."

"Jenkins. He profiled me for you. All those years and all those sessions, he never really helped me. He was just filing a report to you."

"Yes."

"I should be pissed."

"But you aren't," Nero said. "You're intrigued."

There was a prolonged silence, and then Hannah answered. "Yes."

"Good."

"Except you're saying a woman in the prime of her life is the equal of an old blind man," Hannah said.

A cackling noise was immediately followed by Nero coughing for almost half a minute before he regained his composure. "A most interesting observation. However, I know you aren't quite ready yet to step into my shoes, so to speak. We'll have time to work together. For you to learn what you will need. And I fervently hope you will be *better* than me."

"And if I say no?" Hannah asked.

Nero shrugged. "I cannot force you."

"No, you can only manipulate my entire life to this end. How many people like me have you followed and manipulated?"

It was Nero's turn to pause. "I did very little manipulation," he finally said. "Mostly observation."

"How many?" Hannah was insistent.

"Twenty-seven."

"How many failed?"

"Twenty-four. Two have not been, shall we say, activated by circumstances as you were."

"I'm lucky twenty-five? You're running out of possibilities."

Nero didn't respond.

Hannah glanced at Neeley. "What do you think?"

"It was *all* a setup?" Neeley was still trying to comprehend.

Hannah nodded. "There was no need for all those loose ends over ten years ago to be allowed to last so long."

"Most true," Nero said.

"What about Collins?" Hannah asked.

"Senator Collins has become like Racine: a liability. He will be sanctioned."

Hannah leaned back in the deep leather seat. She glanced through the dark glass. She could see Jesse guiding Bobbie to her car. The young man's face was confused, the drug Racine had given him still affecting him. Jesse leaned close and whispered something in his ear and his face split in a wide grin.

Hannah turned back to Nero. "What exactly is your job?"

"The Cellar is the country's bodyguard."

"A bodyguard that uses psychos like Racine and lies and deceit?"

"Whatever means necessary for the greater good. A bodyguard of lies, so to speak."

Hannah opened the door. "We'll let you know."

"The world is changing," Nero said. "It is your time now."

"We'll let you know," Hannah repeated as she exited the car, Neeley following.